In HOBOKEN

Also by Christian Bauman

The Ice Beneath You
Voodoo Lounge

HOBOKEN

a novel

CHRISTIAN BAUMAN

MELVILLEHOUSE

BROOKLYN, NEW YORK

© 2008 Christian Bauman

Melville House Publishing
145 Plymouth Street
Brooklyn, NY 11201

www.mhpbooks.com

Book Design: Blair and Hayes

First Melville House Printing: March 2008

ISBN: 978-1-933633-47-3

A catalog record for this book is available from the Library of Congress.

Printed in Canada

For Diana Finch

God damn everything
but the circus.

—Jonatha Brooke

PART I

Autumn, 1995

THE BUILDING AT SIXTH AND CLINTON

The stink was how they found out. Those seven flights of old wooden stairs, straight up the center of the building, always had a smell and there was nothing you could do. Eighty-five years of burnt olive oil and boiled cabbages and bags of dirty cloth diapers left out for the service—there was nothing you could do. But in the second week of October the usual smell sharpened unusually, over a few days, into something riper, more precise, almost visible. By Thursday morning it was a gagging cloud, rotten ground meat and hairy oranges, and it seemed to come from under the door of Larry Ritzi's apartment on the fourth floor. When the super's thirty-year-old son went in—*Yo, Larry, you home? Yo man, open up. Something reeks, man. Yo. Listen, I ain't call the cops, but I gotta come in, okay I gotta use the key*—he found Larry where he'd been all week, hanging from the ceiling in the kitchen, black vacuum-cleaner cord buried tight in the maroon folds of his neck. Larry's feet were touching the floor, ankles bent with the toes of his high-tops grazing the old linoleum tiles. The first thought the super's son had was it was surprising the feet would be touching the ground and his second thought was *Larry, man, Christ* and then the super's son leaned over his belly and vomited coffee and hard roll on the ankles of his blue tracksuit and own new high-tops.

Four Hoboken police officers and a shift sergeant responded; two full hours of cigarette smoking and coffee drinking and chatting up Mrs. Quatrone on the second floor before they released Larry Ritzi's body to the rescue squad. One of the officers had grown up in the building—although his own dear mother and father passed on now almost ten years, both of them, God bless them—and Mrs. Quatrone stretched to pat Officer DiGiovanni's rough cheeks with her old, open hands like he was still a boy, and insisted on the coffee and a bite—*just some sausage and a little peppers and gravy, nothing to warm it up, no trouble.* Mrs. Quatrone had a lot to say but not much of it about the suicide himself—*a nutter, that one* pretty much summed it.

After lunch, the ambulance team took poor blackened, bloated Larry Ritzi out on a stretcher. They passed Lenora Lupisella, coming home from her morning shift catching dimes on the Garden State Parkway. Lenora— tall to begin with, made taller by the Danish clogs peeking out below her jeans—stepped back on the sidewalk to let the stretcher by, crossed herself despite herself, then asked who it was under the sheet. When it was all said and done the paramedics had to take her, too.

The ambulance brought both dead Larry Ritzi and hysterical Lenora Lupisella to Saint Francis in west Hoboken, the stretcher with Larry off to the morgue and the stretcher with Lenora bound for the ER and a hit of intravenous Valium. The irony was that Larry had sometimes referred to his sometime-girlfriend as Loopy Lenora—in a loving manner, and what do you expect when your last name is Lupisella—but it had always been Larry who was loopy (he'd said the Lithium side effects would drive him to suicide, and hadn't that been a perfect call) and Loopy Lenora Lupisella was a little high-maintenance but no loopier than any of the rest of us floating around on the planet. For Lenora, Loopy was simply a nickname, not a diagnosis.

They kept Lenora in the hospital overnight, and then she kept herself well sedated the rest of the week. She hadn't been in love with Larry, which was fortunate, but they'd known each other years and had a thing now and then when he was more with it than without it. The day before he hung himself, though, he'd really been off his rocker with rants and raves and she'd done some ranting herself then ordered him out of her place on the fifth floor, screaming down the stairs he should do us all a favor and take a flying leap. Larry took her up on it, poor Lenora. In the end she would be fine, but it was no way to start your week.

Thatcher heard about all this second-and third-hand, up on the roof two weeks after the suicide, Halloween weekend, his twenty-fourth birthday. It was a chilly one in Hoboken that night, sky clear and purple over Manhattan, the World Trade Center towers peeking above the steeple of Saint Thomas to the south, Empire State right in front, lit up orange for the season. Everyone had a coat, sitting on folding chairs or right on the silvered tar, a couple guitars out even though it was too cold to play, a cooler filled with bottles of Rolling Rock. Thatcher passed the circulating joint to James; James let his guitar hang from the strap around his neck, re-fired and hit the joint, and said this was all a toast to Lenora Lupisella. Which is when Thatcher noticed she wasn't there. He let his own guitar hang a moment and asked why were they toasting Lenora? James said we're toasting a return to good mental health and karma then told Thatcher the story of Larry Ritzi, which everyone but him already knew. Thatcher raised his bottle to the swift recovery of Loopy Lenora then raised it again to the memory of poor unhinged Larry Ritzi. Thatcher stayed up there on the roof until the Empire State lights went out at 2 A.M., stayed up moving his fingers on the bronze strings of his guitar, stayed up long past the others had left and even an hour past when he put his guitar away. Thatcher stayed alone in the chill—a methodical working through the end of a pack of cigarettes and a flask of Jack Daniels—then came down off the roof and crawled into a sleeping bag on the cold floor of James's sixth-story rat hole apartment. It was raining and raw in Hoboken the next morning, and the TV said it might rain all weekend.

GRAND THEFT SAUSAGE

In Hoboken, this end of Willow Street on an autumn Monday morning is all *Butter on that hard roll?* and *Coffee, regular* and *What with the coffee?* and *Regular, gimme coffee regular* and *Yeah, all right—LISA! Two regular.* It's suits pressing forward for their coffees regular; young suits, this part of town, straight out of college with only three maybe four suits to their name—they change out the ties and call it a new day. At 8 A.M., the young suits are the second shift in for coffee. First crowd was guys who work for a living, coming through at six, seven in the morning; boots and flannel and maybe a coat now on a dark morning like this, usually younger guys in this crowd, too. The foremen wait in their pickups, smoking one of the boys' cigarettes and half-listening to AM radio. The boys all listen to Howard Stern, but foremen have to know about traffic and weather so they're always hitting the AM button—all news, all the time.

By eight, the guys who work for a living have been punched in an hour and the hard rolls and coffees regular are for the young suits. *Paper with that?* and *Yeah, paper* and sometimes *No, keep it, Ralphie, keep it* but fact is the young suits never say keep the change as much as the guys who work for a living. And those guys never actually say *Keep it* anyway; they just walk out, coins scattered across the counter.

Two old crossing guards in black slickers holding up traffic outside Saint Anthony's, yelling gossip over the wind on the first really cold day in November. It's not quite hats-and-gloves-all-day cold, not January cold, but it's wet and the gusts off the Hudson River aren't kidding. It's all get your head down and get to work, it's November now, get to school and get to work—what, are we playing games here?

They're not playing games at Carbone's Diner. Ten suits in overcoats and ties still untied, lined up on stools at the counter. Old Miguel's through the kitchen door like a shot—milk delivery, *Hey sign for this*—and when he's back he's sweating, pissed at the milk interruption, morning's pacing thrown to hell. He's tapping his pencil *tap tap tap*, working down the line of suits one by one, speaking the only English he knows. "C'mon, Okay? We playing games? You ready? We playing games here? I ain't got time for games." *Tap tap tap.*

"I'll give you a fucking game, Miguel," one of the suits right in the middle of the line says, but he's the only one who would even think of saying that, he's older with a white mustache and been eating here since there was a Carbone in an apron at Carbone's Diner (and this suit's tie is already tied because he wouldn't leave the house any other way), and Miguel cracks a grin and laughs, scribbles the order, nodding and laughing, "Yeah, good good good." Then one step to the right, smile gone, in the face of the next guy, a young Wall Street suit barely shaving—"C'mon, I ain't got time for games." *Tap tap tap.*

• • •

Booths line the wall opposite Miguel's counter. James and Thatcher sit across from each other in a booth near the back, opposite sides of a table and opposite sides of a dress code on this Monday morning. Thatcher in two old flannel shirts with his brown barn coat still on even sitting here for breakfast, jeans and black army jungle boots. Thatcher is a picture of skinny, a shaved-head stubble blonde with pouty lips and blue eyes. James, though, with a tamed Jesus mane of straight black hair pushed back off his face, a beard he trims with sharp scissors twice a week, James is done up like the brokers on the stools, in gray suit and maroon untied tie. He's late to grab the PATH train to World Trade Center, his job—day job. James, like Thatcher, has long fingernails on his right hand, for guitar picking, but days James is in charge of PowerPoint presentations for the 108th floor, North Tower. He's worked for this firm two years, first real job out of college; the company does something with statistics for dotcoms. A good view from the 108th floor, if he leaves his cube and walks right then left then down the hall to stand in one of those narrow windows. Some view. He can't see Carbone's Diner where they're sitting now, but he can see the span of Hoboken from way up there.

Thatcher guesses he too will soon enough be wearing clothes like James's on a regular basis—but not today. Today he's in a narrow window all his own, a brief space between four years of reveille and whatever suit-wearing day gig lies before him. He's dressed today for the occasion, for the narrow window. Thatcher had hoped to use the window to sleep in. But James and James's roommate Russell Davitz were loud around the apartment this morning with their hangover groans and their Monday suits and shoes, and then Thatcher was hungry so he pried himself from Jo's warm body next to him in the sleeping bag and came along with James as far as the diner. Breakfast is always a good idea, anyway. Sometimes you just can't sleep in, even when fate says it's your turn to sleep in. Sometimes you just can't, but breakfast makes up for it.

They're forking eggs, potatoes. Thatcher and James sit in their booth, eating like brothers. They're not brothers—Irish death pallor vs. Mediterranean smooth, and a three-month gap between birthdays—but they eat with the fluidity of brothers, creamer to coffee and fork to mouth. They could salt one another's food to a T of taste, if paralysis hit one and a little extra help was required in eating. "Here, I'll get that," Thatcher could say to a nurse, taking the salt shaker from her hand, delivering a precise and measured dose to James's eggs. Or vice versa with the butter on Thatcher's toast. They don't even hold their utensils in the same way, in the same hands, but when you've eaten breakfast together at least twice a week for fifteen years it looks like you do.

Although, Thatcher notices, James eats a little bit stiffer in the suit. *That's you next week, my friend,* he thinks, then thinks, *Fucknuts.*

There is a third option, besides barracks bugle wake-ups on the one hand, and Wall Street rod in ass on the other hand. It is, in fact, the option they're both angling for, and Thatcher's flannel and denim today is the uniform. Option three, you don't work at all. You sleep all day. You change your strings. You write in your notebook. You drive to the gig. You play the gig. You drink the beer. Option three.

Thatcher eyeballs James in his suit, across the table, in their back corner booth. Watches James lifting fork with suited arm. *Option three,* Thatcher thinks. *Suits are temporary. We'll take option three.*

But now it's all about a different kind of hunger. Breakfast. Which, as breakfast usually goes, is gone too soon. Thatcher sighs. The light is an unhealthy glowing yellow back here in the corner, fluorescents flickering off the gray coming through the plate glass up front and the rainy sky outside. Thatcher's fork floats across the table, hovers over James's last piece of sausage, seeing if he'll notice.

"I'll break your arm," James says. "So help me."

Thatcher pouts his pouty lips now, eyeballing James's restricted sausage. Fingers on the fork tensed above James's plate, tendons tightening on a pale wrist.

"No kidding, I'll knock you from here to Canarsie."

Miguel drops something heavy behind the counter, curses loud in Spanish.

"We playing games here?" Thatcher says, and when James looks over at Miguel Thatcher spears the sausage link, pops it in his mouth.

"That's cold, son."

"Hungry, James."

James shakes his head. "That's cold."

"I'll get you another coffee."

Looking for Miguel's old sister who waits on the booths Thatcher sees Marsh, working his way up the aisle. It takes awhile. Marsh walks slow. There's a lot of Marsh to move, and the bulk all goes sort of sideways on a right-hand limp. A slight limp, most days, but there it is. Polio, when Marsh was a boy. Long graying hair on his short round body. He's also slow coming because he gets stopped at each passing booth for a *Hey, how you doing!* Marsh limps slow back through the diner, leaving each passed booth with a *Use it or lose it, right?* or an *I know it, I know it* or the occasional *Come by tonight, we'll talk tonight.* James has said Marsh knows more people in Hoboken than the mayor and the Mafia combined and Thatcher believes it. Finally, Marsh makes it, slides into the booth next to James with his coat still on. He's smiling. Marsh is always smiling.

"Thatcher, Thatcher, Thatcher," Marsh says, laying the six syllables out across the table one by one. He pushes hair from his face then rests his thick arms in front of him. "You're back in the world."

"Good to see you, Marshall."

"It's good to be seen. You're official and honorable and all that now?"

"Not yet. Soon. Mostly. Technically I'm out now. Officially in a few weeks. Looking for a job, day job."

"In Hoboken?"

"In Hoboken."

"Thatcher's in love," James says.

"In love? Young Thatcher's in Hoboken and in love! Wonderful." Marsh is delighted. Marsh is always delighted. "Who's the lucky vixen?"

"Young Lou," James says.

"I am *not* in—"

"Young Lou!" Marsh calls. "Young Lou. A lovely girl." He's nodding his head, absolutely delighted.

"There are problems, of course," James says.

"I'll give you a fucking problem, son," Thatcher says.

"What possible problems could stand in the way of young love?" Marsh says.

James lifts a finger. "Item one: Thatcher's currently sleeping with at least one other someone else."

"Oh, pshaw!" Marsh waves a hand. "Who isn't?"

James nods, point taken. Thatcher lights a cigarette, closing his eyes. James raises a second finger. "Item two: Young Lou is quite gay."

"Again, I say: deep down, aren't we all?"

"Maybe, but in this case, Young Lou only sleeps with girls. Young Thatch here is most decidedly not a girl."

Marsh shakes his head. "I'm disappointed, James. Your logic is weak. Young Lou's ravishing of girls stands not in the way of Thatcher loving her." And now he raises a thick finger. "It only stands in the way of her loving him." He looks at Thatcher. "Son, you're free to love Lou. Let go and let love."

"I'm not in love with Lou. I just met her."

"Thatcher ate my last piece of sausage, too."

Marsh shakes his head. "That's cold, Thatcher. Very cold." He waves his arm at Miguel's sister—*coffee? hello?*—but she doesn't see him. "Let's back up, though," he says. "Who is this 'at least one other someone else' we're currently ensconced with?"

Thatcher opens his mouth but James cuts him off again. "One of them's in a sleeping bag on the floor of my apartment, as we speak. You wouldn't know her. Girl from our high school."

Thatcher drops the stub of his cigarette into the ice in his water glass. "I don't believe this."

"You stole my sausage, son."

Marsh waves a hand at Miguel's sister again, still no luck. He looks at Thatcher. "Hold on. You just met Lou? How is this possible?"

"I just met her," he says, shrugging. "I don't know all these people you know. You know every soul in Hoboken. I don't know anyone. I don't even live here yet."

James's eggs are done and he's reaching for his wallet. "Thatcher calls me last month, Marsh. Middle of the night. Says he's coming north to record a demo, he's booked studio time with Skinny P in Chatham, but he's stuck in his barracks in Virginia until the last minute so can I set up a band for him." James counts bills and coins. "And also he needs a chick singer."

Marsh nods. "Everyone needs a chick singer."

"So I bring Lou to the studio."

Marsh's face lights up. He's delighted again. "And Thatcher falls immediately in love."

"I did *not*—"

"Of course he did."

"—fall in love with her!"

Marsh lays a hand on Thatcher's arm. "We've all done it, young Thatcher."

"Done what?"

"Fallen in love with Lou."

"Oh for Christ's sake."

"She's a very sweet girl."

"Unfortunately," says James, "she has zero interest in you."

"Listen," Thatcher says, "I—"

"Gentlemen," Marsh says, pushing up the sleeve of his coat, looking at his watch. "It'll obviously be hours for coffee and I'm already late for work." This a polite signal more than statement of fact. Unlike everyone else in Hoboken, Marsh doesn't work across the river. He works in Hoboken and he doesn't wear a suit. It's not that kind of job. "I must take my leave."

"See you around, Marsh," James says, throwing his money on the table and standing first.

"You'll be at Maxwell's tonight, gentlemen?" Marsh asks, pushing himself to his feet. Nods all around. "And maybe dinner this weekend? The wife's been a-cooking."

James shakes his head no, points at Thatcher. "Homeslice here doesn't have a car. I'm driving him down to Virginia this weekend to grab his stuff."

"That's an awfully nice gesture for someone who stole your last piece of sausage."

"You're telling me." They moved down the aisle, James's hand on Marsh's shoulder.

Last in the booth, Thatcher leaned against the wall with eyes closed and massaged his temples. Then he lit a new cigarette and waited, hopefully, for a coffee refill. Marsh worked the room in reverse, pressing the flesh and slowly moving the bulk of his body to the door. Outside, James raised collar to the cold and joined the sea of suits for the last two blocks to Hoboken Terminal and the PATH train under the river into Manhattan.

DOUBLE DUTCH AND A REFERENCE CHECK

Two things born in Hoboken, New Jersey—a good representation, as good a place as any to start, what you might tell someone from Goshen, Indiana you meet on a Greyhound bus—two things born here, the memory of both births enshrined on steel signs scattered like jacks around the mile-square city: the great American game of baseball and Frances Albert Sinatra. The former birth disputed by a small yet surprisingly powerful burg in upstate New York, the later birth disputed by none although mostly brushed aside by the birthee himself.

In Hoboken, you know these things. But it's not impressive. Everyone knows *that*, everyone within the sound of this accent. Sinatra yadda yadda, baseball blah blah blah; they filmed *On The Waterfront* over here, that's the old Maxwell House Coffee factory over there—yeah, we've all had a cup.

Stephen Foster, though—who knew? But sure, that was him, Stephen Foster all shacked up at 601 Bloomfield in the cold year of our Lord 1854. Jeanie With The Light Brown Hair was a Hudson River girl.

And Mr. Marconi, ladies and gentlemen, with his transmitters and wireless signals. You might ask where would Frances Albert be without

Mr. Marconi's signal to sing across? Sing all you want, Frank; Marconi made the difference between neighborhood and nationwide.

Right here in Hoboken it all happened. Right here.

$$\cdots$$

Walking back west neighborhood to neighborhood through Hoboken this time of morning is a cold push against the commuter current, Thatcher having to step aside or practically in the street every few seconds for the rush, rush, rushing suits with their coffee and paper and young ladies in skirts and raincoats with sneakers on their feet, their good shoes in hand with an orange juice and PATH transit card. Not many over thirty; once you have kids you move uptown—up past 10th Street is a nice neighborhood for that, or over by Elysian Park and down the end of Frank Sinatra Boulevard.

One small errand this morning: Thatcher needs guitar strings. Two blocks diagonal from City Hall he goes down wet, concrete steps and presses his face to storefront glass. DOUBLE DUTCH the sign reads, an irony of unknown origin. It's dark inside, but Thatcher sees a bald head through the guitars hanging in the window. He tries the doorknob, pushes the door, sticks his head in.

"Closed!" the bald head yells from the counter, hunched over a plate of something and a mug of coffee. "One hour." The bald head looks up, squints, swallows, then says, "Hey. Woody Guthrie."

Thatcher steps in, closing the door behind him. "Hi there Dutch." Dutch owns the guitar shop. He was famous once, briefly, about twelve years ago. Rather, his band was famous. Briefly. It's been said Dutch slept with one of the Bananarama girls. Regularly. They toured Scotland or something together for a month, Bananarama and Dutch's briefly almost-famous group. Dutch says he doesn't remember who opened for whom—

and who cares now anyway, he says. Dutch played a big Rickenbacker in 1985 when no one else played anything like that anymore. Now it's all back in again, double retro. Dutch had hair when he was briefly famous, but keeps his head shaved now because there's not much hair left. It's a good look, though. For him. Thatcher has had to keep his blond hair shaved tight to his skull for occupational reasons the last four years; Dutch is the only person he knows in the real world with less hair than him.

Thatcher goes sideways down the crowded aisle to where bald Dutch sits at his counter, eating a takeout breakfast. Guitars hang from every spot on the ceiling, cover every inch of the walls.

"Want one?" Dutch asks, and Thatcher thinks he means a guitar but then sees Dutch is holding out a piece of toast.

"Thanks, I ate. With Marsh, at Carbone's."

"We playing games?"

There's a loud toilet flushing and a door closing from somewhere in the back, then Bruno coming in, zipping his fly and *Wall Street Journal* rolled under his arm. He's in Dutch's age range, a little younger than Marsh—a good ten years on Thatcher and James—wearing black, all black and neat-trimmed black hair and black shoes, just a little round around the belly and the cheeks, but neatly round, just like his hair. Bruno was on that same tour of England twelve years ago, with Bananarama, but was never a real member of Dutch's almost-famous band. He was a fill-in bass player, just for that tour; the regular guy down with dengue fever from an Asian swing. It was how Bruno met Dutch. Bruno claims a Bananarama bedding as well, but Thatcher wasn't as sure he believed that one.

"Your friend Woody Guthrie's here," Dutch says. "What's your name again, Woody?"

"Thatcher."

"Hey," Bruno says. "What are you doing." Thatcher knows Bruno through James.

"Moving to Hoboken. Trying to set up a day gig."

"Working here in the shop?"

Dutch shakes his head. "Can't even pay myself," he mutters.

"No—office job at the other side of town. Interview later today. Hey, I might need a reference."

Bruno raises an eyebrow, then digs in a pocket of his coat until he finds a business card. "Yeah, alright," he says. "Give them this phone number."

Bruno works for TimeLife in midtown.

"Thanks, man."

"Tell them I'm a V.P., maybe it'll get you somewhere."

"A V.P. of what?"

Bruno shrugs. "I dunno. Editorial services." He was a copy editor, in the publishing arm. He threw an adios at Dutch and made his way toward the door. Thatcher pocketed Bruno's card then began digging through the string box on the counter.

• • •

Back on Clinton Street, Thatcher finds the key on his ring and climbs the endless stairway. Breathless, he lets himself into James's apartment, quiet with the big door then shoes off and padding into the chilly living room. Jo is where he left her, asleep in the doublewide sleeping bag. He can just see the top of her head, thick black hair fanned on the white pillow.

The room is dim, shades half drawn, even the light in here seems cold. Functional, the space—an old yellow couch from James's place when he was at Rutgers, straight-backed wooden chair from the roommate's grandmother or great-aunt. The ubiquitous plastic-framed *New Yorker* print on one wall, a Beatles poster taped up next to it, and a black chalk drawing the roommate made of his girlfriend. James hates the chalk drawing but doesn't know how to ask the roommate to take it down. The Beatles poster is a picture from *Let It Be*, a pissed-off George over the shoulder of a sullen John looking at an insistent Paul with his back to a sympathetic Ringo.

Thatcher drops his clothes down to just his T-shirt, shivering quick in the cold, and crawls in beside Jo.

"Come here," she says, warm and long sleepy arms around him, pulling him in. Jo smells like honey and lotion and is wearing only a T-shirt and underwear. Thatcher has been attempting, on and off, to get into that underwear since he was fifteen. This is an unusual show of determination for him, but she's given him an unusual number of opportunities to try.

He's been close. The underwear—pink and silky at fifteen, white lace at their fifth high school reunion, sensible cotton this morning—has been pulled aside, pushed into, stretched tight. But never completely off, not completely. And, in turn, by strict definition of consummation, they've never consummated.

"Has she with other guys?" James asked once when Thatcher was grousing about his ten-year struggle.

"I don't know," Thatcher said, looking him in the eye. "Did she with you?"

James, caught off-guard: "How did you know about that?"

"What am I, an idiot?"

"That was a long time ago, Thatch. You weren't seeing her at the time."

"Look, did she?"

James scowled, pursed his lips. Then said, "No."

Every time Thatcher has crawled into bed with Jo—whether three years have gone by, or, like this week, every night for three days straight—he is determined that this will be the time. It's not complete self-delusion, he thinks. The signs are all there. Their neverending foreplay is better than most of the consummated sex he's had. Every time he is sure this will be it. Every time he is wrong.

Like, for instance, this morning.

His hands move over her and, eyes closed, Jo smiles, purrs. Moves her hands on him slow. Then, suddenly, "I have to go to work, sweetie."

"Now?"

"Now. I gave you my two days off then called in sick." It was true, she had. They hadn't seen each other in a year and she said she missed him. "But now I have to go. You go back to sleep."

Quick as that, Jo is gone from the sleeping bag, into the bathroom. Thatcher sighs, rolls over. *What am I supposed to do with this?* he thinks. Sounds from a distant sink then she's back from the bathroom, her dark skin tight and goose-pimpled in the cold apartment. Thatcher pulls the sleeping bag over his face.

"For God's sake Joanne just come back in here and let's be done with it," he yells from inside the bag.

She smiles, pulling on a trim black cardigan. "Not until wedding bells, dear."

"Fine—marry me. I'm begging."

Jo walks over and leans down, planting a kiss on the top of his head. "You're sweet, Thatcher." She says. "But I can't marry you." Her jeans are in a ball on the floor; she grabs them, frowning, shakes them out, pulls them on. "Don't think I haven't thought about it, though." She buttons her jeans, then smooths down the denim best she can with her palms. She's a sharp dresser, Jo is. Highly affectionate toward musicians and artists barely able to dress themselves, but personally put-together like a catalogue page. "We just wouldn't get along, married."

Thatcher pushes his face back out of the sleeping bag, watching her hunt shoes, keys, purse, coat, scarf. She comes over when she's all done, leaning down. He meets her lips with his own.

"Come back in here," he whispers.

"Goodbye Thatcher."

"It's such a small thing, Jo."

"Goodbye."

She's in the hallway now. Thatcher yells after her, "I'll be in Hoboken full-time as of next week—I'll call you, maybe come down and see you." Jo has a place in New Brunswick, half an hour south.

She sticks her head back around the corner. "I'm busy next week, Thatcher. I told you."

He remembers. The boyfriend. "The boyfriend," he says.

"The fiancé," she says.

"You're making me ill."

She blows him a kiss. "Don't be ill on James's floor, sweetie," she says.

Then she's gone, heavy door swings shut and a loud click. Thatcher pushes his nose back into the sleeping bag, smelling her. *What am I supposed to do with this?* He does the best he can. Then he climbs half out of the warm green bag, yawns, unsatisfied, looking around. The rain had started again, hitting the window as the wind pushes it in small sprays. The sky outside is a slick gray, a bright gray. The radiator under the window begins to rattle, but Thatcher knows better. It's just a tease. It'll rattle and promise a good fifteen minutes, but it's just a tease and won't make the room any warmer.

DOING THE LORD'S WORK

By late morning Marsh was very hungry.

"I'm very hungry!" he called out, voice filling the wide office. Eight people working at desks and tables scattered around the floor; none of them looked up. Marsh yelled this same thing—"I'm very hungry!"—at about the same time every morning. Still, he always hoped for some acknowledgment. None today. "But I am," he said quietly, tapping a pencil on his desk. "Very hungry."

Marsh pushed himself up from his chair. He thought he remembered a bunch of bananas on the counter in the office's cubbyhole kitchenette. Maybe they were ripe. Marsh liked bananas.

The office was on the fourth floor of an old Hoboken warehouse overlooking the Hudson with—on less rainy days—a view of midtown Manhattan. The original wood floors were intact, stained a muddy blond. The bricked walls painted white and covered with concert posters and banners from FM rock stations in Decatur, Nacogdoches, Bellingham, Allentown, Bellow's Falls. Every available horizontal space had a stack of

CDs or cassettes or, in a few cases, real vinyl LPs and EPs. As independent record companies went, Zippy Records was an anomaly. That is, they were still in business after five years and had a few actual employees. They even paid their employees, usually on or close to on time. The money came from oldies reissues (*Jim Nabors Sings His 20 Greatest Ballads Just For You*) and party compilations (*Breakin'! Electric Hits From the 80s*) sold direct on late-night cable TV. Zippy also had a small stable of original artists: two aging classic rock bands who'd been dropped by the majors, a few studio sidemen from the seventies releasing their own work, and one young vegan folksinger from Northampton, Massachusetts. She'd opened a tour for Ani DiFranco the year before and now sold more albums a month than all of Zippy's aging classic rock bands combined. She didn't sell more than Jim Nabors yet, but close. (The vegan folksinger had been to the office recently and Marsh had pulled out a spreadsheet demonstrating her impending takedown of Jim Nabors. Marsh—who'd enjoyed two or four pints of Guinness at a Brooklyn radio station lunch that very day—offered the vegan folksinger this unsolicited advice: "A few less pictures in the press of you and your boyfriend arm-in-arm and a few more of you and...well, any woman, really, and you'll toast Nabors in no time flat.")

In the little kitchenette, bananas were found. Marsh snapped one free, stripped down the sides, took a bite.

"Not hungry anymore!" Marsh yelled around a mouthful of banana. He swallowed and walked back to his desk, eating slowly. "Crisis over." Only Claudia, the secretary, looked up. She smiled and Marsh blew her a kiss.

Marsh did Zippy's radio promotion. Once past the important but not insurmountable fact that he would rather have been the one *being* promoted, he liked his job. It helped that he liked his job. It also helped that he was good at his job. The ever-thoughtful Marsh had considered—in a late-night, beer-drenched, confessional with Bruno—that liking and being good at promoting very probably spelled doom for one's own chances at artistic success. Successful artists, Marsh observed, rarely were able to match their own socks. Still, happy with day-to-day victories, Marsh persevered in both his job and his personal pursuit of rock and roll.

Marsh swallowed the last bit of banana, dropped the empty peel in his waste basket, lowered himself carefully into his chair. His left leg, never a cooperative member of the body electric, had been grouchier than normal of late. Marsh had been moving with caution since he left the hospital post-polio when he was six; caution reigned just a little stronger now until he could figure out what new ailed his limb.

Marsh pushed a stack of CDs to the side of his desk. He still wasn't quite used to what was on his desk these days. This was the new tack of Zippy's esteemed skipper, and Marsh was the man involuntarily implementing it—Jesus rock.

A smattering of rain splashed the wide warehouse window over Marsh's desk. He looked up briefly, considered the rain, then shuffled the paper and discs on his desk.

Zippy's boss and owner was a Deadhead lawyer named Calvin Begley. He'd gone deep South the year before, visiting distant family on his wife's side, and had stumbled on what he quickly became convinced would be the ticket to his fortune—bigger than Jim Nabors re-releases and vegan folksingers combined.

"Jesus rock?" Marsh had asked, eyebrows up. They'd been sitting right here at the desk, Calvin back from his family trip, breathless with discovery.

"I see an entire third division of Zippy within a year, Marsh," he'd said. "And it could be bigger than everything else we're doing." Arms spread in a white starched shirt, he looked evangelical himself, a rich, WASP, pseudo-Buddhist businessman delivering a new Gospel. Marsh opened his mouth but Calvin cut him off. "You should have seen it, Marshall.

A stadium. A fucking football stadium, SRO. The bands all hats pulled down over their eyes and Seattle-grunged like a bitch. Kids dancing and carrying on just like a regular show—except they're doing it all for Jesus. It's a goddamn money machine."

"You know, Calvin," Marsh had said, "in my little hometown in Ohio, folks generally didn't use words like 'fucking' and 'goddamn' in the same sentence as a mention of the Savior. 'Money machine' you might hear from time to time with the name of the Lord, but usually not '*goddamn* money machine'."

Calvin slapped Marsh on the arm. "That's it, that's the thing. That's why I pay your salary, Marshall. Because what do I know."

So Zippy Records was now officially in the Jesus rock business. Calvin had flown back South and signed four bands in two days. They'd rushed the kids through the studio ("Not so easy to do," Calvin had confided in Marsh, "when they won't snort coke") and now it was Marsh's job to figure out how to sell the product.

Marsh picked up the phone, dialed James's number, changed his mind and quickly hung up. He picked up the receiver again and called Bruno. If you were close friends with Marsh you could expect at least one call a day. Young James and Old Bruno (as he frequently referred to them—Marsh and Bruno were in fact close in age) were not only Marsh's friends but also sometime co-workers (Marsh booked the music at a Hoboken club called Maxwell's and both James and Bruno tended bar there from time to time) and—if the new plan with Thatcher and Lou went forward—they were all about to be bandmates. This close of a connection upped contact to a possible three or four calls a day. James he'd already spoken to twice this morning, not counting the conversation in Carbone's Diner, so it was Bruno he called now.

"I've got a list of Christian stations, AM and FM, nationwide," Marsh explained. "But here's my question."

"Good morning, Marsh," Bruno said. "I'm fine, how about you?"

"I'm doing the Lord's work. And what I need to know is: can I sell Jesus rock to a straight rock station?"

Silence on the line, Bruno thinking a moment. "You mean in regular rotation with AC/DC and Blue Öyster Cult?"

"Bruno, Bruno, Bruno," Marsh sighed. "Not there, of course. Somewhere lighter. Listen-at-work. Adult contemp. You come out of local news, do an ad for Stinky's Shrimp Shack, hit the weather, then here's a nice Michael Bolton, here's a little slice of—I don't know, Marc Cohn. And then here's some great Jesus rock to round out the set."

"Isn't Marc Cohn Jewish?"

"Oh, for Christ's sake."

"Well, exactly."

"Okay, not Marc Cohn. Paula Abdul. She's upbeat. She's positive."

"So—the set is Michael Bolton, Paula Abdul, then Jesus rock?"

"Sure."

"I don't think anyone would notice."

"See, that's what I'm thinking."

"Is the stuff any good?"

Marsh shuffled through the stack of CDs on his desk. "Well, this one band's pretty good. Sort of. I mean, it's relative. Who are we comparing them to? Los Lobos? Then, no. No good. But Michael Bolton? Yeah," Marsh said, "they're alright. Better than Bolton."

"How bad is it? Really."

"Look," Marsh said. "I got to go. Can't talk to you all day. I've got a job. I'll see you at Maxwell's tonight."

And he hung up.

DULL RUBBER IN A STRONG WIND

You can't stay naked all day. Even guitar-slinging soon-to-be-ex-soldiers with time heavily on their side need to get it together at some point in the morning. Thatcher made it through most of *Oprah*, then crawled out of his sleeping bag, turned off the TV, and pulled on a pair of jeans. James's little apartment was very quiet. Thatcher went into the kitchen and grabbed a beer from the fridge, drank it while looking out the window at the wet street below. Feeling better, he retrieved the strings he'd bought that morning out of his coat, opened another beer, went searching for where he'd laid down his guitar case.

You could, Thatcher thought, learn a lot about someone by knowing what kind of strings they used. The kind of strings, how often they changed them, and how they changed them.

Six strings on an acoustic guitar. There are twelve-string guitars, of course, but that's a commitment Thatcher couldn't even contemplate. James had an old twelve string he'd bought the summer they were sixteen and way into David Crosby. They took it out for a spin every now and then. But really, a twelve string is an instrument for people with an extraordinary amount of time on their hands. And six strings manages everything most mortals need a guitar to do.

Originally, guitars were strung with gut, which led directly to modern nylon-string guitars. Nylon strings are no good for nobody. In his humblest of opinions, Thatcher held out that anything you could play on a guitar sounded better on anything other than nylon strings. Nylon strings sounded like dull rubber in a strong wind.

"There's a whole world of classical music played on nylon-string guitars," Marsh had said to Thatcher and James once, sitting over pints in Maxwell's. Night of the first time Thatcher met Marsh. "Consider that before being so dismissive."

"I don't want to know about that world," James said. "Do you?"

Marsh had considered, then said, "Not really."

If you have an acoustic guitar and a sense of pride you use phosphor-bronze strings; four steel strings wrapped in the phosphor bronze, two high strings of plain steel. Cats playing a lot of leads tend toward light strings. Most fingerpickers and folksingers tend toward medium gauge. Thatcher didn't know anyone who played on heavy strings. He also allowed, though, that he didn't know much.

James bought his strings in bulk, shipped from someplace in Canada. He needed to; he changed strings a couple times a week on his main guitar, changed them daily if he was gigging two or more days in a row. James could change six strings and tune perfectly in less than ten minutes, five if he'd slept well. Thatcher, on the other hand, needed half an hour, a couple of cigarettes, and a cup of coffee or a beer to change his strings. In the army he'd changed his strings once a month. If he was gigging he considered himself ahead of the game if he got them changed weekly.

In high school and right after, James and Thatcher had tried to start a band with another kid, a guy a year older named King Papas. King Papas was tall and Greek and got in people's faces about things. He played a big Taylor jumbo. He changed his strings daily.

"Yo, man," he'd say to Thatcher, "you got to take care of business more often. James changes his strings every day."

"James is a far better guitar player than me," Thatcher said. "Far better than you, too."

King Papas moved to Boston shortly after this conversation. Boston was where the new wooden music was really coming out, the avant-impressionist songwriters—the scene was exploding. Northampton, Portland, Burlington, and, more than anywhere, Cambridge, Somerville: the greater galaxy of Boston. King Papas had pretty much never liked too many people in the greater galaxy of New York anyway, hadn't liked *anyone* in Hoboken, and one day he packed his guitar case and moved to Boston.

"I'd rather eat shit," James had said.

Didn't matter to Thatcher; he was in the army at the time and wasn't going to Boston or Hoboken or anywhere for that matter except by deployment order. He filled his notebooks with lyrics, played an electric guitar with a pick-up band Saturday nights when he could at a bar in Virginia Beach and his acoustic guitar sometimes at a club in Annapolis, and stayed drunk most of the time.

But this is the real deal again, now, Thatcher thought. *Back in the swing, not hit or miss.*

Unlike both James and King Papas, Thatcher had only one acoustic guitar and one electric guitar and no desire for any other, in place of or even in addition to. His electric was a piece of shit, a Fender Mustang, but a good enough time. His acoustic guitar was his baby. It was his late father's, a black Gibson. He pulled it from the soft case, took it now into James's bedroom, sat on the bed, lit a cigarette. James would bitch about the smoke, but fuck him anyway. Getting all assed up about a piece of sausage and talking shit about being in love with Lou. Fuck him anyway.

Thatcher blew a mouthful of smoke into James's pillow. He felt bad about it right away and dropped the just-lit cigarette into a half-full beer bottle next to James's alarm clock.

Thatcher quick spun the tension off the strings then popped the pegs one at a time with a quarter. Pulled the strings, wiped the guitar down. Reached into the hole, unclipped the 9-volt that powered the pick-up. Your pick-up dies on you once at a gig, you don't again forget to change the battery on a regular basis. He lit another cigarette and began stringing the phosphor bronze.

As long as he didn't feel rushed, Thatcher liked changing strings, and wondered if that's why he was so slow at it. He enjoyed the ritual. He liked the tools needed (wire clippers, plastic spinner, pitch pipe); he also liked that, in the end, you didn't need any of the tools. He preferred to have them though; he wasn't much good at doing a first tune on new strings by ear. If nothing else, he needed the pitch pipe. Thatcher tensioned the low E string, puffed the note from the pipe, adjusted.

• • •

The black Gibson, his late father's guitar, had been a present to a man just younger than Thatcher was now, from either Grace Slick or Joni Mitchell; the story changed depending who you talked to. Thatcher preferred to think it was Joni Mitchell but figured the reality was closer to Grace Slick. If the story was even close to being true at all. He'd first heard the story reading a twenty-year-old copy of *Sing Out!* and even there the tale was third-hand. Thatcher thought it just as likely, if not more likely, that Randolph—the young man in question, Thatcher's father, supposedly—picked up the guitar in a pawn shop. He'd been a big fan of pawn shops, Randolph. Thatcher was in possession of a train watch Randolph bought at a pawn in Reno, and a black walking stick from a pawn in the Haight.

The watch, the walking stick, the guitar—along with a very small trust that Thatcher had cashed when he was eighteen to buy a Datsun he'd wrecked three weeks later—this was all he had of his father. Which was fine with Thatcher. Just fine. Randolph hadn't left behind anything of a family of origin; his parents and grandparents were all dead, he'd no siblings. Even Randolph's songs (and the profits from them) weren't his to leave behind. They were owned by a curly haired producer named Wilson who lived somewhere in west Jersey horse country. Randolph left behind a watch and a guitar. And the seed he'd planted in the womb of a momentarily star-struck college student named Mona Smith—lawyer, feminist, author, all these eventually, in a later life, but a giggling, stoned-to-bejesus freshman backstage volunteer who gave her virginity to the almost-famous long-haired balladeer in late 1969, a short three weeks before he drowned himself in a Berkshires lake.

Sperm, watch, stick, guitar; some legacy.

Well, Thatcher thought, you can't take it with you, right? Randolph hadn't lived long enough to make anything to take. All he took with him was the cinder block he'd tied to his ankle.

It was thought Randolph's second album would have been huge—the bare tapes Thatcher had acquired of some early sessions showed some promise of that, maybe—but the first album hadn't sold particularly well before his death. It was a crowded year, 1969. The irony was if he hadn't died no one might know who Randolph was at all. But he did die, perfectly timed between an obscure first and planned-for second album. And now you could find the one well-known tortured black and white picture of him on posters in better head shops nationwide, and hung on dorm-room walls in sensitive schools like Amherst and Mount Holyoke. And that one record, of course, selling just enough year after year to pay for the curly haired producer's home in Bedminster.

Randolph had been a young drunk—and an unpleasant, difficult drunk at that, it was said—but not a bad guy sober. It was Mona Smith's Bryn Mawr dorm room where the procreating was done—sober of alcohol but wrecked on black hash—and when they woke the next morning, both of them fairly blind with pain, Randolph hadn't bolted. He'd stayed a few hours, accepting cups of tea from the plug-in kettle. He left Mona his phone number and address and told her to stop by if she was ever in South Hadley, Massachusetts. He lived on a big farm there, he said, with some people he didn't know well but who seemed cool enough. Two weeks later Mona wrote him a letter with some news. A week after that, Randolph was dead. It was fairly obvious fairly quickly the two events had nothing to do with each other—that is, word of coming unplanned child on the one hand, a suicide on the other—but still, it freaked her out. How could it not. One week after his death the guitar, walking stick, and train watch showed up at Bryn Mawr. The attached note said simply:

Mona, Pass these on, in whatever way seems best. Sorry. —R.

"They were friends," Thatcher had explained to James when they were in junior high school. Thatcher hadn't told anyone else who his father was. James was perhaps his only friend who knew who Randolph was, anyway. Thatcher had explained the situation to James in the way Thatcher knew it: "They were friends, you know. He came through from time to time. Shit happened."

Thatcher's silence about Randolph was in fact born of Mona's lead. The bio on the cover of her first book—published when Thatcher was six—said nothing about being the mother of the son of a dead one-hit wonder. The cover bio was a long one, and would get longer with each subsequent book, but the paternity of her child was not a part of it. Thatcher grew up as the child of Mona, period.

．．．

From the kitchen, Thatcher could hear James's bird clock squawk out top of the hour. The clock was loud and annoying. They'd found it one morning sticking from the top of a trash can down Observer Highway. Thatcher had pulled the clock from the can, held it to his ear.

"Works," he'd said, and James put it in his knapsack and carried it home. Trash day was always a good day in Hoboken. This particular trash day had been about two years ago, not long after James had moved to town, Thatcher up from the army for a long weekend. It was the weekend Thatcher first met Marsh and Bruno, and the weekend he'd acquired his nickname.

"Folksinger, huh?" Bruno had said. They'd just toasted introductory pints, in the front room at Louise and Jerry's on Washington Street. "Joanie and Bobby and diamonds and rust, etcetera etcetera?"

"Fuck that," Thatcher had said, wrinkling his nose. "I go to the source." He'd reached down into his gig bag, pulled a yellow paperback held together with a rubber band. *Hard-Hitting Songs for Hard Hit People*, by Woody Guthrie and Pete Seeger. The book usually raised eyebrows. To their credit, Marsh and Bruno gave nary a blink.

"Woodrow Wilson Guthrie. Hometown of Okemah, Oklahoma," Marsh said, turning the paperback over in his large hands. "Just to the left of the middle of nowhere, Okemah. We passed through there once on our way to L.A.—maybe ten years ago?"

"That's about right," Bruno said. "Ten years." As with Dutch, Bruno and Marsh had also shared beer-hall stages and conversion vans.

Thatcher leaned forward. All he'd heard was they'd been to Okemah. "Shut up," he said.

"Really." Marsh nodded. "Three water towers in Okemah. Right in a row. Painted HOT, COLD, and HOME OF WOODY GUTHRIE."

"That's the place," Thatcher said.

Bruno sipped his beer, tilted it toward Thatcher. "So they're letting Communists in our noble U.S. Army now, are they?"

"Nobody knows what a Communist is anymore," Thatcher said. "Let alone knowing Woody and Pete."

"Damn shame," Marsh said. "On both counts, I think. Makes for a considerably more boring world." He ran his palm over his hair. "Woody was in the service, too, you know."

"Yep. Got torpedoed. Pulled out his guitar and kept playing. That's what it's all about, fellas. That's why I dig him."

Marsh nodded, raised his glass to Woody, drank, then said, "Course, maybe you dig him because it gives you license to misbehave."

Before Thatcher could reply he was called up on stage by James to sing one, and by the time he got back to the table the conversation had moved on. But from that point forward Marsh had introduced him around Hoboken as "Woody," secretly pleasing Thatcher to no end.

In James's bedroom, Thatcher twisted the peg on the high E, last string up. One thing he didn't know much about was where Randolph's taste had been, what had formed him. He played acoustic guitar, of course, springing up in that great singer-songwriter second-coming-of-folk-sort-of era with Joanie and Bobby and Stringbean Taylor and the Chapins and the like. But what Randolph had listened to as a kid, dug as a teenager— Thatcher had no idea. Where the guy took his cues, or why he'd even first picked up an ax. No idea. Who put it in his hands. No idea.

Which was okay with Thatcher. Meant he could own his own tastes.

Thatcher took his time changing the strings on the black Gibson, drank another beer, then pulled down the shades and took a nap.

Cold rain or no, it was marketing day at Sixth and Clinton. Mrs. Quatrone went to market same day every week every month every year since before her husband died and that was thirty years ago. That qualified as good routine.

The wire push basket she kept folded behind the refrigerator. Mrs. Quatrone pulled it out now, popped the basket into place, pulled it behind her down the long hall from kitchen to her front door. She bundled there, coat and scarf, plastic hair wrap and rubbers for the rain. A small lady, almost seventy-five years old. Dressed for market. She knocked once on the bedroom door next to the front door.

"Won't be an hour," she yelled.

"Love you, Ma." A man's voice, from behind the door. Her son. The painter. In a few weeks he'd be doing the shopping with her and then a few weeks later for her, as the cold settled colder, then ice caked the sidewalks. But she liked to do the shopping and preferred it alone and would hold out as long as possible. Same every year. Five, six years ago he might be out here already, all over her with *C'mon Ma, let me at least pull the basket, it's too cold for you,* but it wasn't too cold for her, not yet, and he was old enough now—forty-two, could you believe—to understand, give her space while there was still space to give. He was a good boy, he was. Her son. The painter.

Mrs. Quatrone opened her apartment door, pulled the basket out onto the landing, looked up and down. Quiet. A quiet day, in here. The air still and cool on the landing; musty, too, a little. Decades living in the same building, she didn't notice the cooking smells anymore, and the other smells of living. Those odors just didn't register anymore. But the must, when it came—the white tang of must she always smelled. Mrs. Quatrone wrinkled her nose. The apartment door closed behind her.

Mrs. Quatrone owned this building at Sixth and Clinton. Not many souls knew that. Not anymore. The boy, Philip DiGiovanni, for instance, the policeman who'd come when the nutter hung himself, the good boy who'd grown up here; he'd know, of course. He'd've known her husband from when he was a boy and the Quatrones had lived in the super's apartment down first floor, before she'd taken this nice one up here on the second. The boy Philip, he knew Mrs. Quatrone owned the building. But not many others. No one living in the building now, she thought.

"No one," she said. "Not one person."

The current super and his stupid son—they certainly didn't know. That guy was super number three since Mr. Quatrone had passed. It was kind of a game to her now, having less and less people know until finally no one knew including the guy who ran the building. She hadn't intended it, but once she realized had found the benefits. Her son thought it was funny; he never let the cat creep from bag. It was no one's business anyway, Mrs. Quatrone thought. And when tenants knew where the buck stopped, when they knew whom to complain to—Mary, Mother of God. The running around had been bad enough when Mr. Quatrone was just the paid super. When he'd bought the place—oh, my water pressure this and his noisy radio that and *there's a law, you know, there's a city ordnance about this very thing!* Too much. Now, the tenants called the super, the super yelled at his stupid son, the stupid son fixed the pipes. There was an agency collected rent and supered the super; they sent Mrs. Quatrone a check once a month. A good thing, all around. She was too old for late-night phone calls and her son did his best painting at night.

Her son, the painter. It pleased Mrs. Quatrone beyond measure to provide this life for him. How many could pursue their true talents? How many actually possessed any talents at all? Mrs. Quatrone thought not many. The world was lit dull with dim bulbs. But her boy—she didn't know where he got it. Not from her. Certainly not Mr. Quatrone, God rest his soul. But from wherever it came, he'd been smacked with it full on. A lightning bolt, Mrs. Quatrone thought. There was no one getting rich from the building at Sixth and Clinton, but Mrs. Quatrone wanted for nothing and her son could paint all his days.

WHAT'S A GORUS?

Napped, showered, and clean of tooth, Thatcher dug in his duffle for the collar shirt he'd brought. He shook it out, tried to smooth the larger wrinkles with his palm. From the dark cave of James's room he pulled a tie and set to knotting it. James's digital clock said almost three; the job interview was at three thirty. He'd have to hurry. Out in the kitchen James's roommate Russell Davitz was just home, drinking from a carton of orange juice. Thatcher stepped into the kitchen and Russell eyeballed the tie.

"Sharp, man," Russell Davitz said, wiping his mouth.

"Yeah?"

"Oh, yeah."

Russell Davitz was a sharp dresser. He had one drawer with nothing but socks and another with nothing but socks still in the wrapper. Twenty or more pair in each drawer. Thatcher had never seen anything like it. Russell Davitz worked for a ticket wholesaler, the main reason James picked him from the fifty-some applicants who'd answered the roommate ad he'd placed after the last roommate moved out. Turned out Russell wasn't quite senior enough yet to score really good freebies—the Dead, perhaps, or maybe a Knicks game—but twice he'd paved the way for a free trip to the Monster Truck Rally. Last time Thatcher came north from the army Russell Davitz had treated him and James to a pair of nosebleeds at the Garden for "Disney on Ice." He'd thrown in a small baggie of mushrooms for palatability expansion.

Thatcher touched the tie knot with his fingers. "I'm wondering do I need a jacket?"

"Like a sports coat?"

"Yeah."

Russell Davitz thought about it. His cheeks moved as he thought, first one up then down, then the other. Finally he said, "Wait a minute," and went back to his room. Thatcher dug through the freezer, looking for coffee then making a pot. Russell Davitz came back with a black sports coat. "Try this on, sharp guy."

Thatcher pulled the jacket on. The sleeves hung inches past his fingers, the shoulders hanging off the sides. Russell Davitz made his cheeks move again. "Okay, no," he said. "Never mind. You don't need it. You look sharp—a major dude. Russell the Love Muscle says so."

"Well, okay."

"A major dude, trust me."

Thatcher poured a cup of coffee and stepped into the bathroom, checking the mirror. Not quite convinced of major dude. He thought he looked like a convenience-store night manager. Not much he could do about it now. The only decent thing he owned was his dress uniform and he wasn't going to a job interview in uniform. Thatcher drained his coffee, brushed his teeth again, went to find his coat.

Outside, the rain wasn't so much falling now as hanging in the air, suspended in a cloud of chill mist, sprayed from tires of passing cars, dripping from power lines. Cold enough to show breath. Thatcher walked with hands down deep in coat pockets. He was going far west and north, a part of Hoboken he didn't know. The signs in store windows went from Italian to Spanish as he walked. He hummed under his breath, "*Goodbye to my Juan, goodbye Rosalita—Adios mis amigos, Jesus y Maria....*"

The building was where the address said it should be, on a corner just a block from the city limit and freight-rail tracks. It looked like an old hospital but smaller. Two workmen had a ladder up on the long plain front of the place, and from across the street Thatcher could see they were replacing the name. The letters were metal; glued or cemented or something to the wall. The two men were almost done. So far, the shiny new letters read:

BEGINNINGS BEHAVIORAL HEA

The former name had been much longer. The shadow of the old letters lay across the wall clear as day. Not too attractive, Thatcher thought. They should've covered that. The old name was the one Thatcher had been looking for, from the ad he'd found in the veterans' job newsletter:

MID-HUDSON COMMUNITY MENTAL HEALTH CENTER

Beneath the new and old names was a double black gate through the brick wall. Thatcher crossed the street.

The gate led not directly into the building but a small garden, a walled outdoor entrance courtyard with three trees and some benches. Ten or so people milled around, smoking. None of them sat on the benches, wet from the rain. They all seemed to be doing a good job of not looking at one another. Thatcher checked his watch; he was five minutes early. He lit a cigarette and joined the group's mutual isolation project, staring at the tree in front of him.

Halfway through his smoke the small courtyard cleared. By some hidden signal he hadn't caught, they all stubbed their cigarettes and walked into the building. Thatcher followed with his eyes; men and women, but only two or three women. The way they'd been deep in their aloneness out here Thatcher had assumed they had no connection, but the group movement to the doors was too much for coincidence. The last one in line, a middle-aged man with a tan barn coat and brown slacks, went through the door.

As the door closed Thatcher saw there was one more person out here, who hadn't gone in. He was sitting on a bench by the door, the only bench situated close enough to the building to avoid the wet. He didn't so much sit on the bench as own it, square in the middle, ballooned in thick gray sweats and worn black high tops on his feet. He sat with one hand resting on a knee, the other holding a cigarette. Hair wispy thin and eyes pinched deep in the splotchy red dumpling of his face, he looked right at Thatcher.

"Drugs," the man said suddenly.

Thatcher wasn't sure who he was talking to. "How's that?"

"*Druuuugs*," he said, and hooked a thumb over his shoulder, pointing into the building. "All them. On the jobs program."

"Is that right." Thatcher looked away, smoked his cigarette.

"Come here," the guy said, and beckoned. "I don't want to shout."

Thatcher blinked, unsure, then walked over. The fellow patted the bench next to him, offering a seat. Thatcher waited for the guy to move over but he just looked up and patted again. Not wanting to seem rude, Thatcher sat down. He had a hard time saying no, Thatcher did. It created problems in his life. He wished he could say no now, but couldn't. There was barely room to sit, pressed against the gray sweatsuit and an odor of flesh and onions. "It's dry," the man said, and Thatcher saw then that only one of his eyes was glued in right. The other eye flew up sideways and didn't seem to be connected to anything it was looking at.

"Blind over there," the man said, catching Thatcher's gaze and waving his free hand in the direction of his head. "Other one still works." He blinked, good eye and bad. "Diabetes," he said. "Blew it out."

Thatcher didn't know what to say but nodded.

The man took a deep drag off his cigarette then hooked his thumb again behind him, where the smokers had walked in the building. "They all had to do the pee-pees and it didn't work out."

"I'm sorry?"

"You know, the pee test. They all failed their first test and got to come here once a week for group."

"They all work here?"

"No, no. They had to do the pee test wherever they work, and got sent here when they got caught. For group."

"Oh." Thatched nodded.

"They all come out together during break to smoke." The man made a show of flicking ash off his cigarette. "They're kind of funny. Keep to themselves."

"Well, I guess—"

"They have to stick with it six months, coming here for group. They get to keep their job, then."

"Well. That's good."

"Yeah, that's good. My name's Orris."

"Orris?"

"That's right. Like Horace, but not." He stuck out his hand.

"Hi there, Orris. I'm Thatcher." Thatcher shook. Orris's hand was like a moist meat coffin.

"Hi Thatcher. I don't know no one named Thatcher. Kids call you Scratcher in grade school?"

"Yes."

"That's too bad. They called me Gorus."

"What's a Gorus?"

Orris shrugged. "I don't know. That's what they called me."

Thatcher checked his watch, stood up.

"I have to go. Nice meeting you."

"They'll treat you good in there, Thatcher," Orris said. "It's a good place. Good people, mostly."

"I'm here about a job."

"You failed the pee test?"

"No, a job working here. I'm applying for a job."

Orris narrowed his good eye. The dead one twitched up and down. "Yeah?" he said.

"Clerk—records clerk."

"Oh. Alright then. Good luck, Thatcher."

"Good luck to you, too, Orris."

"Okay."

• • •

The associate director's name was Herman Jeffries, call me Herm, newly minted MBA from Trenton State hung on the wall. Soft of build and puffy from Cheetos and the lazy roundness of recent double fatherhood. His tie was black with a picture of Bugs Bunny. He told Thatcher he was thirty, though it hadn't been asked. Herm's thin, neat hair wasn't so much blond as absent of color. He sipped from a can of Diet Coke while they talked, and when it was finished he gave it a slight crush then stacked it on a small pyramid of empty cans at the side of his desk. Later in the interview he reached into a desk drawer and pulled out a fresh, warm can. The soda fizzled on his fingers when he popped the can, and he jammed the better part of his hand into his mouth to lick it off. It looked to Thatcher like he was reaching for something in there.

"We're a traditional, hospital-based community mental health center, Thatcher," Herm said, wiping fingers on his pants leg. "A few blocks removed from the main medical hospital." He waved vaguely toward the window set high on the wall. The office was very small and Thatcher suspected—correctly, as it turned out—the office had been a janitor's closet not long before. "We're independent now, though. Growing, growing."

Thatcher asked about the workmen outside and the name change.

"That's part of it. A new beginning for us, and it's reflected right there in our name." He drummed his fingertips on the desk. "It's cleaner, too, don't you think? The name?"

It was cleaner, no arguing.

"That whole, 'mental health' thing," Herm said, painting quotes in the air with his fingers. "Carries bad images."

"You're still a mental-health center, though?"

Herm nodded his head, just once, grudgingly. He leaned forward and explained in a patient, teaching manner: "It's a paradigm shift across the industry, Thatcher. 'Mental health' is so"—he bugged his eyes and clawed his hands—"crazy sounding. 'Behavioral health' is much more reflective of the cross-spectrum of positive therapies offered here."

" 'Behavioral' sounds a little Orwellian to me." Thatcher said then laughed because he thought he was down with Herm. But Herm didn't crack a smile.

"I'm not sure I understand what you mean, Thatcher."

Thatcher stared, blank, caught. He opened his mouth but didn't know what to say. Herm didn't drag it out, though. "Let's talk about your qualifications."

Thatcher had no qualifications; none relevant to the job, anyway.

Still, Herm hired him on the spot because Thatcher was a veteran and they needed at least one of those on payroll to qualify for continued state funding. Their previous veteran, a fifty-four-year-old black maintenance worker who'd lost a foot to a Vietnamese toe popper in 1968, had died in his sleep of heart failure two months before.

"In his sleep," Herm said. "Just didn't wake up the next morning."

"We should all be so lucky," Thatcher said.

Herm gazed somewhere over Thatcher's shoulder and drained his warm Diet Coke.

TIME TO PLAY B SIDES

If the day's weather was a customer at Carbone's Diner, Miguel would have labeled it a game player. Holding steady with the cold, that was no problem, but drizzle this and shower that and drip drip here then icy fog there—*what, are we playing games?* At four o'clock the games stopped and the gray sky let loose, a punishing torrent that forced pedestrians off the sidewalk and, for a few moments, cars to the side of the street. In the associate director's former-closet of an office, Herm Jeffries glanced up at the little window as the rain hit hard enough to cause him to wonder if the window would hold. Out in the courtyard Orris had a premonition. He was always good with stuff like this, weather and the mood of women and other shifting natural forces. Nothing with his joints or knees like he heard some people say. He just knew. Cigarette halfway to his mouth he paused, raised his round head up on its thick neck, squinted his good eye while the other eye wobbled. He ditched his smoke almost before he knew what he was doing, heaved himself off the bench, making the door with the first smack of rain. "Yeah, yeah, yeah," he mumbled. Orris watched out the window forlorn as the remains of his cigarette died wet. Prices were a mile high these days—what a waste.

Across Hoboken, sitting at his desk beside the warehouse window, Marsh watched Manhattan disappear. The city was there, sort of, across the river—roots of skyscrapers mostly visible most of the day. Then it was gone, poof, nothing to see two inches past his own window pane. Marsh was on the phone when it happened, on hold with a receptionist from a Christian contemporary radio station in Akron. Christian contemporary—CC they called it in the trade, so you might never know it had anything to do with Jesus. When the receptionist came back on the line Marsh said, "Holy moly, it just started raining here, Jayne."

"It's raining here, too, Marshall."

"No, I mean like *raining*," Marsh said. He was staring out the window, mesmerized. Then remembered he was on the phone and she was waiting for him to speak. "I'm from Ohio, you know," he said. "Originally."

"I remember that," she said.

"You do? That's so sweet of you to remember."

"Listen, Marshall, if you're looking for Mr. Mailer, he's—"

"I am."

"He's not in."

"He's never in when I call."

"Well—"

"Never you mind, Jayne. I think I'll watch the rain."

"Alright, Marshall."

The phone clicked off in Marsh's ear. He replaced the handle in the cradle and looked out the window for a long while, trying to remember the bridge to Harry Nilsson's song about rain in the city. It never came to him, but the rain finally let up and by then it was time to go home.

In Manhattan, James rode out the storm in his cube on the 108th floor, unaware he was riding out a storm. Miles from the nearest window, he had absolutely no idea it was raining.

On the west side of Hoboken, Thatcher slogged back to Clinton Street through the rain, soaked to the skin before he got a quarter block and he had eight blocks to go. The gutters backed up and overflowing, crossing every street was the fording of a cold New Jersey river. He considered at least he was wet and, in theory, employed. But it didn't help much. The rain stopped—suddenly, completely—at Sixth and Clinton, ten feet from the front door of James's building.

"What is this?" he mumbled into the upturned collar of his coat. "Some kind of a sick joke."

Thatcher was inside less than an hour, showered and changed and clean of tooth again. By the time he was back out the door with guitar gig bag over shoulder the skies were cold but clear, dim and chilly twilight, all the suits rushing home, Thatcher stepping through puddles on his way to the bus.

YOU PUT THE "HO" IN HOBOKEN

If commute you must—and eight million a day do—going home nights on the PATH train from World Trade Center to Hoboken isn't too brutal. Crowded, alright, this time of day. Packed so you can't move, sure. But that's New Jersey, it's all relative. There are longer commutes, deadlier rides home. NJ Transit to Trenton; Good God. Driving the GWB to Fort Lee and I-80 beyond; have mercy. The PATH; well, pay your buck, what the fuck. It's just under the river.

James doesn't even try to find a seat, this time of day. Slip in the door, sidle over, grab the overhead rail. It's all slamming elbows and assholes, but less than fifteen minutes onboard, who cares. Don't breathe too hard and steer clear the sneezers. Actual illness leads to a waste of valuable sick time, sweet precious sick time, and you can get sick on the PATH this time of year, you bet you can. Hold your breath, hold the rail, and hang on those fifteen minutes.

The PATH, she rolls back and forth, back and forth, picking up that dark and weightless underground speed, steadying out faster she goes.

PATH doesn't rattle like the NYC subway, she rolls. Her cars are cleaner, too. That's something, anyway.

"*Ho*boken, laststopHoboken." Then again as she pulls into the old blue-tile underground station: "*Ho*bokenstation, laststop—leddemoff first, leddemoff first—Ho*bo*ken."

Crowded, the evening rush-hour commute. Packed. But later nights—that's a better story: the late-night station, waiting in a silent hollow echo and drip drip dripping from the tunnel cave beyond the platform; ten minutes, twenty minutes, lean back in the shadows and wait.

The night train comes with a wait, but late nights the PATH is a shiny railed limo in and out of Manhattan. Empty and spacious, your smooth, cheap cruise below the Hudson. Couples coupling sometimes in the front car or back, deep kisses, hiked skirts, furtive glances. Never a cop on the PATH, so it's just whether you care what a fellow rider sees or hears.

"I got laid on the PATH last night," James said to Thatcher on the phone once, calling down to Virginia.

"Laid?"

"Well. Close to it."

"You put the 'ho' in Hoboken, James."

A pause across the phone line, then, "I think that's the sweetest thing anyone's ever said to me."

But not evening rush hour, no. Not the commute. In the commute, we're all fish in the stream. Pushing and rubbing and pressing in all the wrong ways.

"Leddemoff first, leddemoff first—*Ho*bokenstationlaststop."

From the inside out, then. Released from the open doors of the PATH and packed up the stairs to the street. James follows slow, hands in overcoat pockets and head up. James allows the world to flow around him. He watched his father tackle life like this, and it looked comfortable, looked like it might fit. A smooth stone in a rushing eddy, all that torrent racing by. James slides, unaffected. Sliding by, taking her slow and rising up into Hoboken.

• • •

Hungry, James thinks. *Could be hungry.* There's a cart at the top of the stairs and James hands over a folded dollar for a dirty-water dog with kraut. That's a one-buck, four-bite snack that'll carry you two hours if you need it. James needs it; if he eats an organized dinner at all it's never before ten. He rubs his fingertips to check for stray kraut in the beard he's been cultivating, then turns for home. It's full night, dark streetlight orange on the rain-beaded backs of dispersing commuters. James walks home slow, diagonal. Second and Washington. Fourth and Bloomfield. Fifth and Willow. Sixth and Clinton. The big old building on the corner. Lobby key out, James turns the lock, holds the door open for a guy from the fifth floor.

"Howyousedoin."

The guy barrels past James then down the block. They'd had a beer together on the roof one night, maybe a year ago; just happened to be up there at the same time. The man owns a cell-phone kiosk in a mall, Short Hills or Far Hills. One of those Jersey hills, who can keep them straight. *Pastures of plenty,* James thinks. *Cell phones, anyway. Like someone could actually afford one of those.*

James begins the long walk up the central stairs to the sixth floor. His perspective is a little different than Mrs. Quatrone's. No one ever moves in or out of this building, seems like to him; too damn hard to truck couches and sideboards up or down these stairs. Better to stick it out or just die; you'd have to have a damn good reason to move. James was here when the paramedics took poor, dead Larry Ritzi out on the stretcher. Those guys were sweating, by the time they got down. And it was Larry Ritzi himself who told James a story once how a guy checked out, up on the sixth floor same as James. He wasn't that old, but had some kind of thyroid thingy, couldn't keep the weight in line. Packed it on, well over four hundred pounds. Checked out one night, daughter found him next day, and they didn't even try carrying him down these stairs. "Tied him up," Larry said, "lowered him down the middle. Took nine cops and paramedics to hold the rope."

"How'd they get him over the banister?" James had asked.

"Cut the banister out of the way. Rolled him off the landing, fixed the banister."

And it could be true, James thought. He'd never seen signs of the banister having been cut, but hell it could be true. Life was funny. Death was too, sometimes.

Larry Ritzi was dead now, poor Larry. Hefted down the stairs and out of their lives.

"Hello, James," a voice from the second-floor landing. Quatrone come out for air, tall and wide in paint-smeared carpenter pants and no shirt on. The chest of a Roman wrestler, he's a rug of thick, curly black hair, chest and back and arms, thick black mustache, round head trimmed tight and balding forehead gleaming. "That's some suit for a rock star," Quatrone says. "How about a beer, rock star?"

"I'd love a beer."

"C'mon, then." Quatrone turns toward his open apartment door. "You hungry?"

The door opens to a long, dark hall, quick whiff of garlic and olive oil from Mother Quatrone's kitchen at the end of the hall, then gone as Quatrone stepped into the front bedroom he used as a studio. He closed the door behind them. The faintest whiff of garlic in here, but mostly paint and thinner. Quatrone reached into a deep metal pail on the floor and pulled two green bottles of Peroni from ice, twisting the caps and handing one over.

"Salud." They swigged deep. *This beer,* James thought, *is the best thing that's happened to me today.*

Quatrone belched, wiped a hand across his hairy chest. He painted topless for a reason. It was hot as balls in the little room, radiator in the corner banging and clanking, heat rolling in waves off the metal. No one else in the building got heat like this. It was annoying to be in it, but up in the cold of his sixth-floor bedroom James sometimes fantasized about Quatrone's studio radiator. It was, James knew, because of Mrs. Quatrone, Quatrone's Mama. She might as well have owned the building. Loopy Lenora had told James that Mrs. Quatrone had been in the building longer than the super, been in Hoboken longer than most had been alive, a retired schoolteacher who counted the current mayor among her former students. She liked it hot and you didn't argue with her. Quatrone's father—Mr. Quatrone—was dead since he was ten; Quatrone had painted in this heat forty-some years and thrived on it. The man was dripping sweat, and James tried to keep a distance. He had to lose the overcoat, though, and did, folding then dropping it in a corner, pulling his tie free and shoving it in his pants pocket. They both swigged again, emptying their bottles. Quatrone pulled replacements, popped the caps.

"What do you think?" he said, then belched again.

The canvas was small, and James leaned in toward the easel for a look. Quatrone was in a naked period, had been almost a year now. Fat, pleasant, human-looking things with cone breasts or flagpole johnsons jutting at ninety-degree angles. They had no faces but the men were all hairy thick and bore a certain resemblance to the artist. This canvas on the easel was man and woman, paw in paw, riverside it seemed.

James took a swallow of beer, contemplated the painting. Shifted his head around for new perspectives. He didn't rush to answer. "I like the fish," he finally said. There were hints of purple in the river water behind the couple. James had learned Quatrone liked you to look for what he wanted you to see.

"Beautiful," Quatrone said, pleased. "The fish. They seem right, don't they?"

James didn't know but didn't say so. It all seemed alright to him.

• • •

James was genetically as Italian as Quatrone—Naples vs. Florence, but who's counting. Not Hoboken-Italian but Brooklyn-Italian, though, James's family; Bay Ridge. His parents had been thick in the outward migration of the sixties and seventies—places like Brooklyn and Hoboken are for immigrants, and the grown children like to put distance from that—and a suit and a tie on James's father had got the family away from Brooklyn and immigrant grandparents and as far west as Gary Ridge, New Jersey. Now the grandchildren had all gone back: James in Hoboken, his older brother in Astoria, little sister just graduated NJIT and now on the Lower East Side.

Funny old world, James thought. *Funny old circular place.*

James's father had helped him move into the apartment at Sixth and Clinton. Breathless at the top of the six-flight haul, the old man had rubbed his trim beard, looked around the landing, said, "I worked my whole life to keep you out of this."

Tonight the apartment was empty—Thatcher off to his gig, Russell Davitz out with the ladies (plural; Russell Davitz never stepped out with less than an entourage). James didn't turn the lights on, going in. He preferred dark. It was his place, he got around by touch as much as possible. Dark, quiet. Cold—especially compared to Quatrone's place—but cold was okay. He popped one shoe then the other, wingtips and oh Christ how they hurt his feet. But, you know, everyone's got to eat.

There were a lot of songwriters and guitar slingers—especially the ones who hung around with Geoff Mason across the Hudson in Greenwich Village—who didn't work or tried to work as little as possible or tried to pretend they didn't work. And that was okay, James thought. But not yet for him, maybe. Cautious, cautious. No one wants to land on their ass. (Thatcher seemed to land on his ass more frequently than James thought absolutely necessary, but it didn't seem intentional; not completely, anyway. Not usually.) James did some traveling with the guitar, more and more as time went by—up to Massachusetts, mostly, and a few clubs inbetween—but not enough yet to live on, not enough yet to justify a resignation. He didn't like his day job, who did, but—you know, cautious. If the job got in the way of music, he'd quit. That very moment. He was sure of it. Until then, James gave them his days and lived on the nights.

In the dark, halfway down the hall, he pulled his socks, pulled his belt, left where they fell. James wasn't particular about housekeeping. In the bedroom he wrinkled his nose—*fucker was smoking in here*, he thought. Most of their lives they'd known each other; James was pretty sure he was just as likely to die from Thatcher's cigarette habit as Thatcher was. In general the smoke didn't bother him. But in the bedroom? Man. Cold, son. James reached for the light switch, hovered, then changed his mind and kept it off. He crossed the room and wrapped his hands around the smooth wood of his Ibanez.

There were four guitars currently in the collection. One of them, a sweet Alvarez with rose inlays on the fret board, was a recent purchase. Still, James tended to reach for the Ibanez. He didn't name his guitars or any stupid shit like that, but still. Of the beautiful things a guy can wrap his hands around in his life, there are only one or two that imprint on your mind and if you're lucky enough to keep your touch on it, you do. The Alvarez was not just good looking, it was a better guitar. Indeed, from the day he'd brought her home James had made the Alvarez his gig guitar. But on his own, especially in the dark—he just liked the way the Ibanez felt under his palms and fingertips.

He sat down on the edge of his bed, guitar in lap, thought about it a minute then stood again and put the strap over his neck and shoulder. He could see a little bit now, his eyes adjusting, pulling dim scraps of street-light from behind shaded window. He could see his shadow in the mirror. He strummed once, to see where he'd left the tuning. CGDGBD. Good shit. He cracked his knuckles, took a breath. The strings were cool under his fingertips. "Eleven Little Roaches," baby. Let's go.

James's father and mother took no end of delight in their son's talent, close to retirement now both of them and only too happy to drive ridiculous distances to make every gig that it wouldn't be embarrassing for them to be seen at. James's father liked to sit up close to the stage and watch his son's fingers move across the fret board. It was like a dance, and so very foreign. No one in the family knew where James got it from. There were no musicians they knew of in the blood, no known organic or even environmental influences.

"It's easy to see with you," James said to Thatcher once, not terribly long ago, somewhere dark over pints. "You're genetically predisposed to be musical."

Thatcher had waved a hand, dismissing the comment. "Have you ever really looked at me?"

"What do you mean?"

"I don't look a thing like Randolph."

"That doesn't mean anything. You're clearly his—you inherited the talent."

"I don't know, James. I'm a passable guitar player. I can't sing harmony for shit."

That was true, James had to agree—the boy was irritatingly incapable of harmonies. "But," he said, "you're fine singing melody, and you can write."

"Go take another listen to Randolph's first album, James. I'm not so sure my writing came to me from that side of the supposed, possible, theoretical family tree."

"Whatever." James had thought about it all for a minute, then said, "It's just funny in my family. You go back even a few generations, you can't find any musicians."

"Three generations ago your family was picking olives—how are you to know one of them didn't pluck a little mandolin from time to time?"

"Yeah, I'd like to think so, anyway."

Thatcher had scratched his nearly shaved-bald head then and said, "You ever think about what people don't know, though? I mean about their born-with talents?"

"You lost me, son."

"Well, like how is it someone finds out? You, for instance. You had no one in the family, so it didn't come to you by watching someone play. But I could take a pen and draw a map of James, showing, okay: 'here are the Beatles and I like them' and then 'here's an old guitar and let's see if I can make a sound with it' and then okay 'that sounded pretty good maybe I'll take a lesson.'"

"Your point here is eluding—"

"My point is what if you hadn't had that path? What if it just hadn't happened that way? You grew up in say Mongolia, and there was no Beatles and no old guitar."

"What then?"

"Exactly. That's my point. What then? Because you're the same guy. Born with the same equipment. So there you are, shoveling camel shit out on the Mongolian steppe, a master acoustic guitar picker who has absolutely no idea he's a master acoustic guitar picker."

"Damn."

"Yeah. I mean, check it out—Richard Starkey is a young lad in Liverpool, never gets sick, though, never spends a year in the hospital or home or whatever, never gets bored because he's sick so never has reason to look for ways to pass the time so never picks up a pair of drumsticks."

"No Ringo Starr."

"Right. Or, no—of course he *is* Ringo Starr, he just doesn't know it. He's got the solidest backbeat in all of northern England but has absolutely no idea. Becomes a barber, leads a happy but uneventful life, retires on the Isle of Wight, all the time with no idea what he's capable of."

"Maybe there's one of those in my family."

"And that's my point. Happy Giuseppe out in the olive field—he thinks he's an olive picker. Turns out he's one of the best guitar players the world has ever known, but he doesn't know and never touches a guitar once his entire life. The son of his son moves to America, and then the son of his son is—"

"Me."

"You."

"Sweet."

"See, that's a better story than possibly, maybe, rumored-to-be-the-son-of-a-dead-balladeer-and-his-one-time-feminist-lover, isn't it?"

James had ruminated on that a second, then was forced to admit Thatcher was right: Giuseppe the olive picker was the better story.

And here tonight in the dark bedroom, James had three hours before he'd have to head out to Maxwell's for dinner and then the first rehearsal with this band they were trying to put together. Three hours. A beautiful thing. "Eleven Little Roaches" done, he reached out to the end of the neck and began twisting the tuning pegs, CGDGBD to DADF#AD, on to "Suite: Judy Blue Eyes."

There was a rattling of wind outside the window, the shade shaking with the force of it through the thin glass. In the dark, eyes closed, James didn't see it and he certainly couldn't hear it. The rain had started again, but just like in his cubicle buried high and deep in the World Trade Center, James had no idea. He had three hours he could keep the Ibanez between himself and the world.

OUR TALENT, OR THE BLUES IN G#

The NJ Transit commuter bus cleared Hoboken from the northwest, not far from Beginnings Behavioral Health. Slow negotiation through a crowded Weehawken neighborhood, up the Turnpike, then off into sub-urbia. The towns laid out in circles of collars up here: dark blue, light blue, then white collar. The farther the whiter. Short-sleeve accountant's white off the Turnpike, starched button-down attorney white rising from the sprawl into the Jersey hills. The bus route skirted a corner of Gary Ridge, starched-white childhood home of Thatcher and James. The next town was Elmswood. The Elmswood bus stop was a deli in a strip mall. Thatch-er watched through the steamed window of the deli as the bus pulled away, ordered a coffee at the cramped counter, then used the payphone in the corner to call the number he'd been given. The woman who answered said someone would be by shortly. Thatcher hoped so, he was hungry. He wandered back toward the counter to ask for another packet of sugar and caught the skinny kid there with third finger planted squarely up left nos-tril. The kid looked at Thatcher, gave a hard push on the digit, then turned and ambled to the other end of the counter, wiping finger across apron. Thatcher figured maybe he didn't need that sugar, anyway.

The gig was a big one, a good one—monthly concert series held in Elmwood's plush community center. Thatcher was the opening act, a thirty-minute slot that paid well because the series had a grant from the county arts council. The fact this suburban bedroom had an arts council with grants to give said a lot to Thatcher right there. Thatcher thought his mother sat on the arts council's board of directors, but wasn't quite sure. He also thought she almost certainly didn't know he was playing here tonight, but wasn't quite sure about that either. Thatcher hadn't seen his mother in six months, maybe.

The headliner for this concert series always came from the same small spattering of older almost-rans—artists who'd managed to push, pull, or shove one song up the charts any number of years ago and still managed to sell one or three hundred seats a night on the strength of that, trimmed down to acoustic guitar because they couldn't afford a band, calling themselves folk now and sometimes even dressing in flannel and jeans to look the part.

Thatcher was opening for one of these tonight. A guy Thatcher thought of as The Talent. That name—The Talent—was what Nate Goldman called the guy. Nate was The Talent's manager. He called everyone on his roster The Talent or Our Talent. For Thatcher, somehow the name stuck particularly to this guy. The Talent had covered one of Randolph's songs in 1975, rising to a not-too-shabby Number Eight on the Billboard charts the week the American embassy in Saigon had been evacuated. Thatcher was five in 1975, too young to remember either event. He did remember singing a Paul Simon song that summer; up at Brown with his mother, the Rhode Island beaches all awash in "Slip Sliding Away." Little Thatcher thought it a funny song, and would try to make himself glide across the hard-packed surf-edge sand, singing out the chorus.

But Nate Goldman on the phone a few weeks ago: "Well, Thatchery, I was trying to tell these granola-crunchers that Our Talent personally wanted to see you opening the bill for him—but it's talking to a brick wall, these people. I got my way, but sweet Christ how these cocksuckers argue."

"Your Talent doesn't know who I am, does he?" Meaning Son-of-Randolph, which no one was supposed to know, and meaning Son-of-Mona, which it was possible to know.

"Of course not—what am I? But listen, you really need to start re-thinking that whole your-own-man thing—"

"Yes, you've said that before."

Nate grunted. Paused. Then, "You want the gig or no?"

"Of course I want the gig. Does it—"

"Fifty bucks and dinner."

Fifty bucks and dinner—pencils down. Thatcher had traveled three times as far for much less.

• • •

"We're all just *so* excited for the show tonight."

The woman wore a Blue Fish dress under an unzipped red parka. The gray in her hair was dyed, badly, something Thatcher never would have noticed—either the dye or the quality of the job—except Jo had pointed out two examples of the same as they walked down Washington Street the previous day. The woman's car was a Volvo and smelled like cats.

"Very exciting," Thatcher said.

There were times, he knew, it was in his own best interest to make polite conversation. The army had made him very out of practice. And he questioned whether one gig in Elmswood, New Jersey justified a retooling of his social graces.

"Mister Goldman was very enthusiastic about you," she said.

She said "Mister Goldman" the way a nun might mouth "Mother Mary."

"That's very nice of him."

"The show has been sold out for weeks, of course."

The woman shifted down into second to make a turn, grinding gears obliviously.

The woman giggled then said, "I just can't believe He's coming tonight. There's just something about Him that makes people love Him so."

The Talent. Thatcher wondered if this woman was aware she was referring to a singer in a Biblical manner.

"He's a great one, for sure," Thatcher said. Making conversation now; good, good. "Have you ever seen him play before?"

"No!" she exclaimed, whipping her head wide-eyed toward Thatcher in a way that made him distinctly uncomfortable. "Can you believe it? Never." She put her eyes back to the road. "I actually had tickets once to see Him, in 1976, but I was pregnant with my son and we couldn't make the concert. I was *so* upset."

"I bet."

She mentioned the song, then. The Number Eight. Randolph himself had only managed to get one of his songs to Number Fifteen (pre-suicide, anyway; two in a row went to Number Four and Six, respectively, in the six weeks following his death). The Talent, though. Well, he'd had better luck with Randolph than Randolph had.

The woman was still talking. "—and then He fell off the face of the earth. I'm *so* happy He's touring again." She glowed.

He didn't fall off the face of the earth, Thatcher thought. *His label dropped him.*

This immediately followed by, *Don't be an asshole, Thatcher.*

"It must be so *exciting* for you to have the backing of someone like Mister Goldman. Like I said, we on the committee had never really heard of you, but he was just *so* enthusiastic, we could hardly say no."

"Oh, and I sure do appreciate that, ma'am," Thatcher said, digging in his pocket for his cigarettes, then pushing them right back down again. "I really do appreciate it. And hey, is it true there'll be a little bit of dinner before the show?"

"Yes! We always have a little dinner for the concert volunteers right after the sound check. It's so nice, giving them the opportunity to sit down with an artist. No one on the staff gets paid, of course, so it really is wonderful to give them this opportunity. When else do you get a chance to pick the brains of such a talented songwriter?"

She downshifted again, noisily, and pulled into the church parking lot.

"Oh, and you're invited to eat too, of course," she added quickly. "And—I'm so sorry—what's your name again?"

Thatcher smiled.

• • •

The Talent had still not entered the building after Thatcher sound-checked, and the sound man was nervous. His name was Otto, and he asked Thatcher if he'd mind checking levels for The Talent's mike. A Dorkestra T-shirt stretched over Otto's belly, and Thatcher liked him immediately. He liked anyone who made him sound as good as the sound he was hearing from the monitors. He moved over to the mike set up for The Talent and began singing into it, John Prine's "Paradise," a song the Dorkestra covered on their first album. Otto looked up and smiled as he twiddled with his knobs.

The concert volunteers gathered in the community-center basement for dinner, a tofu stir-fry, to the unhappy news that The Talent was running late and unfortunately wouldn't be able to join them for dinner. Thatcher thought this might bring the mood down, but in the absence of The Talent they were almost as happy to gush over Thatcher—something told him the main talent du jour rarely showed for dinner. Thatcher hadn't played for a paying, *listening* audience—as opposed to a drunken, nonlistening audience—in almost a year, maybe more, and had taken the opportunity of The Talent's absence to soundcheck for almost half an hour, unheard of for an opening act. Happy comments flowed down the dinner table toward him, from those who had been there during soundcheck.

"Thanks," Thatcher said, stuffing some tofu in his face. "I haven't played out in a while."

A tie-dyed old man next to him asked what he'd been up to.

Without missing a beat, Thatcher came back with, "In the studio, you know. Very busy with that. New album and all."

It's like riding a bike, he thought, smiling around his stir-fry. *Acting Like The Talent 101.*

The man had a bean sprout stuck in his beard. Thatcher wanted to reach over and pull it out.

• • •

It was terrible.

There were close to three hundred people crowded into the community center's hall, all there to sit through The Talent's set so they could hear two songs—one of them the Number Eight from 1975, penned by Randolph in 1967. Thatcher was a late addition to the bill, his presence hadn't been warned on any of the posters, and when he took the stage he walked into a wash of polite but restrained, bored applause. He slung guitar over neck and shoulder, approached the microphone, smiling at the crowd, squinting into the bright lights. He couldn't see past the third row and decided this was a blessing—the first row was a line of women who could be twins to the volunteer who had driven him here tonight. They stared like zombies, and his smile grew so wide he thought his face might break.

He strummed down once on the strings. Changing strings and meticulous tuning for naught—they were incredibly, horribly, out of tune.

Sweet bleeding Christ.

His smile reached the tips of his ears now, and as his left hand made for the tuning pegs he leaned into the microphone and said, "Hi." It echoed around the room like a lonely bomb. No response. Nervous twitter of feet, a crying baby from the back of the room, a muffled cough from near the front of the house.

He tried talking while he tuned—*hey, friends, my name is Thatcher, I'm with you tonight to start the show…*

No response; uneasy smiles from the first-row line of death.

I got a couple old songs you might know, couple things I wrote—about what I've been seeing in the world.

Thatcher's words bounced back at him off the walls in a flat echo of indifference. The strings refused to cooperate.

What's going on here, folks, is I'm practicing some of that ancient Chinese art of Tu Ning.

A thunderously silent absence of laughter.

Yeah.

Close enough for folk music. Thatcher started playing, simple country blues in E (on capo four, which in fact made it blues in G#, one of the lesser-used blues platforms)—a little adapted scrap of Woody to start things off, he almost always started a gig with this thing, earning his Hoboken nickname.

Ain't no one here can sing like me, way over yonder in the minor key.

Couldn't be easier.

Way over yonder in the minor key, ain't no one here can sing like me.

Couldn't sound worse.

Thirty minutes crawled by in thirty hours, nerves feeding into mistakes that fed into more nerves that fed into a sudden and overwhelming loathing of everyone and everything in this room—certainly, he was sure, they must loathe him. Who wouldn't? When he was done with his last song, he turned from the microphone without a word, unplugged his guitar, made for the stage door. He saw the sound man, Otto, eyes down as Thatcher passed, fiddling knobs, trying hard to look at anything except Thatcher.

He walked alone into the center's empty office, the closest thing they had to a green room, put his Gibson in the case, zipped it, found his coat. The car ride from the deli, he remembered, had been five or six blocks, very walkable. If he hustled he could make the 8:55 bus back to Hoboken.

• • •

Our Talent was a tall man, almost six and a half feet, short blond hair, blue eyes, a swingin', easy gait—worked on diligently in front of his mirror so long ago that He had now, in His fiftieth year, forgotten it wasn't natural. He ambled onto the stage and toward the mike in two easy strides, waving His hand above His head at the audience as they rose to their feet cheering wildly, and yelled, "How y'all doing?"

And the New Jersey crowd yelled back that they were, as a matter of fact, doing just fine.

The Talent turned to take a shiny Martin from His road manager, slung the strap over His neck, gave two quick strums, and they were off.

• • •

Stepping through the back door, Thatcher heard The Talent's opening notes—Randolph's song. Thatcher stopped in his tracks, holding the heavy wooden door open with his shoulder.

That's mine, he thought. *Motherfucker.*

He listened, fingers tugging hard on his shoulder strap. He listened, and then he changed his mind.

No, it isn't, he thought. And walked out, door swinging shut behind him.

PUSSY DRINKS AND THE PRICE OF TEA IN CHINA

Hoboken's east side is loosely anchored by the PATH train running into Hoboken Station on the south and Maxwell's on the north with Washington Street spanning the eleven-block distance between. The PATH is the two-track Port Authority commuter subway. One track runs straight under the Hudson River to Christopher Street in Greenwich Village then up to Chelsea then midtown at 33rd Street. The other track goes down through Jersey City then across to the twin towers of the World Trade Center at the bottom of Manhattan.

Maxwell's is about as far from Hoboken Station as you can get on Washington Street, which helps keep the jackasses away. The bars on the south side of Washington Street—even the locals' bars—overflow with jackasses Friday and Saturday nights: Jersey kids who parked in Hoboken, downing the evening's first drink (or last) on the way into (or out of) Manhattan. And lately, with the new money in town, skipping New York altogether and sticking to Hoboken for the drinking.

Maxwell's is eleven blocks up, though; a solid fifteen-minute walk, a commitment most college drunks aren't willing to make when there are so many cheaper and louder bars right next to one another downtown. Occasionally a gaggle of jackasses will make it up to Maxwell's—lost, maybe looking for a frat house at Stevens College up the hill. Four or five guys and peroxide-blond girlfriends, all of whom would be named Lisa. They'd invariably try to order Jell-O shots or a round of sex-on-the-beach. If it was a music night and Marsh was hosting, he'd holler the order across the room: "Pussy drinks, we got any pussy drinks back there?" If James was bartending, or any of the musicians who made up the majority of Maxwell's revolving staff, an order like that drew a curt "Fuck you."

Locals who lived in the Maxwell's neighborhood—and it was a pricey neighborhood, these days—came during the week for the food, a pretty good bowl of soup, maybe mashed potatoes and whatever was grilling, pork chops or steaks or could be ribs in the summertime. And they came on music nights for Marsh—not Marsh's music, mind you (many regulars didn't even know Marsh played; contrarily, most musicians didn't know he worked for a record company), but Marsh's presence. If you could float on a blunt, round, crippled body, Marsh did it. On his good days, you only saw the limp if you made yourself watch. Alive in the moment he floated between tables, greeting by name and if he didn't know the name you became Charlie or Jack and that was good too. The wave *hi* that morphed right into the hand pushing the long hair behind his ear, laying his syllables out slow and happy as he talked, making a fool of himself in jokes as he gent, gent, gently poked at everyone around him. Maxwell's wasn't Marsh's bar (any more than Hoboken was Marsh's town or New Jersey was Marsh's state) but Marsh was Maxwell's (like Marsh was Hoboken's and Hoboken was decidedly New Jersey) in a way vital and unbreakable.

Those who walked to Maxwell's from Hoboken Station, or paid the cab fare, were music fans. The back room—a narrow, black box with a riser on one end and a capacity for about a hundred tightly squeezed, sweaty, standing audience members—was filled Thursdays, Fridays, and Saturdays. Tuesday nights Marsh ran an acoustic showcase in the front room. He called it Folk & Fondue although the fondue was a bad idea that hadn't lived past the first week he'd done it, some seven years before. The name stayed, though, because Marsh liked it.

The back room of Maxwell's was a niche room. That's how you get a hundred people to fill a room in a region where there's more live music in five square miles on any given night than on the rest of the East Coast combined. Maxwell's didn't book much in the way of metal—"Please God, no more," Marsh would say, heaving a bag of demos from Jersey hair bands into the dumpster—but they were a good room for reunited or reconfigured punk bands, British or otherwise. The new anti-folk groups coming out of the Bowery were starting to pack them in. Any singer-songwriter who got play on WFUV and no other station was always a sure bet, especially if their name was Ben or Julie. Rockabilly was good for a night or two a month. Ska was picking up, and the local Skanatra was filling every room in town including Maxwell's. And retro swing bands were surprisingly popular until they became too popular and started attracting people who ordered pussy drinks and then Marsh stopped booking them.

For bands at that certain spot on their way up or way down—or who lived in that spot perpetually—Maxwell's was a good room. Some of the bands on their first nights in, especially bands from the Midwest, were somewhat surprised when it came to their attention halfway through the night that not only were they not in New York City, they weren't even in New York State.

"New Jersey, huh?" more than one frontman has said, usually agreeably, into the Maxwell's microphone. "Well okay then. New Jersey."

• • •

On a bench outside the propped-open fire exit from Maxwell's back room a slim girl sat smoking a clove cigarette. It was almost 1 A.M., twenty minutes after the end of the show, the night dry and cold. The streetlight overhead made her face shine a little. She had a long, curved neck, a smiling face under a bob of brown hair. She dropped her cigarette and was crunching it under her hiking boot when she saw the figure turn the corner from Washington Street onto Eleventh Street and come down the sidewalk toward her, guitar case strapped across his back. She waved then, stood and hugged him.

"Hi, Lou," Thatcher said, surprised and pleased to find her arms around him. She smelled warm, like sandalwood. And the clove smoke. Lou pecked his cheek, then stood back.

"James said you had a gig tonight," she said. "That's a good one, too."

"Big room. Biggest I think I've ever played."

"Did you knock them dead?"

"I knocked them dead, alright," Thatcher said. "Dead bored. Dead tired. Dead on arrival."

"Aw, you were great. I'm sure."

"No, really. I wasn't."

"Oh, Thatcher," she said, putting a sympathetic arm around his shoulder. "Poor Thatcher."

"What can you do."

"Win some, lose some."

"Exactly."

"Well, this will be fun," she said, and led him to the door. "Take your mind off things."

In the back room the night's band had already broken down and loaded out, audience gone, floor littered with cigarette butts and empty plastic beer cups. Bruno and Marsh were up on the bare riser, pulling instruments guitars out of cases. An older, darker version of Lou sat dangling her feet off the riser, dressed all in black except for green Doc Martin boots. The same pretty face as Lou but rounder, the same short haircut. Lou's sister Mary Ann, she had hooked up with Marsh a few months before as a singing partner. They'd been trying out a duo—first at the Tuesday Folk & Fondue then a handful of trips across the river for unplugged nights at Cornelia Street and Postcrypt—and had so much fun Marsh decided maybe it would be even better as a band. That's where the conversations had started, anyway. Thatcher hadn't met Mary Ann yet—he'd only met Lou a few weeks ago, and then just once in the studio recording his demos, although they'd talked on the phone almost daily since. Mary Ann was leaning back on her fists, humming something.

James pushed through the double doors from the front room, two dark pints in his fists. He handed one to Lou, nodded at Thatcher.

"How was the gig, son?"

"Great." Thatcher pursed his lips. Then said it again, "Great."

"Good."

"Yeah. Good."

Mary Ann had stepped down from the riser. "You're Thatcher the soldier," she said, and stuck her hand out formally. He shook and she said, "Let's get beer," and pushed through the swinging door into the front room. Thatcher followed.

By the time first rounds were drunk and guitars tuned it was almost 1:30 A.M. They put themselves into a loose circle in the middle of the room, eyeing one another. Thatcher couldn't decide whether it reminded him of Old West gunslingers or lonely hearts at an eighth-grade dance. He put a cigarette to his lips, saw a sneer pass Bruno's face, and let the smoke hang unlit. Marsh coughed. He was the only one sitting, his eyes drooped half asleep. Marsh had a wife and a kid and a house and wasn't much for late nights anymore. He'd needed an arm-twisting to make it tonight, and this was his project.

James strummed an open chord. "You awake, son?"

They all laughed.

Bruno turned on his amp, plucked his bass on James's chord, then said, "Well, this is really something. What do we have here?"

"A rock and roll band, I guess," Lou said, and strummed a seventh over Bruno. "Right?"

"Some band."

Everyone laughed again. Bruno began running a scale. "What—we got, five, six frontmen in this band? We have bass"—he bent a note here—"but not a drummer? Six frontmen, no keys, no drummer. Some band."

"We'll find a drummer," James said.

"It's a *nouvelle* band," Marsh said. "A *nouveau* band."

"No, it's Fleetwood Mac."

Mary Ann yawned. "Are we going to play something or can I go home?"

Bruno raised his eyebrows and said, "See, it *is* Fleetwood Mac."

"Let's go," Marsh said, and he nodded at Thatcher, winked, and began playing. Thatcher found the chord and Marsh put his head back to sing—a good, rich, rock and roll voice from that big, broken body.

She's the kind of girl who always looks excellent
Holes in her jeans and a Cleveland accent

A fast song, it was the song that had led them all to be in the room tonight, trying to be a band, a song written months ago in the front room of Maxwell's: those first lines penned by Marsh on a napkin, shoved down the bar to Bruno, then picked up and carried on by James.

Perfect little teeth, she's a terrible dancer
Roll that top down, drive a little faster
Mean as a rumor, beautiful at breakfast,
and all she is now is gone.

"Perfect!" Bruno had yelled that night, shaking the napkin at James. "See, that's the way to do it! In and out, baby. First few lines, then right to the chorus, right to the hook."

"I know," James had said. "I'm the guy who just took it to the hook, remember?"

"That was an accident. Those songs you write, takes forever."

"Dude, I just wrote this. I took it to the hook."

"And it's perfect."

Next verse.

She looked good on my arm, better on another's
Walking away she reminds me of my mother

Thatcher pulled the biggest triangle pick he owned from his case and lost himself in the strum, smiling as they all sang.

Loves to make you sweat, loves to make you crawl
Telephone ringing right off the damn wall.
Could make a priest kick a hole in a stained-glass window
and all she is now is gone.

ALL THINGS BEING THE SAME

The idea was for James to take off work Friday, wake up at 5 A.M., throw Thatcher in the old Subaru and motor southbound on the NJ Turnpike by 6 A.M. Newport News, Virginia by lunch. The truth came closer to an 8 A.M. wakeup, 8:30 breakfast at Carbone's (*"I wouldn't know a game if you put it in front of me, Miguel—now howsabout that omelet?"*), and a 3 P.M. arrival at the Greyhound bus depot outside the gates of Fort Eustis. They switched drivers here, Thatcher easing behind the wheel and digging for his green ID card. At the far end of the depot lot four kids stood in jeans and light jackets, all with no hair, each of them standing behind a packed green duffel. James pushed his sunglasses down and eyeballed them, fingering his beard.

"They look nervous," he said.

"They are nervous. They should be nervous."

James took one of Thatcher's cigarettes from the pack on the dash and hung it unlit from his lips. Thatcher took a last look across the backseat for visible beer cans or other MP gate bombs then strapped his seatbelt on.

"They're just in from basic training, wherever they did it," Thatcher said. "Waiting for the van to come take them through the gate."

"Yikes."

"It's not so bad, really," Thatcher said, dropping the emergency brake. "Especially stationed here. Hard part's over for them, they just don't know it."

"The hard part is over? What if they get sent to war?"

"Yeah, well. There's that."

Past the gate, Thatcher drove south by the hospital and through the lower-enlisted family quarters—which, to James, resembled graffiti-less public-housing projects; which, Thatcher explained, they were—to a small, neat trailer park. Old Airstreams, new doublewides, brief and plastic picket fences around two of them.

"We're a long way from Hoboken, baby," James said. He slouched down lower in the passenger seat.

The trailer park was the only place on post with true integration of class: trailers were a good choice for career soldiers; relatively cheap to buy and the army would pay to move them when you transferred posts. But small posts like Fort Eustis only had one trailer park. So you had sergeants dwelling next to lieutenant colonels; specialists next to warrant officers. Thatcher pulled in front of an old brown trailer; it belonged to a major and his wife who'd shipped to Hawaii for two years and left the trailer behind. They'd rented it to the soldier who'd been the major's assistant, a young female corporal named Parker Calton. This was about a year ago, and Corporal Calton was moving in with her fiancé. They were planning on reenlisting after the wedding; the trailer would be a perfect first home for two married soldiers. Thatcher, the former fiancé in question, turned the key and let the engine die. James pointed to the pickup truck in the spot next to them.

"Trouble?" he asked.

"No," Thatcher said. "That's not Park." Thatcher checked his watch. "She's still at work. That's Deal. Parker's new boyfriend."

James's eyebrows went up.

"Nah, it's good," Thatcher said. "Me and him used to fish together. He's good people."

James—jeans ripped, lengthening hair and beard, double earrings and a smell of patchouli about him—couldn't remember feeling more out of place. He kept a few steps behind Thatcher on the path to the door.

Deal was on the couch. Thin, tall, he looked to James a lot like Thatcher. He was in uniform, relaxing with a beer and Rikki Lake.

"Yo, man," he said when they came in.

"This a bad time, Deal?" Thatcher asked.

"Perfect time, man. Perfect." He pointed toward the window. "Parker threw your shit in the shed. It leaks some when it rains, but I went out and pulled a boat tarp over everything."

"Thanks, Deal."

"No troubles, man." Deal raised his beer can in James's direction. "Hey," he said.

James said hey.

The loading was easy. Under the tarp in the shed were two duffel bags, a few boxes. It filled up the Subaru but they were able to close the hatch.

James turned around to a blue Ford Fiesta pulling in next to them, a brown-haired young woman in camouflage behind the wheel.

"But of course," James said, took it as a cue, and slipped back into the passenger seat of the Subaru. He recognized the pretty soldier in the Fiesta; Thatcher had brought Corporal Parker Calton to Hoboken twice. The second time, early this past summer, James had thrown them an impromptu engagement party at Albert's Steak House on Washington Street. Thatcher had got so drunk he'd passed out across the table and Parker and James had played darts for an hour until he woke up.

Thatcher drummed his fingertips on the roof of the Subaru. His face had gone red. He saw Deal looking out through the trailer's kitchen window. Parker got out of her car without closing the door.

"Just, uh—" Thatcher began, but she held up a hand and cut him off.

"Don't even bother. Just grab your shit and go."

Her car door still open, she walked right past Thatcher, toward the steps up to the trailer door. In the three or four possible scenarios of how this might go and what she might say to him, Thatcher had not considered her saying nothing to him. He called after her, "Park, look—I just—"

Parker stopped walking and turned around. Her hands were on her hips and, Thatcher noticed, shaking.

Thatcher pressed on: "We both know it wouldn't have worked, Park. We both—"

"You're fucking-A right about that," she said, one hundred twenty pounds of fierce Minnesota in her voice. She looked Thatcher in the eye. He took a step forward.

"If it means anything, I think—"

"Fuck you, Thatcher," she said. Over her shoulder Thatcher saw Deal take a drink from his can of beer, watching the proceedings, waiting to see if military intervention would be necessary. "You know what's wrong with this?" she asked. Thatcher could think of a million things, easy, wrong with this, but kept his mouth shut. "I'll tell you what's wrong with this," she said. "Twenty phone calls this month, all those messages you left me, with your bullshit sensitive voice and all your bullshit excuses…" Thatcher felt himself turning red again. "Not once in any of those messages, and not once that one time we actually talked together—not once did you ask me how I was doing. Not once did you ask me how I felt. Didn't once ask how *I* was doing."

Thatcher stood silent a moment, staring, then put a hand up to his forehead and said, "Oh, Parker, I'm—"

"Blow me, Thatcher," Parker said, then spun around and stormed into the trailer, door slamming behind her. Thatcher stood where she'd left him, standing next to her open car door, staring at the trailer. He waited for her to come back out and when she didn't he closed the door of her car, opened his, and got in behind the wheel.

"That went well," James said. He had another of Thatcher's cigarettes hanging unlit from his lips and it bounced as he talked. "All things being the same."

Thatcher turned the key to start the engine, sat unmoving, then killed the engine again. He sat another minute, then started the engine and backed the car out. Down the road he finally spoke.

"I don't know what's wrong with me, James."

James—who'd seen Parker in a yellow bikini sunbathing on his roof in Hoboken, and who'd found himself in awe as she drunk him under the table—wondered the same thing, but kept this to himself.

"Some things just aren't meant to be, my friend," James finally said, patted Thatcher on the shoulder, and closed his eyes. They stopped for a six of Meister Brau on their way out of Tidewater, cracked the first and toasted, settled in for a long drive back to Hoboken.

SUNDAY IN THE PARK WITH MARSH

Sunday afternoon blew cold off the river. Elysian Park, on its little hill, gave up the last autumn vestige, long-fallen leaves blowing through the iron gates of the park and across Hoboken's Hudson Street. A full playground, though; swings up and back and little coated bodies swooshing down the slide. Kids don't mind about cold. City kids especially never care so much about the cold. Apartments are small and Sundays are long and legs got to move. City dogs can't stop going outside a couple times a day just because winter's coming; city kids can't either.

Marsh and his son Dash had an informal standing play date with six or seven other kids and their dads or moms, just about this time every Sunday. Some people go to church on Sunday morning—most of the oldsters, of course, and some of the squeaky-white young Republican couples moving into the new high-rises down Observer Highway and over into Newport and Jersey City; these people went to church on Sundays. Marsh and his boy Dash went to the playground.

They crossed Hudson Street and Marsh held the iron gate open for the boy. Dash popped through and took off, gone, toward the jungle gym. Six years old. Amazing, six. Six-year-olds don't feel cold. Six-year-olds feel more things than they let on, but they only feel cold when it's convenient.

Marsh, though; well. Marsh pulled his scarf higher and followed slow behind his son. His leg was getting worse as the season progressed and he couldn't figure it. Polio as a kid, then thirty-odd years of pushing his big body on a mostly painless limp. Now for some reason something was wrong, the limp harder from an ache he couldn't place or explain away.

Ahead of him, Dashiell hit the bars of the jungle gym with both palms open and swung himself up. *Imagine*, Marsh thought. *Imagine that.* Another little boy, a five-year-older called Rickie or Dickie or something, ran across Marsh's path, stumbled on a pavement crack, and fell right in front of him. Marsh waited for the cry but it wasn't that bad a fall. No cry. Marsh reached an arm down, wrapped his big hand around the kid's upper arm, pulled the kid up.

Rickie or Dickie moved to run but Marsh held tight a second.

"You're Dickie?" Marsh said.

"Rickie."

"Yeah, Rickie." Marsh set his face stern. "You got that ten bucks you owe me, Rickie?"

Rickie's face opened wide. He sputtered. Marsh kept his face tight but loosened his grip. Rickie fell away, looked back once, then ran to the jungle gym.

"Nice kid," Marsh said. Dash, at the top of the jungle gym now, turned to look for his father, saw him, and waved hard. Marsh waved back. "Look out for that Rickie," Marsh yelled. "He'll rob you dry."

"What?"

"I said, 'I'll be over there'." He pointed to a row of benches but Dash was already otherwise occupied, pulling Rickie up the bars of the jungle gym. "Nice kid, that Dickie," Marsh said to himself.

Lou had entered the park from the other side and she beat Marsh to the bench. She had two steaming Greek take-out coffees, and handed one to Marsh after he settled himself on the bench.

"The Lord's blessing on you, youngstress."

Lou kissed his cheek, sat down next to him. "That's a bad limp, Marsh."

"I've had that limp longer than you've been alive." He pulled the plastic lid and blew on the coffee.

"It looks worse today. Is it worse?"

"No," he said, and sipped the Greek joe. He reached over and tapped the pocket of her jacket. "What you got for me?" Lou pulled a cassette tape out of her jacket, stuck it right into the pocket of Marsh's coat.

"Nothing fancy," she said. "Just alone on my four track. But it's enough to practice."

"I'll practice my little heart out," Marsh said. "I promise." They were all learning each other's songs now, the ones they hadn't known anyway, figuring which might be best for the band. "Do we have a name yet?"

Lou shook her head. "Not really."

"We could go with that—Not Really."

Lou laughed. "The Not Really a Band band. Perfect. And I like James's idea, Free Beer."

"Free Beer at Maxwell's tonight," Marsh said. "That'll pull them in."

"Exactly."

Across the playground Dash had abandoned Rickie and moved on to a group of girls hanging out by the swings.

"Six years old, Lou," Marsh said. "Just imagine."

Lou was shielding her lighter from the wind, firing up one of her clove cigarettes. Marsh breathed deep, trying to grab it second-hand. He lay his head back, breathing the cold morning and a wisp of clove. A gaggle of geese crossed the sky. Twenty years in the greater metropolitan area, fifteen of them specifically in Hoboken, Marsh didn't think he'd ever seen geese crossing the sky here before. Geese were an Ohio sight. Autumn geese; arcing over cornfields and cheerleaders. Of which his body was built for neither, making his home state a rough place for him.

Thinking Ohio made him wistful. Marsh sipped his coffee, steam and frozen breath swirling up. Lou had her clove going; the smoke swirled into the mix.

"I remember six," she said, exhaling.

"Six is an awful long way back for me, girlie."

"Six is a long way back for anyone over eight, old man—don't beat yourself up."

"What do you remember about six," Marsh said.

"I remember my sister dragging me down the stairs. She was wearing red pajamas. The back of my head hit each step on the way down and I had a massive bump back there for a month."

"Mary Ann dragged you down the stairs?"

"No, Helen." Lou was the youngest of five girls, Mary Ann a year ahead of Lou. Helen had been two years ahead of Mary Ann. She'd died early the previous summer, in a car accident on Cape Cod. Helen had worked at the Hoboken Public Library and she sang Sunday mornings at Saint Peter's in the city. She'd only been twenty-seven when she died. The library closed the day of her funeral. So did Maxwell's.

"What ever had you done to Helen to warrant such abuse—stolen a Barbie?"

"No, Helen was too old for Barbies. I took a tube of her red lipstick and drew all over a picture of Bobby Luciano she had taped to her mirror."

"I'm having a hard time picturing Helen dragging another human being down the stairs."

"You didn't know Bobby Luciano—he was pretty cute."

"Who got in bigger trouble, you or her?"

"Actually, we both skipped. Mom gave us two choices: either keep our mouths completely shut when Dad got home, or face the firing squad equally and together."

"You chose wisely."

"We chose wisely. I wore a hat for a week so he wouldn't see I was a lump-head."

Marsh laughed at the vision of that, and then he put his arm around Lou—she was holding her jaw very tight in that way you need to do sometimes. She put her head on his wide shoulder and they sat like that for a while.

"What do you think of this little experiment of ours?" he said later.

"I like it," Lou said simply. Marsh nodded. He liked it, too. "I like all of you," she said. "It's a little funny. Not built like a real band. But we're all a little funny."

"So there you go."

"So there you go."

"I like our new Woody Guthrie," Marsh said.

"Me too. Thatcher's a good fit, I think." She dragged on her cigarette, thought for a minute. "I wasn't sure what James really thought, but I think it's all good."

"Wasn't Thatcher James's idea?" Marsh said. "Aren't they blood brothers or bonded Injun scouts or something?"

"Blood brothers and bonded Injun scouts doesn't necessarily mean happy bandmates."

Marsh grunted at that. "True enough."

MATTHEW BRODERICK AND TOOLS OF THE TRADE

Thatcher figured no other institution could approach the slow-blood, thick-papered bureaucracy of the United States Army. They gave the army a run for their money at Beginnings Behavioral Health, though; sure enough. Monday morning, the dark tools of clerkdom were all here on a long work table, like little bureaucrats neat in a line: two-hole punch, three-hole punch, standard stapler, industrial stapler, staple remover (two of these, one black, one brown), Wiro binder, label kit, electric pencil sharpener, cup with freshly sharpened pencils standing tall, pencil eraser, Wite-Out, highlighter, and—at the very end of the table, business end up, delivery end perched over a green recycling bin—an electric paper shredder. A clear progression across the table, a progression in the life of paperwork: punch it, staple it, fold it, file it, unfile it, rework it, throw it out. Standing beside the table, Thatcher ran his fingertips across the plastic veneer. The paraphernalia of his new profession made him uneasier than even his army rifle had.

Monday morning. Crack of the morning, crack of the week. First day on the job. Thatcher's training came from the clerk he was replacing, a nervous young woman named Dee. She'd been promoted to a secretarial job, administrative assistant to Herm.

"Mister Jeffries," Dee called the man. "The associate director. I'll have the desk outside his office."

There was a fluster about Dee, perpetual low panic. She'd been promoted more than a month before but hadn't been allowed to take up her new duties until a replacement was hired. The whole situation made her anxious. She wasn't hiding it well. Dee tapped and turned and talked then pressed her lips then talked again. Thatcher stopped asking questions, whether or not he understood what she was saying. Dee clearly wasn't in an answering mood.

The two were alone in Thatcher's new domain, Dee's late domain, the records room. The work table stood in the middle of it all, an old wood desk to the side—computer terminal very out of place on the desk, rising centered from a sea of papers and black binders. Another desk, metal and smaller, on the far side of the room. There was a window, at least, over-looking the walled courtyard at the front of the building where Thatcher had smoked the day of his interview. The shades were drawn. Judging from Dee's complexion Thatcher guessed the shades were usually drawn. He'd finally realized Dee couldn't be much more than his own age, but that hadn't been his first impression. His first impression, the way she'd been sitting behind the wooden desk when he first entered the dark room, had been of a matron. Once he got past that and took a look he realized it was a fairly young woman hiding in those gray clothes. A curvy one at that.

"These are the main records," Dee said, and laid her hand on a bank of steel file cabinets filling one whole wall side to side and floor to ceiling. Three of the four walls were steel file cabinets. There was a step on wheels for the higher drawers. Dee flicked her wrist, taking them all in. "The Day Hospital program, in-patient program, group and singles therapy patients." A quick flick to point out two cabinets whose labels were marked in red. "If they're here for drugs or liquor and nothing else, they go in there."

Thatcher tried a question. "What if th—"

"Brains trumps booze. If a patient's here for regular treatment but also sees a substance-abuse counselor, they go in the regular file."

She was quick, Dee was. When questions failed, Thatcher tried taking notes. It was obvious Dee thought that took too long and finally he just gave up. He followed her around the room for an hour, nodding and smiling. Or trying to smile. It was very difficult for him to keep his eyes open at this point. They'd done a Sunday-night rehearsal at Maxwell's and finished around 3 A.M. James began the work week by calling in sick. Thatcher assumed calling in sick his first day might not go over. The now ex-soldier in him sucked it up and suffered.

"Did you hear what I said, Thatcher?" Dee had a big brown folder in her hand.

"Yes, ma'am," he said automatically, before he could stop it from leaving his mouth. Dee gave him the funny look everyone up here gave you if you used a word like "ma'am." It was army-instilled and, Thatcher realized, would have to stop. Especially directed toward any woman under fifty.

Dee said what she had to say about the big brown folder then turned and talked and pointed and turned and pointed again and then she was done.

"Well," she said. "Well." Her hand went to her cheek. She looked Thatcher in the eye. "Good luck."

Thatcher was surprised she said it, found the words almost touching. "Thank you, Dee," he said, shaking her hand. "I'll do my best." Her hand was warm, unexpected. He said, "Be sure to come back and visit me here from time to time."

Dee made a small mumbling noise at that. She reached over the desk, picked up a thick paperback novel (a cat filled the cover; Thatcher tried but failed to glimpse the title), and then she was gone. Out the door, gray slacks swooshing in a fussy walk down the hall and up the stairs and down another hall to sit at a desk outside a former janitor's closet. To assist Herm. There was a prestige to it; up to this point only the director had a personal administrative assistant. Small office or no, Herm was moving up in the world and Dee had been plucked from the depths of the records room to answer his phones while he did it. Her footsteps sounded on the shiny hospital tiles down the hall to the stairway and then she was gone. Thatcher looked around. It was all too much. He needed coffee. He put his cigarettes in his pocket, closed and locked the door behind him, and headed out for the first official coffee break of his new job.

· · ·

The daily tasks of the new gig were straightforward enough. There would be filing and organizing and label-making aplenty. Punching and stapling galore. Once a day a formatted report to fill out and forward electronically to the State Office of Something or Another in Trenton. But mostly the job was consulting the daily schedule of programs and therapists, drawing the files of the patients involved, placing the files in the appropriate cubby on the far side of the room. When the staff was done with the files they would drop them on the work table, and Thatcher would have to ensure they were updated correctly and then refile them.

"I can do this," Thatcher said into the phone. He leaned back in his desk chair, an old wooden swivel model with iron wheels and the seat worn smooth and perfect. "It's an alright deal, I think. For me." The phone wasn't as old as the chair—it had buttons and extensions—but the handpiece was heavy the way Thatcher remembered from the old house in Gary Ridge. Administrative staff weren't supposed to make or take personal calls from institute phones but Thatcher thought it would be alright to make one call to let James know he couldn't make or take personal calls at the new job. "Twenty years of school and then they put me on the day shift," Thatcher said.

"Sounds pretty good," James said, "except for the no phone part."

"Yeah."

"You got e-mail?"

"What's e-mail?"

"You don't have it. How about a fax machine?"

"Right here on my desk. I don't know how it works."

"Give me the number."

Thatcher read James the number as a gaggle of men—a sweater vest and button-down, two black sports jackets, one polo—entered the room, all of them arms drowning in thick patient files. These weren't the simple therapists who'd wandered in and out since Thatcher had taken charge of the room; these four were staff MDs. The shrinks. Thatcher hung up the phone on James.

"Good morning, gentlemen," Thatcher said. Wordless, the doctors dropped their files and left. "And a fine day to you, too," Thatcher said to his empty room.

• • •

Dee had quickly, vaguely explained the center's hierarchy, in her own way ("Do what the doctors say, bring the nurses whatever they want because they can't leave their floors, don't worry so much about anyone else"). In truth, the hierarchy was a much more solid map, one it wouldn't take Thatcher more than a few days to chart: Support staff—like Thatcher, like Dee—existed on rung two, a step above the janitors, Jackson the maintenance man, and Mr. Scapaletti, a retired Jersey City police sergeant who served as the center's security guard on the days when his agida allowed him to leave the house. Above these gentlemen, rung two had a mini-hierarchy, with Thatcher solid bottom, the night receptionists next, day receptionists higher, the three back-office accounting ladies square-even with the day receptionists, and the now two administrative assistants leading the pack. Dee had moved within striking range of the top of rung two.

Then came the professional world. Rung three was for staff with no or low graduate degrees, mainly the day program staff—your psych-major BAs, your CSWs—those who generally wore sneakers to work and sometimes jeans on a Friday. The nurses lived on rung four; LPNs first, RNs second, the expansive, barking, fifty-year-old nurse practitioner Rosealba dominating the rung. The more credentialed therapists and substance-abuse counselors were on rung five (LCSWs mostly, and a few other impressive-sounding alphabet strings), and the psychologists stood high atop all on rung six. (Here on six, the PhDs privately considered themselves a step above the PsyDs; the PsyDs privately considered the PhDs professional equals who'd foolishly spent twice as much money achieving essentially the same degree.)

The center's nonclinical MBA director—a tall, manly woman who commuted in from Park Slope and was rarely seen by anyone during the day—and the associate director—Herm, who'd originally been hired as finance manager then quickly arranged for a title upgrade—theoretically ruled from rung seven; mostly, though, they had little presence outside of meetings.

Then there were the shrinks. The four doctors, the psychiatrists, the MDs. They weren't even really on the ladder. They floated, more a spiritual force in space rather than a solid presence in the center. (One of them, Dr. Jenkins, had not long before been the director. The hospital board had informed him one day they were relieving him of that title to free him up for the patient time they knew he craved more of. Dr. Jenkins—who, quite happily, hadn't seen a patient in five years—watched as the female MBA arrived and moved into his office, then he had gone home. He came back to work the next day—and had come to work every day since—but still had not seen a patient. "I'm supervising," he told the MBA, and she simply smiled and decided to wait out the last eight months on his contract.) On a map, the MDs would fall below the administration, but in fact they lived apart, made their own schedules, followed their own rules, and attended no meetings (the surest sign of true power there is).

Below all these rungs, below the ladder itself, lower even than the night janitors—one of whom was more than slightly brain damaged from a car accident on the Pulaski Skyway some eighteen years before—were the patients.

• • •

Thatcher brought a stack of the patient files back to his desk and opened one. Signatures were a priority, he'd been instructed. Thatcher was to be guardian at the gates of signatory assurance. He found the dictation sheet where the therapist or MD wrote the day's notes, scanned down, saw the scrawl of signature. Check. One down. He glanced over at the cover page, a box marked DIAGNOSIS. There was a note scrawled: PARANOID SCHIZOPHRENIA WITH GRANDIOSE IDEATIONS. Thatcher thought that one over. The reading at this job, at least, promised to be interesting.

The door opened and a round, pink face appeared, looked around then drew back again. A second later the door opened wide, filled with Orris, the big man from the courtyard on Thatcher's interview day. He wore what looked to be the same gray sweats as a week before.

"Congratulations, Thatcher," the man said, nodding his head.

"Thanks."

"Orris, remember?"

"I remember. Hi Orris."

"Heard you were starting today. Thought we'd come see how you were doing."

"Doing great." Thatcher stood up. Patients, he'd been told, were not to be in the records room. For any reason, Dee said. At any time.

Orris stepped in. There was a small man behind him. Slight, with thin black hair in a careful comb-over, wearing a very dated but very neat banker's suit. The man had a narrow mustache, black glasses, and an old leather briefcase in his right hand.

"This here's Bill Pin," Orris said. "Bill Pin, this here's Thatcher."

"Hi Bill." Thatcher waved with the pencil in his hand. "Listen, I don't think you fellows are supposed to be in here."

Orris ambled across the room, looking around with his good left eye. The right one seemed to be looking, too, at other things.

"Never been in here," Orris said, then whistled through his teeth. "Lots of stuff."

Thatcher glanced nervously at the door, sure a staff member would come through.

"Listen, Orris, I—"

"Matthew Broderick," Bill Pin said suddenly. He was looking at Thatcher with a small smile on his face.

"What's that?" Thatcher said, watching with alarm as Orris picked up a patient file from the drop-off pile on the work table. "Hey, you can't—" But Orris had already put the file down. He turned and leaned onto Thatcher's desk, taking in everything on it.

"What're they paying you, Thatcher?" he asked, a question so socially disarming and unexpected that Thatcher could think of nothing but to answer it.

"Nine bucks an hour," he said.

Orris whistled through his teeth again, long and loud. "Big time."

Thatcher didn't know if he was kidding or not so kept his face very straight and said nothing.

"Nine bucks an hour, Bill Pin," Orris said. "What could you do with that."

"Matthew Broderick," Bill Pin said.

Orris looked at Thatcher and said, "Bill Pin's got you all set." Orris's eye thing was creating difficulty for Thatcher. He didn't know where to look. The right eye was looking at him, but the jiggling left one demanded attention, too. Two eyes in two directions, and two Day Hospital patients who weren't supposed to be in the room.

"Guys," Thatcher said, "you're really going to have to—"

"Everyone's a star with Bill Pin, Thatcher," Orris said. "Isn't that right, Bill?"

Bill nodded, smiling. Orris picked up a pencil from Thatcher's desk. He waved it at Bill Pin. "I've never seen him make up his mind so quick, though. Usually it's like a few days."

Thatcher looked at Orris. He was so tired. "Hey, Orris, I—"

"What do you think of your name?" Orris was leaning across the desk again. Thatcher couldn't tell if he was eyeing him or the desk or what. It was disconcerting.

"What name?"

"Matthew Broderick. What do you think? Great fit, huh?"

"What's a great fit?"

"Your name. Bill Pin gives everyone a star name. Dr. Jenkins, he's Alan Alda. Rosealba is Roseanne Barr. Bill Pin says you're—"

"Matthew Broderick," Bill Pin said. He was grinning ear to ear now, holding his briefcase in front of him with both hands on the handle.

"You think I look like Matthew Broderick?" Thatcher said.

Bill Pin shrugged. "Well. It's in the nose, that's all."

"Bill Pin looks at details," Orris said. He was off Thatcher's desk, hovering over the work table again.

Thatcher was very anxious now, but Bill Pin was raising his voice a little bit.

"It's just the nose, just from the nose."

"You think I have Matthew Broderick's nose? I don't look anything like Matthew Broderick."

"I can change, you know. I could change the selection." Bill Pin had stopped smiling now. His face drew down, concerned.

"Hogwash," Orris said. "Bill Pin's never changed a selection before. Thatcher, you just don't know your own nose, is all. Bill Pin calls it, that's where it stands. Don't you change nothing, Bill Pin."

Thatcher nodded, worried now he'd upset the man. "Yeah, really, what do I know, Bill. You can—" And that's when Orris apparently found what he was looking for, shot his thick hand and forearm out surprisingly fast, and swiped a thick patient chart off the work table.

"Gotta run now, Thatcher," he said and hustled out the door, gray sweats moving in a streak.

It took Thatcher a second to realize what he'd seen—he was *so* tired—then his heart hit his mouth.

"Hey, wait!" he yelled, and vaulted over his desk in a near-perfect obstacle-course GI jump, but the less-than-perfect landing turned tragic as his ankle buckled on the floor and he went down, face first. "Orris!" he yelled.

"Here, Matthew," Bill Pin said, offering down his hand, but Thatcher pushed himself up and was out the door, looking left and right, but no sign of gray sweats in the hall, no sign of anything. "Orris!" he yelled again.

"Yeah, it's okay then," Bill Pin said from behind him. "You watch those jumps, you gotta take care of that nose." The little man was in the hall with

Thatcher now. "The ladies must go nuts over that nose, huh Matthew?"

"Where'd he go, Bill?" Thatcher said.

"Who?"

"Orris. Where'd he go?"

"Orris gets around a lot," Bill Pin said. "He's always around somewhere." He looked at his watch—a fairly decent-looking Rolex, Thatcher couldn't help but notice. "Well, ta-ta. Must run." Bill went left down the hall. "You keep good care of that nose, Matthew. You and the ladies—boy, they must go nuts for you."

"Holy shit," Thatcher mumbled. "Holy fucknuts."

He went back in the records room. The shadows were long out the window, dark in the corners of the room. A patient had just stolen a chart. A patient—no, two patients—had been in the records room, and one of them had stolen a patient file. "First day," Thatcher said. "First fucking day." He wiped his mouth with his palm.

On his desk the fax machine whirred into life, a greasy piece of white fax paper pushing out the thing's ass. Thatcher stepped over, pulled it free. It was from James, across the river at the World Trade Center. A quick-sketched marijuana leaf and scrawled note: HEY WOODY GUTHRIE, IT'S 5 O'CLOCK…MILLER TIME, BABY.

Thatcher sat down heavily in his desk chair and tried to think what might be the best course of action.

PIMP DADDY CALLED

The new band—sort of a band? almost a band? they still needed a drummer—managed three rehearsals over the next week, an impressive number
considering, as Bruno was wont to point out, they still had no gig to work
toward.

"Gig, schmig," Marsh said to Bruno, exasperated. "You want a gig?
I'll shit you a gig."

"That'd be a neat trick."

"Done," Marsh said. "We're playing the back room at Shannon
Lounge."

"When?"

"Two weeks from Wednesday."

"And when did you line this up?"

"I haven't yet. Not a problem. Not a factor. Two weeks from Wednesday. Shannon Lounge. You be there." The two were onstage in Maxwell's
empty back room, the two old men of the band, pulling tubes from a tube
amp. James, Lou, Thatcher, and Mary Ann were at a table near the sound

board, playing through a few hands of post-rehearsal poker. Marsh stepped to one of the mikes. "We're playing Shannon Lounge," he said, his voice amplified and bouncing off the walls. "Two weeks from Wednesday."

"Excellent," James said, drawing a card. Mary Ann half turned in her chair to look over at Marsh.

"Does it pay?" she asked.

Bruno rolled his eyes. "What do you think," Marsh said, backing off the mike.

"I think it should and probably doesn't."

• • •

The next morning, Thursday morning, Thatcher found a thick patient file leaning against the locked door of the records room, a note taped to it. One word, scrawled in black ink: SORRY. Clearly the stolen file, clearly the thief's own handwriting. Orris and the file had both been missing three days. Thatcher had decided the best course of post-theft action was do nothing and his decision had paid off—in three nail-biting days no one from the staff had come complaining of a missing file. And now here it was back. Thatcher picked it up, looked at the label to see whose chart Orris had borrowed. He blinked. It was Orris's own file. Thatcher smiled. Sometimes when you least expect it the world makes sense.

Up three nights rehearsing, up every morning at dawn for work. Thatcher kept an electric alarm clock on the floor next to his mat in James's living room. When it went off Friday morning Thatcher threw it so hard against the wall the thing shattered into a spray of black plastic and circuit board. Russell Davitz, passing down the hall toward the shower, said, "Yeah, man. Fuck it up, sharp dude." After work Thatcher came home and fell asleep on the couch, woke up to darkness, ten o'clock. He dressed and headed for Maxwell's.

"My brother," James said, eating a burger at the bar.

"My brother from another mother."

"You look like shit."

"I think I'm losing weight."

James ran a napkin across his beard, raised his finger for another pint. "Did you check the machine?"

"No."

"Two messages for you. Geoff Mason called. I couldn't tell what he said."

"Yeah—no, I heard that one. I couldn't tell either." Geoff Mason was an almost-famous songwriter and folksinger who lived on Houston Street in Greenwich Village. Mason wasn't quite old enough yet to be the grand-pappy of the scene, but he was edging into Uncle territory, at least. New York's original industry-rebel songwriting Uncle. Mason and Thatcher went through life hiply pretending they weren't quite fond of one another, which, in fact, they were. "Yeah, I'll call him," Thatcher said.

James bunched up his napkin and wiped ketchup from his lips. He took a sip of beer then said, "And Pimp Daddy called for you."

Pimp Daddy was what James called King Papas, their former high school trio mate.

"What'd he say?"

"I never know what Pimp Daddy say. Pimp Daddy talk too fast, son." James belched. "I didn't listen, anyway."

James and King Papas hadn't spoken in more than a year.

"I'm going up there this weekend. Boston."

"I know. You told me."

Thatcher shrugged. "He invited. What the hell."

"Sure. What the hell."

James walked away, leaving Thatcher his bar stool. *What the hell*, Thatcher thought. *It's a gig. He invited.*

Joanne had left a message earlier in the week, maybe she'd be able to stop by Maxwell's Friday night. Maybe. Thatcher drank pints and played with toothpicks and when Jo walked through the door around midnight he was pleased bordering on relieved. She wore a white men's dress shirt unbuttoned low and tucked into gray slacks. Thatcher stood from his stool to kiss her, that long hair flowing all around him. Pushed back into the corner of the bar, she whispered, "I'm so glad you're not in the army anymore."

They played pool with James and his current girlfriend—Melissa, from down the shore—for an hour or more, before James and Melissa-from-down-the-shore slipped away. It was nearing last call, the crowd thinner. Jo stole one of Thatcher's cigarettes, lit it, put her arm around him with a dream smile. "I'm dreading this drive home," she said.

"Stay. I don't get on the bus for Boston until late tomorrow night."

"Can't. First meeting with the caterer at nine in the morning."

"Yikes." Thatcher drained his pint. "How's the fiancé doing with all your planning?"

"Punctual," she said. "He's very punctual."

"It's an admirable trait," he said.

Jo kissed Thatcher on the cheek. "My car's over on Bloomfield," she said. "Walk me, and I'll give you a ride home."

• • •

Melissa-from-down-the-shore had to make a phone call (to a roommate? a hairdresser? a grandmother? Unclear, really, and James had lost interest in the explanation) so James walked her to the pharmacy to use the payphone. Leaning against the magazine rack James saw Thatcher and Jo pass by on the sidewalk outside. That was one he'd never understand. Well, maybe *understand* wasn't the right word, it was easy to *understand*—Jo was a whole lot of fun to be around—but the way it dragged on. Ten years now? Ridiculous. They were clinging to something; James wasn't quite sure what.

Personally, James wasn't a big one for clinging. Onward always seemed best. Melissa, he'd met her in August, when he was down playing a few nights on the boardwalk at 11th Street in Ocean City. Hung out, traded numbers, hooked up in Hoboken this fall. That's the way life ought to be. None of this reliving your past or holding on to history or whatever it was Thatcher and Joanne were doing.

Onward, James thought. *Let's keep it moving.*

THE THING ITSELF

Before Quatrone stepped out Friday evening—two of his paintings were hanging in a group show at William Paterson, opening tonight—he'd had coffee with his mother, thick almost like candy with half-and-half and sugar enough to make the spoon stand up straight. It was to his mother's taste, this coffee. His, too, of course—he was her son—although he didn't drink it this way out of the house so much. But home, it was good. Bitter burnt espresso beans underneath as the base of the whole thing, but not so you'd know except for the resulting wake-up. The final drink—*the thing itself*, his mother would say, talking as much with her hand as her voice—was as close to bitter as New Jersey is to Iowa.

At the kitchen table Friday night, his carpenter pants pressed and a bright red tie for the occasion, Quatrone sipped his coffee. He was pretty sure he'd spent more time in this room since birth than any other room he could think of. It was good, this kitchen. Good light in the day, well-lit and warm at night. Here on the belly of autumn, nowhere better to be on an evening. In a ceramic bowl on the counter, a bunch of green bananas sticking up, and the tops of two eggplant.

"Eggplant," he said, laying his wide, hairy hand down across his mother's wrinkled one. "Eggplant makes my stomach rumble."

Mrs. Quatrone took note, and that was all that needed to be said about it. Quatrone himself didn't even know he'd just put in his Saturday lunch order—or, maybe he did—but Mrs. Quatrone now knew what she would do to fill the hour between her son leaving tonight and the story she wanted to watch on channel 11 at nine. Mrs. Quatrone set coffee aside, hustled her boy out the door, and moved on the eggplant.

• • •

The process wasn't complicated, but it was precise. You don't deviate. Everyone wants to deviate on things, make it their own. But some things, they're just not your own. They are what they are. Take your fancy restaurants on Washington Street—they deviate, because by deviating they think they make it their own, and when it's their own they can charge more.

Some things—it is what it is. Like a good recipe. Mrs. Quatrone, when she was learning, first year married, she deviated. That was a mistake. There is no deviation. It is what it is and you make the thing right or don't make it.

Eggplant, for instance. How can you make it better? There is no better. You make it and you eat it and it's good or it isn't good depending on you, but you don't make it different. You just make it.

For Mrs. Quatrone, there is only one way to make it: you wash the eggplants first, nice and purple, scrub them in the sink, pat dry, then slice them down with the big knife. Lay the slices, push down with a cast-iron pan on top to squeeze the water out. You flour the slices, dip them in the egg, then take your big bowl of breadcrumbs and push the slices right through the breadcrumbs itself. Right through, cover them good. Take the cast-iron pot, heat the olive oil, fry them nice, then lay on paper towels to drain the oil. You get your ham, your ricotta, your mozzarella, you roll them tight.

What is there to deviate? And what could you possibly add to that? Nothing.

It is the thing itself—you just cook it right.

BOULEVARDIERS

The Saturday late-afternoon sky glowed golden bright over the Hudson River and New York City, the air chilly but that sun felt good. Thatcher and Geoff Mason were on Christopher Street, walking east through Greenwich Village, side by side, not fast. When you walked with Mason you never walked fast; Geoff Mason didn't walk as much as stroll. "Like a *boulevardier*," he'd growl, in the scratchy, pretty Mason growl. "That's how one *walks* the city. Like you've no place else better to be, ever." Mason with his gray hair and sharp blue eyes bright on a face just beginning to crease, hands buried in the pockets of green corduroys. Mason never had anyplace better to be, ever, than the space he occupied at any given moment.

They were a couple of *boulevardiers* now, Thatcher and Mason, letting the sidewalk crowd flow around them on Christopher Street. They didn't speak for a while, then Mason said, "I don't understand why you got a job."

"Have to eat, Geoff."

"But a job." He spat the word, a curse, vile poison; *boulevardier* noting a blemish of *feces caninus* on his sidewalk.

"I know," Thatcher said. "I owe some money, too. This and that. A chunk to Uncle Sam."

"Tax debt?" Another whiff of soiling shit.

"Some of it taxes. I filed wrong while I was in the army."

"But you went to war, no? There must be some sort of provision. Even the IRS isn't that uncivilized."

Thatcher shrugged. "There's a provision. I calculated it wrong."

"Fucking folksinger."

"Yeah." Thatcher squinted.

"What about your estate?" Mason said, and they both chuckled. Thatcher's estate, their joke—Mason was one of few in the world who knew Thatcher was Randolph's son. Mason also knew who owned Randolph's copyrights, and the extent to which Randolph had left anything behind. "Why not go across Jersey and ask that fat bastard Wilson to pay your taxes? Least he could do."

"Yeah," Thatcher said. "No."

Mason had been friends with Randolph, back in the day. One of only three people Thatcher knew—other than Thatcher's mother and Nate Goldman—who'd known the moody, doomed young singer-songwriter. Mason had split bills and bottles with Randolph at the old Kettle of Fish and the Bitter End the summer before Wilson had dragged Randolph out of the Village and recorded him. Mason had warned Randolph to take Wilson's contract to a lawyer and Randolph—fierce drunk in Chicago now, living on the floor of the studio where Wilson was recording him—had told Mason he was a jealous prick and Mason said I'll see you in hell and Randolph hung up the phone. They didn't speak again and Randolph was dead within eighteen months.

"How about your mother?" Mason said. "Doesn't seem like Mona's poor."

"We don't talk much."

"She has a new book."

"I like fiction. I've never read any of her books," Thatcher lied.

"This new one's making waves," Mason said. "Trying to keep the world safe from pornography."

"That's a shame," Thatcher said, and they both laughed.

"Well, someone needs to help take care of that debt for you. No folk-singer should have to get a job."

"Do you pay taxes?"

"I make it a point to never earn enough to owe taxes. You get a job, you'll owe even more taxes."

"Need to live somewhere. Have to pay rent."

"You and that major-seventh James you play with can't scrape up enough from gig money to pay rent?"

"Not in Hoboken."

Mason grunted. "So why live in Hoboken?"

"Never mind. And James plays a whole lot more than major-sevenths."

"Immaterial. No one should ever play a major-seventh. Ever."

"Entire careers have been spun around major-sevenths, Geoff. Very successful careers."

"My point exactly," Mason said, and Thatcher laughed despite himself. Geoff clapped him on the shoulder. "You need a rent-free chance to save up some capital, Thatch. So why not Mona? Surely a few months in Castle Mona wouldn't kill you."

"Surely not," Thatcher said. "But it's not really Castle Mona. It's Castle Stanley."

"Who's Stanley?"

"Husband of Mona."

"Oh, right," Mason said. "Issues?"

"Issues."

"With which one? Stanley? Or Mona?"

Thatcher nodded and said, "Yes."

They passed the Ridiculous Theatre at Sheridan Square then Mason stopped and opened a double door into the brightly lit lobby of a law office. A young woman sat behind the reception desk. It was all so out of place with the law and order and serious wood paneling it took Thatcher a moment to realize the young woman was Anna, Mason's girlfriend. Anna was pale, thin, tall—taller than Geoff, taller than Thatcher—and when she stepped on a stage to sing she sounded a lot like the pale, thin, tall, famous young songwriter Mason dated five years before (in advance of her current fame—Mason never dated anyone more famous than himself). This similarity wasn't Anna's fault, though. She was a good singer, a good writer. Anna was Thatcher's age, maybe a year older. They were both young enough that being a year apart in age still sort of mattered—some bizarre extension of a high school rule—although it was all academic to Thatcher: they were both easily twenty years junior to Mason, maybe more. No one really knew Mason's age.

"My dear." Mason swept around the desk and planted kisses on both her cheeks. He winked at Thatcher. "Another one with a job."

"Someone has to pay our rent, Geoff," she said.

"*Touché.*"

"Hello, Private," Anna said. "It's been forever since we've seen you."

"Corporal," Thatcher said. "I was promoted a few times."

"Are you out now?"

"Mostly out."

"Isn't that like being a little bit pregnant?" she asked, and Mason laughed out loud.

"Not quite," Thatcher said. "The army is complicated."

Geoff pointed to a large yellow envelope on the desk. "For me?" he asked.

Anna nodded and handed it to him. Photocopied flyers for an upcoming show. Geoff peeked in the envelope then said to Thatcher, "The girl with the office equipment—she's the one you stick with." He turned and bowed low. "A hot meal will await your return from the salt mines, my dear."

"I certainly hope so," she said.

Mason kissed Anna on both cheeks then stepped to the door, peeking in the envelope again. Thatcher leaned over the desk to kiss her cheek goodbye, too, and was pleasantly surprised to find her lips on his. His face flushed red. Anna winked at him.

"*Adieu*, Corporal. Don't stay gone so long next time."

• • •

Geoff's New York apartment was a fourth-floor walkup, a former cold-water tenement flat from the days when the Village had been more Italian, less Bohemian. You could get hot water in the sink now, but the toilet was still down the hall, shared with the three other flats on the floor. The window in the kitchen/living-room combo looked out on an air shaft. The bedroom was completely filled by the bed. Geoff lived and wrote here during the week. Weekends he was either on the road for a gig or with his four kids at his ex-wife's farm Upstate.

They sat in the two old easy chairs, Geoff leaned back and balancing a glass of cabernet on his knee, Thatcher sitting forward, almost off the chair, to accommodate the guitar he held. It was Geoff's Martin, beat and worn but fret action slim as an eyebrow. Thatcher's notebook was open on the floor at his feet. He leaned over the body of the guitar and flipped a few pages.

"That's pretty much it," he said, and Mason nodded.

"Quite a—" and he coughed as his voice cracked. He took a sip of wine, tried again: "Quite a handful of work for a year." Mason's speaking voice went from scratchy pretty to just scratchy when he had wine in him.

"I had a lot to write about."

Mason nodded. Closed his eyes, frowned, then opened them again. "It's not all great," he said.

"I know."

"It's not all bad, either." He coughed again. "Nothing was really *bad*. You're past that." Mason swirled his wine. "Two were really good."

"You think?"

"Yes, I think. Do you know which ones?"

"The first two I played."

Mason nodded. "I'll bet they're the last two you wrote," he said.

"No, but close."

Geoff shrugged. "What are you doing Tuesday night?" he asked. "It's time you came back to church."

For fifteen years, songwriters—folk, pop, rock, whatever—had been coming to Geoff's apartment on Tuesday nights. From the amateur to the obscure to the famous, all were usually welcome. You played your newest song and the group critiqued. Fiercely critiqued. When Thatcher was seventeen, a senior in high school—and still unknown to Mason as Randolph's son—he'd been in a trio with James and another kid from their town, a tall, muscular Greek kid a year older named King Papas. Three kids from the same Jersey town into acoustic music, in 1987—not common. The trio took the bus from Gary Ridge into the city one night to play the open mike at Cornelia Street Café. A guy who looked like a vacationing dentist came up after they'd played and took Thatcher aside. He'd introduced himself as Nate Goldman. "I'm a manager."

"I know who you are," Thatcher had said, heart rate accelerating. Goldman was a legend, an old-school legend, who'd started his career while still in college, in the 1940s, following Pete Seeger around like a puppy dog and offering a management contract to every Communist folksinger and black blues belter Seeger turned him on to. Goldman's day had essentially passed, but his management stable—his Talent—was still impressive.

"Yeah, well—I can't manage you three kids, so don't piss your lederhosen." Goldman had grabbed a card from his pocket and a pen and scrawled something on the back. "You know who Geoff Mason is, smarty pants? Yeah?" He gave Thatcher the card. "Here's his address. You guys—whichever of you guys writes the words—you go to his place Tuesday night, any Tuesday night, tell him I sent you. You can't sing for shit but you got some good words."

James was at Rutgers within a few months, but Thatcher and King Papas made Geoff's apartment a religion. Thatcher ended up in the army, and King Papas ended up in Boston, but there was a time they never missed a Tuesday night. In the four years Thatcher was in the army he never came back, even when he was on leave. He visited Geoff if he was home, and wrote often, but never came by on Tuesdays.

"So why don't you come?" Geoff said again. "Bring both those songs."

"Okay, maybe."

"It's not a death sentence. Do what you will." Mason reached for the bottle on the floor, filled his glass and then filled Thatcher's. Thatcher took a long drink of the wine.

"You know what it is?" Thatcher said. "I just—I just don't have a connection with those people anymore."

"What people? Which?"

"The people who come here. The New Yorkers."

"You mean your friends?"

Thatcher rolled his eyes. "Some of them. My friends are in Jersey."

"So why don't you like New York writers? Because they only write about life as a New York writer?"

Thatcher rolled his eyes again.

"Yes, well." Mason tapped the stem of his wine glass with his fingernail. "We're not as elitist as you think, and you're not as worldly and of-the-people as you imagine. Just come on Tuesday and sing your fucking proletarian drivel."

Geoff grinned, stood, drained his glass in a swallow and placed it carefully on the kitchen table. He went through the door and down the hall to the john, wobbling slightly. Thatcher looked at the two empty bottles on the floor. They'd drunk a lot of wine. He was pretty sure one of those bottles had been half gone when he got here, but still. He stood and leaned Geoff's guitar in the corner before he did any damage to it.

There were five framed pictures hanging in the corner. Geoff didn't hang a lot of flashy stuff up, like some might. Just enough, Thatcher thought, to maybe remind himself of who he was when he got drunk. Thatcher smiled at that, and leaned in to look at the framed pictures. Mason and his brother with guitars on a stage somewhere in Germany, looking about Thatcher's age. Mason and Van Ronk and Paxton. Mason and Nate Goldman, arms around each other, standing next to old Pete and a roomful of crusty Village Communists. Mason in the spotlight onstage at the Bottom Line, a very young Randy Newman at the piano behind him.

"People know who he is," Thatcher said aloud, staring at Mason's face in the picture. The sound of his own voice made him jump, but he said it again anyway. "They know who he is."

Rumor was this tiny flat was a ruse, that Mason was loaded. It might be true—Thatcher had never been, but King Papas said the farm Upstate was sweet—but if there was money it didn't come from the thirty-year labor of lyrics. And to Thatcher, it just didn't matter. Mason did what he wanted, and people knew who he was.

The apartment door closed, Mason back in the room. He cleared his throat then said, "Will you see the King while you're up north?"

"He got me the gig."

"You tell him I said Boston is for pussies."

"I'll do that, Geoff. Count on it."

• • •

By the time Thatcher got back to the street it was winter dark, the sidewalk a completely different crowd now—hungry, on the prowl. Thatcher had the Boston bus to catch up at Port Authority, but no time soon. He headed off in the general direction of the West Village but not directly there. It was easy, in the Village, to not walk directly anywhere. Up this street and down that and over here and around this small block. He didn't feel like a *boulevardier* now, though; just a little drunk—aimless and lonely.

If he had to be in New York, Thatcher preferred the West Village. Over by NYU, Bleecker and MacDougal, he had to admit, it freaked him out a little. He spent very little time thinking about his late father—not hard to do with someone dead before you were born. But the center of the Village, that was Randolph's territory. Those were the clubs he played. And it was, well, weird. Best just to stay away. The West Village was nicer anyway. Better yet, keep going west—cross the river to Hoboken. Far as he knew, Randolph had never gigged in Hoboken. Hoboken was Thatcher's. From the first time he'd come up to visit James in his new digs he'd felt it, embraced it. That's why he'd moved in.

But this was the Village; and here was the White Horse, where he used to stop every week with King Papas for chili and a pint, and Thatcher stopped there now for a half pint. He squeezed between bodies to yell his order to the bartender, grabbed his glass and popped back out into a warm bubble of empty in a corner near a pay phone where he drained the glass then left. It was too crowded to smoke, even. It's always more crowded when you don't know anyone in a room.

Most of the bars down here opened to the sidewalk, even in this weather. Thatcher finally got back over on Christopher Street where all the bars were of a type, places to be seen, and it wasn't for him but he was cold and wanted another drink so went in to one, leaned against the bar and ordered. He waited to be seen but wasn't—invisible in old jeans and older overcoat. He swallowed his drink and moved on, next door, another drink, then next door again, another drink. An hour slipped. It was colder outside between each bar, more crowded inside. He couldn't afford this and didn't know why he was doing it—he didn't have the money, and still had to pay for a twenty-dollar bus ticket to Boston tonight. Thatcher carefully inventoried his wallet: forty-one dollars, twenty-seven cents. He ordered another drink.

A boy came up to him in the fifth bar, smiling drunk. Thatcher fumbled around the math then realized he was drunk, too. Slow on the uptake he was, sometimes.

"What are you doing?" The boy draped his arm over Thatcher's shoulder.

"Waiting to be seen."

"Not dressed like that, you'll never be seen like that."

Thatcher lit a cigarette.

"Well, *I* see you," the boy said.

"You do?"

He nodded.

"Are you sure?"

"Yes." The boy had a funny way of clipping his words. He took Thatcher's cigarette from him and smoked it. "You seem very sad. No one will see you if you look sad."

"That's something," Thatcher said. "Hadn't thought of that. You're right, though." He noticed his words slurring. "I just—" He took his cigarette back, inhaling deep. "All my life, I think all my life, I've just been waiting to be noticed, waiting to be seen. And tonight I thought, 'Well, if I can't be seen in there, of all places, then I'm just invisible.'"

"You are invisible."

"I am?"

The boy nodded. "You're invisible, alright." He smiled. "I see you, though. No one else here does, but I see you. That's something, no? One person's better than nothing, no?"

"You think?"

"I think so."

Thatcher stood up and his barstool went flying out from under him, spinning and falling over to the floor, an angry yell from someone he couldn't see.

"I'll walk you home, baby," the boy said. "Where you going?"

"No, that's okay," Thatcher said. "Really. I'm drunk."

"Me too."

"Yeah, I gotta go. Gotta catch a bus. Hey, are you sure you can see me?"

"You're right there."

"You sure?"

"I'm sure."

"I have to go."

"Okay, baby," the boy said. "You stay warm out there in that ugly old coat."

• • •

His bus to Boston didn't leave until 11. He thought the long walk might sober him up. Thatcher was crossing 21st Street—halfway up to the Port

Authority terminal—when he remembered his guitar and duffel bag, stashed in the back room of Marge's Grill for his afternoon of *boulevardering* with Mason. The road to remembering was a cloudy and tangled process, but his beer thoughts had run something like this:

For a handful of blocks he hadn't thought at all, just walked and wallowed drunk in the dark. Then he'd got to thinking about this new band he'd joined and then specifically of Lou, and how much he liked her. Just really, really liked her. Not like James called it. More like a sister, like a sister from another mister. And then he'd had to stop and laugh on that one awhile—a sister from another mister—stopped to laugh in the middle of the empty Chelsea sidewalk—his sister from another mister—and he lit a cigarette and smoked it, then started walking again. He'd hung out with Lou for a day just a few weeks ago; they took the PATH from Hoboken to the Village. Lou had a gig that night and carried her guitar in its clunky hard case and Thatcher had wondered if she was going to carry the thing all day. Lou winked and showed him a bar a few blocks south of the PATH on Hudson and they'd had a beer in a room filled with women. Lou introduced Marge herself, and then Lou spoke the name of Thatcher's mother and pointed at Thatcher and said to Marge, "That's her son," and Marge herself had come around the bar and hugged him like her own child. When Lou put her guitar in the back room for the afternoon old Marge herself told Thatcher he was welcome to utilize the storage space from time to time, too, if he didn't mind pushing his way through a surly estrogen crowd and they'd all had a good laugh and sure enough Thatcher had dumped his stuff there for his afternoon with Mason and it was crossing 21st Street tonight that he remembered.

He stood in the middle of the street, staring through the windshield of a taxi stopped at the light. "Fucknuts," he said. "Drunk again."

Thatcher's breath puffed with the words. The taxi driver wore a red ballcap. Hands gripped on wheel, he stared at Thatcher.

"Yeah, I know," Thatcher said. His stroll was over. To get his stuff and get to the bus on time he'd either need a cab down or the subway up. He'd spent any money he could have used on a cab. Thatcher turned and began jogging downtown—*a boulevardier no more*, he thought. *Just a fucknuts on the run.*

CRYPTS AND CLIENTS

James caught the PATH from Hoboken Station, under the river then up to 33rd Street at Madison Square Garden—end of the line. He transferred to the 9 train to get up to 118th and Broadway on the Columbia campus. Big cathedral there, down into the basement, the catacombs. The old Postcrypt. A long, narrow, subterranean cavern of stone, wine-jug candles and a narrow platform stage. James pressed in, moved sideways, excusing himself as he went, made it to the far side. There was a booth there and James paid the $2 donation for a free bottle of Rolling Rock. No seats left, so he leaned against the stone wall and drank his beer. Onstage was a young guy, built thick and head wrapped in a red bandana, telling funny stories between songs about living in his van with his dog and did anyone want to meet the actual dog and everyone should feel free to stop by the van tonight and say hi to the dog; the van was parked up at 121st Street. The guy's songs were very funny and very long, too, and James worked through two $2 free beers over the guy's last three songs. Well, James thought, that's folk music. Love it or leave it.

It was Lou he was here to see, and from the response at her introduction more than half the audience as well. She came out in a purple sweater and jeans, smiling shy, lips pressed and silent as she tuned, then a simple hi that brought another quick round of applause. She waited for silence until she struck her first note. (You had to wait for silence at the Postcrypt, there were no mikes, no amplification. The stone acoustics rang beautifully, but you couldn't do it fighting any other noise.) Lou opened with the song everyone knew. Someone at WFUV had got a hold of a simple stripped-down demo she'd done and they'd been playing it every morning for two weeks now. "That's the song you should close with," James had told her on the phone the day before, and he almost laughed out loud when she played it first. *Nice,* he thought. *That's my Lou.* She called him up for the second song, and then again at the end of the hour for her last song. They sang together perfectly, Lou and James. There are some things you just know, and James knew they sounded perfect together.

"Thanks," she said after her set, in the Postcrypt's lounge, and he gave her a hug.

"You killed."

"Yeah," she said, the shy smile again. "I think so."

• • •

James hadn't seen him but Quatrone had made the gig, too, ruling a small table in the back corner, eating the $1 free popcorn. He loved this stuff, the live music. Besides having to go somewhere for his paintings—like last night—Hoboken music played elsewhere was about the only thing that could entice him out of Hoboken. Quatrone simply could not stand New York. But he'd go for something like this. Especially for Lou. She was worth a small journey. Quatrone smiled and tapped his foot, mouth moving silently to the words even though he didn't know any of them. He'd gussied up for it, too, in a collar shirt and black pants and shoes. He spied James across the room and tried to get his attention but James was gone in the back with Lou after her set and Quatrone didn't much feel like swimming the crowd to get to them. He wanted to paint tonight, anyway. He strolled slow back to the subway, whistling Lou's final number as he went.

Home, Quatrone went quiet down the apartment hall to the kitchen to make some tea. He was a day artist, almost always, but some nights he just got the urge. This was one. He'd felt it all afternoon, that pull toward the empty silent of night and expanse of time to work, that fuzzy-headed tiredness that on most days would distract him but sometimes, on some nights, took his brain directions it wouldn't normally go.

"Goodnight, Mama," he said, sticking his head in her bedroom door as he brought his tea to the studio. Mrs. Quatrone was sitting up in bed, eyes closed, a magazine dropped in her lap. "You go to sleep now," he said. The old woman's eyelids fluttered and she waved a hand at him, shooing him, then whispered goodnight.

• • •

Five blocks north of Beginnings Behavioral Health, Orris sat on a bench on the porch of an aging three-story house sandwiched between two truck warehouses. It was late; Orris wasn't quite sure what time and how late— he never wore a watch, he couldn't find one that would fit comfortably on his thick wrist and besides he figured he'd likely lose a watch pretty quick anyway—but he knew it was late. He wasn't one for being up late, this was way past when he liked to be horizontal and done for the day, but he didn't feel well and even bed didn't sound good to him. So he sat out here and smoked.

Not that'd you'd know it was late from the sky, an orange so bright it lit almost as good as day, all those lights from the city and highway behind and the big lot lights around the warehouse next door. Bright as day out here, a sick and orange kind of day.

It was a downside to living here, the perpetual light. Had to keep the blinds down nights or there'd be no sleeping at all.

Although, Orris thought, *maybe keeps crime away.*

Half full, Orris was. Or tried to be.

He smoked.

It wasn't a bad place. Orris had lived here five years, Bill Pin almost as long. Best place so far. The house had room for five others, but for now Orris and Bill had it to themselves. The house ran pretty smooth, even with just the two of them. Sometimes Orris had to open the whoop-ass can or the dishes didn't get done. But him and Bill Pin worked most things out. Other roommates might upset the symmetry. And Orris had had thieving roommates, too. One thing about Bill Pin: he was no thief.

Orris had done some thieving of his own recently. Felt bad about it, too. That file. Old Thatcher seemed like a nice enough guy and Orris hoped he hadn't gotten into any boiling water over it; wasn't his fault. But Thatcher was new and Orris had been waiting a long time for the chance at this. He'd put the file back. Hadn't heard anything so figured no one was wiser, just Thatcher and Thatcher had the file back now.

It was a thick one, the file. His own. He'd been dying to read it since the thought occurred to him two or three years ago. Had asked around, tried to do it official. But they'd have none of that. No looking in the file.

"But it's my file," Orris would say. "That's me in there. How can I be sure you're getting it all right if I can't see what everyone is saying?"

No dice.

Just didn't seem right.

But he'd read it now. Whole thing. Took a magnifying glass and a dictionary and a lot of patience but if Orris had one thing for sure it was patience. And time to burn. Old Bill Pin had come into Orris's room the night he was digging through it all. Bill had squinted and shuffled some of the papers then said, "It's an awful lot. You should just not worry about it."

"Don't you worry?" Orris said. "Don't you care what gets said about you?"

Bill Pin shook his head. "Doesn't matter, really, if you think about it." And with that Bill started thinking and stood there thinking for a few minutes. Orris had watched him a moment then gone back to his reading.

Well, he'd read it all, now. Or all that was in that file. Turns out that file was only the last two years. The label said "File 6." He really would have liked to seen what got written when he was younger. That File 1 must be a fat boy, too.

Orris sighed, dropped his cigarette butt in the can he kept out here. He thought now maybe Bill Pin was right. Maybe it hadn't done him any good to read all that. Maybe he'd been better off without. Too late now. Horse out of the barn.

Orris stood with a grunt, went back inside. Bill Pin was on the couch in the common room, watching the TV.

"You take your heart meds, Bill Pin?" Orris yelled as he came in, and Bill jumped a little and nodded.

"Okay then." Orris put his hands on his hips, looked around the room. Getting messy. He might have to kick some butt on ol' Bill Pin tomorrow. You couldn't live messy.

"You going to bed, Orris?" Bill Pin asked.

"I think so. Yeah, I am."

"Okay. Goodnight then."

Orris waved, turning off the light as he made for the stairs. Bill Pin stayed on the couch, sitting upright, bathed in the TV glow. He watched movies most nights. Sometimes he fell asleep, sometimes he didn't. But he had to keep up with the movies, and with groups all day and the house chores in the afternoon, night was the only time left. Nighttime was movie time.

"Goodnight, Orris," he said again, but Orris was halfway up the stairs and didn't hear him.

BEDS AND BASEMENTS

Retrieving his guitar and duffle, Marge had passed Thatcher two bagged bottles of Grolsch over the bar. He'd killed one on the subway and made it down into the dark sewer of the Port Authority Terminal with ten minutes to spare. Now leaning against a pay phone across the hall from the bus line, Thatcher popped the ceramic cap on the second bottle and chugged deep.

Earlier tonight, in conversation about his debt, Geoff Mason had asked Thatcher about moving into Mona's place for a few months, to save up some dough. Thatcher had been vague in his answer because in fact he *had* been offered board in Castle Stanley, the last time he'd been home on leave, a few months back.

"Sounds great," James had said on the phone when Thatcher called to explain the situation. "It's a four-bedroom house, right? Plenty of room for everyone to stay out of everyone's way."

"Stanley says he set up a bed for me in the basement," Thatcher had said.

"Where?"

"The basement. Near the furnace, he says. In case it gets cold."

"It's an unfinished basement in a four-bedroom house," James said. "He put a bed in the basement?"

"So I can feel free to come and go as I want."

"Stanley said that?"

"Coming and going," Thatcher said. "It's what I do best."

"My brother," James had said, "have I mentioned the luxury of a sleeping bag in my living room?"

Offers of rooms aside, Thatcher had also insinuated to Geoff Mason a reluctance on his part to just take money from his mother. It wasn't quite like that, though; Thatcher wasn't so noble. Not nearly. In truth, he didn't ask Mona for the money—some four thousand dollars, an amount almost impossible for him to even contemplate—simply because he knew she wouldn't do it. Again, there was Stanley to consider, and Stanley wouldn't hear of it—you made your own way in this world, slept in your own bed, tied your own shoes, fought your own battles, rolled up your own sleeves, picked your own nose, dug your own basement. No way would Stanley approve paying off a bill caused by the laziness, incompetence, or neglect of the debtor. No way.

Beyond Stanley, though, Mona could be financially generous, but particular and selective in her generosity, and a credit debt or tax bill would in no way meet the standard. There would be nothing tangible for her after she wrote the check, nothing physical she could point to with satisfaction. She had offered, and Thatcher had accepted, other, more solid, charities over the years. She'd paid for a few plane tickets. Purchased and shipped to Virginia an extraordinarily expensive couch when he'd moved in with Parker (never mind what they'd really needed and asked for was a refrigerator; never mind Parker had sold the couch when Thatcher skedaddled a few months later). The best thing Thatcher's mother had underwritten was a piece of plastic he drew from his wallet now, balancing his Grolsch precariously on top of his duffel as he did this. It was the only plastic he carried in his wallet, a phone card, preapproved forty dollars a month. When the forty tab was crossed (usually around week three of any given month) the card stopped working. On day one of a new month, it worked again. Hard to beat. It had kept him in touch from Virginia. Not so much with his mother—she was seldom home so he seldom tried calling—but the small circle of people whose phone numbers he'd memorized over the years. Lou was the most recent name added to his list. Some names, like James, like Jo, went back years, even if their numbers had changed. Thatcher looked at his watch. Eight minutes to bus departure. He felt dark. Dark and drunk.

Drunk again, he thought. Thatcher swigged the Grolsch and dialed his old number. Parker's number.

Down in Virginia the phone rang and rang.

He'd read recently that what a caller heard through his phone wasn't the actual sound of the callee's phone ringing. It was, in fact, a recording, a stand in. It seemed so obvious, Thatcher couldn't believe he hadn't known this information before. Still, he hadn't, and the knowledge now made him uneasy. The ring was like an imaginary runner, in baseball or kickball. Not a real thing, just a shadow, standing in and taking credit. Down in Virginia, Parker's phone rang and rang and Thatcher stood drunk at a pay phone in the basement of Port Authority Terminal, listening to a recording generated somewhere in the bowels of the New Jersey headquarters of American Telephone & Telegraph.

It was Saturday night. Almost eleven o'clock. *She's not home*, Thatcher thought. *On duty, or out for the night*. He looked at his watch again. Five minutes to bus. He lit a cigarette, the phone ringing in his ear.

Maybe her and Deal are in bed, ignoring the phone. Deal had actually been Parker's boyfriend before Thatcher stole her away. They'd all stayed friends, Deal was casual like that, real nice like that. It was why it was so easy for Thatcher to stay calm when he and James had found Deal in Parker's trailer the weekend before; it seemed the least Thatcher could do, to return that favor.

Man, I'll bet they're drunk and going at it, Thatcher thought. His face was turning red, standing, swaying, at the pay phone.

One night, about a year ago, when they'd all been drunk and Deal was over, Thatcher had turned out the lights and Parker had ended up making out with Deal, while Thatcher first just watched then slid his hand down her shorts. The next morning—Deal and his truck gone, painful sunlight slicing into the bedroom—Parker had exploded, repeatedly punching Thatcher in the chest, screaming at him.

"Goddamn it," she'd said. "How could you let me do that? Goddamn it. That was so mean to him."

Thatcher said he hadn't seen anything mean about it.

"You jackass," she said, really angry now, hitting his chest again, "it's not fair, not fair to him. It's like a tease—it's mean."

"Who's the tease?" Thatcher said. "You're the one who lets him hang around all the time."

She'd slapped him then, across the face. The conversation hadn't gotten any better from there that morning.

Much later that day, after a few afternoon drinks, they'd mellowed and mended and ended up back in bed together. Eyes closed afterward, Thatcher whispered in her ear: "Did you like kissing him again? Did you love that?" The moment broke hard, and Parker rolled over, her back to him. She'd started crying.

"I love *you*, fucker," she said. "Don't you know that?"

He did, though. He did know that. And he loved her back.

It didn't seem to help one bit.

The phone rang and rang. Not one for answering machines, was Parker. Thatcher looked at his watch again then hung up. He lifted the receiver and, after two fumbling tries, dialed Jo's number. Someone picked up after two rings. It was a guy, a guy's voice, sounding pissed-off but he gave the phone to Jo.

"Hello?" she said.

"What are you wearing?"

"You're drunk."

"Was that the fiancé?"

"Yes. What are you doing? I thought you were in Boston?"

"Leaving in two minutes. I'm at Port Authority."

"For God's sake."

"Did I just get you in trouble?"

"Over what? No. He's oblivious to life. He's in the kitchen now."

"I wish I was in your kitchen, Joanne."

"You're drunk, sweetie. I have to hang up now. Go to Boston."

"Listen, I—"

"Good night, Thatcher," she said, then hung up.

Only ten people got on the bus. Thatcher sprawled across two back seats and was asleep before they cleared Port Authority. He slept restlessly for a little more than an hour, and woke somewhere in Connecticut.

• • •

Thatcher had entered the world of sexual relationships with a stumbling crash by shedding his virginity the summer he was fifteen—as it is with these things, later than he would have liked, sooner than actually expected. It was 1985, the year Mona married—a blow to the legions of American women who'd assumed she was impervious to men. In fact, Stanley had been living in the house almost twelve years by this point, but only Mona's immediate circle of friends knew it. When the marriage took place ("tax reasons," Stanley said, an irony not lost on Thatcher now), *Page Six* found out and ran a jabbing paragraph. It was a slow news week, apparently, because the story hit the AP wires. American women despaired.

Thatcher was less than pleased with the turn of events himself. Stanley had always acted like he owned the joint (it turns out he did, in fact, own the joint, but that wasn't the point), and the marriage did nothing to ease his strut or soothe intrafamilial relations. For a man who spent the better part of a decade telling anyone who would listen that the institution of marriage meant nothing, he sure acted as if it meant something now. He attempted, for the second time in Thatcher's life, to formally adopt Thatcher. The first time, when Thatcher was seven, Mona had talked the matter down; she'd just published her book on parenting as a single mother. This time, though, Mona was all for it. Thatcher expressed his dislike of the idea by disappearing for most of the summer. Not technically running away, just not coming home except to sleep and sometimes not that, either. Stanley got wrapped up in work and the matter eventually melted.

Thatcher financed his summer out of the house by working at Bunratty's Inn as a dishwasher. When one of the prep cooks was busted dealing coke, old man Bunratty moved Thatcher into his slot, chopping vegetable and helping an ex-con line cook named Max. The dishwasher replacement mid-July was Danielle. A solid girl, Thatcher's age but almost six inches taller, broad and with a square jaw; kept to herself, she washed plates and pots methodically, powerfully, pushing steel wool through baked-on cheese and burnt rib sauce like it was so much butter. Danielle was quick on the dish machine, unloading and delivering clean product around the big kitchen on her dishwasher's cart every half hour like clockwork through the night. She never failed to smile at Thatcher when she came around. He smiled back, but they never talked beyond that.

Thatcher let his eyes rest on a waitress named Lucy. She was twenty, no more than five foot tall, dark hair in the tall perm all the girls had then except it looked good on Lucy. She drove to work in a 1980 red Honda

Prelude, an impossibly sexy car. He'd sat in it once, when she'd tossed him the keys and asked him to run out and retrieve her extra shoes or apron or something. The car smelled like smoke and dark perfume and he let himself sit back in the passenger seat a minute, eyes closed, wondering what it might be like to take a ride with her. Lucy wore short black skirts and black stockings when she worked, and Thatcher imagined the skirt would ride pretty high while she was driving.

"She got a killer butterfly tattoo on her," Max the line cook said to him one night, following Thatcher's eye as Lucy left the kitchen. "She got a kid, too. You know that? A rugrat." Max was grinning wide, ladling liquid butter over scallops in a broiler pan.

Thatcher skipped for a moment what Max had said and took the logic back one step.

"You guys are dating?"

Max busted out laughing. "Dating? I didn't say nothing about dating. I said sometimes she invites me over and when I do I come home through the back door."

Thatcher had one of those moments of panic when he knew he was in over his head. He smiled and nodded knowingly and went into the walk-in for something he didn't need.

Whether what Max claimed was true or not Thatcher never found out, except for the part about the tattoo. He saw proof of that. One Saturday night around eleven or so Max sent him out to the bar to get a pitcher of Bud from Big Jay the bartender. Big Jay wasn't behind the bar so Thatcher went down the long hall to the storage room where they kept the kegs and cases of wine. The door was cracked and Thatcher happened to look before he put his fist up to knock and yell for Jay. And there they were, Big Jay had Lucy up against the wall. Her waitress blouse was open, her arms around his neck, and Thatcher saw the tattoo, bright butterfly over a dark nipple. He watched them move, Lucy with her eyes closed and breathing hard, Big Jay not making a sound. He was almost fifty years old, Jay was, twice divorced. He was looking down at what he was doing.

Thatcher backed from the door and returned to the kitchen in a cloud. He passed Danielle by the dish station and without thinking or forethought said, "Hey, got a second?" She nodded and he said, "C'mon, I have to show you something." She grabbed a dish towel and dried her hands and forearms as she followed him.

Thatcher went back through the dining room, through the bar, then down the long hall. He was a few feet ahead of Danielle and snuck a quick glance as he passed the storeroom. Big Jay and Lucy were still there. He turned and nodded his head. Danielle stopped and looked, her eyes growing wide. Thatcher had already moved on down the hall, to Bunratty's deserted office. He knocked, waited, then opened the door and went in without turning on the light. Danielle was in the doorway a few seconds after him.

"Thatcher?" she said.

"C'mon," he whispered, and she closed the door behind her. They kissed awkwardly—Danielle had to lean down, Thatcher had to stretch up. Her mouth was wet and tasted like Doublemint gum. They both lost their aprons and, after some fumbling, both of their checked kitchen pants dropped to their ankles. Thatcher didn't know where to put his hands, just moving them up and down across the wide, clammy expanse of her skin.

They did it on the floor. Awkward, quickly.

Once they'd done it, Thatcher had a hard time thinking of anything else. He caught himself watching Danielle all week, catching her watching him. They never said anything about it. They'd never talked before and nothing changed in that afterward. But he found himself thinking about what happened all the time—the smell, especially. When Thatcher caught Danielle looking his way he would smile. She always smiled back. Late on the next Saturday night he worked up his nerve and went over to the dishes station. He said, as nonchalantly as he could muster, "Want to go hang out?"

Danielle didn't so much look at him as nod, a quick series of nods. She was up to her elbows in dish water.

"I'll meet you over there in a few minutes?"

The nod again, her face flush and red. When she came back to the dark office five minutes later they were somewhat less frantic than the first time, but not much. They were unclothed, on the floor, and done all in just shy of five minutes. Danielle grunted when he thrust, eyes closed tight, and panted deep heavy breaths when they were done.

"Oh, man," he said, panting along with her.

They kept at it for a few weeks, meeting in Bunratty's office Saturdays around closing. He tried using his hands and she seemed to like that although she never actually said and he never felt like he knew what he was doing. The only time Danielle said anything at all was when once he tried to put his face between her legs, something he'd seen in the pages of *Hustler*, an image he hadn't been able to get out of his mind. Thatcher got down there, pressing his face into all that wet flesh down there, but she pulled him by the hair.

"Stop," she said.

They never talked in the kitchen, just their small smiles and ducked heads as they passed. He thought to himself once, "I'm having sex with her," and it was close to the happiest thought he'd ever had.

It was about that same time that Max said to him, "You're poking the dishwasher, aren't you?" Danielle had just come by with a load of clean sauté pans.

"What?" Thatcher said, his face betraying him.

Max smiled with his teeth and nodded his head at Danielle, making her way back across the kitchen to the dish station.

"No!" Thatcher said. "What, are you kidding?"

Max just whistled.

Thatcher couldn't get his quick, secret times with Danielle off his mind, but he never told anyone—not James, not any of his friends. He denied it to Max. And Max, of all people, would have high-fived him. But he couldn't. He couldn't even talk to her. This was pathetic and he knew it—who doesn't talk?—but there was nothing he could do.

And it was about that time he stopped appreciating what he had and started wondering what else he might get.

When school started back up in September he met James at his locker at the end of the first day. James was standing next to a dark-skinned girl with long black hair and the boldest chest Thatcher had ever seen on someone his age.

"Thatch," James said. "Meet our new good friend. Just in from Chicago, exiled with us here in the badlands of New Jersey."

"I'm Joanne," she said, and smiled.

When Danielle kissed Thatcher that Saturday night in Bunratty's deserted office it was Jo he was thinking of. As it turned out, it was the last time he went in the office with Danielle. It was, though, just the first of many, many nights his head filled with thoughts of Joanne.

• • •

The Greyhound bus pulled into Boston terminal just before 4 A.M. Thatcher was awake the last half hour, watching the headlights and the dark rain-soaked streets of the city. He supposed he wasn't sober but he felt a little better. Relative to as much as one can feel better curled in a Greyhound bus seat with face smashed against window. At 4 A.M. Thatcher stepped from the bus, greeted by no one. King Papas had promised to be there but Thatcher knew better. The King didn't do 4 A.M. Thatcher gathered his guitar and duffel and figured out which city bus route he needed. His headache was coming back.

King Papas lived with two roommates in the left half of a double in Cambridge. At 4:45 Thatcher set his guitar down on the front porch and quietly turned the front-door knob. Locked. He tried again, just to be sure. Locked. He walked around back. Locked. Tried the front door a third time, simultaneously not believing and not surprised. Locked. Past the point of caring, Thatcher pulled his coat over his chin, covered himself with an extra sweater from his duffel, lay down on the porch and went to sleep. When King Papas found him three hours later there was a light frost on Thatcher's clothes.

WE GOT FAT MATTRESSES

Quatrone didn't know it was morning until the dim glow of sunrise lightened the studio window. It took him by surprise; his eyes moved quick from the window to the clock to his canvas then back to the window again. Then back to the canvas. He yawned, explosive, and agreed with himself that it was definitely time for bed. He dropped the brush on the newspapered floor where he stood, then walked down the hall to his room. Quatrone drew the shade, shed his clothes, slipped between sheets.

Back in the studio the shade stayed open, windowpane lightening and brightening as the sunrise minutes ticked. The canvas on the easel was a larger one than he'd been doing of late; Quatrone was pretty sure he was moving out of the little stuff he'd been focusing on for a year or more. It felt good to stretch again, to extend the muscles in his arm to reach across the canvas. Felt good.

On the canvas, the shapes weren't all quite there yet. Quatrone wasn't done, not by a long shot, and this was all just cover for now, all back and back. The colors were purples and a light green mostly, and the thick oil paint glimmered as the sun passed through the window and laid on it, the paint drying slow and hardening.

Four floors up the light passed through the window of James's room. He was alone under the sheet, asleep but it hadn't been long. The light of morning didn't bother James's sleep any more than the dark of night ever got in the way of his walking. He'd sleep through it. His Ibanez leaned against the wall, and the sun through the window finally reached the guitar, bright and sparkling on the still, steel strings, warm on the brown-yellow wood.

Nine blocks northeast, Marsh lay awake under a blanket in his bedroom. His wife Carla was up early and he could smell coffee from the kitchen. Dash lay curled in a ball at the foot of the bed; he came in most nights around midnight and crept up onto the mattress with them. Marsh never had the heart to kick him out. The morning light played across the boy's face and his crazy, thick hair; crazy hair for a six-year-old. Marsh loved the kid's hair. He watched the light glow on his boy's hair and his cheeks, and lay still, not moving, trying to be quiet with his breathing. Marsh's leg seldom hurt when he was in bed like this, floating on a mattress, pressure off the leg and everything else.

AGAIN WITH THE DEEPENING IRONY

In Cambridge, near Boston, the apartment King Papas shared was nicer by building and by decoration than James's Hoboken place. Almost adult, even. But somehow (though this seemed impossible) even colder. This morning, anyway. Maybe it was just residual from the porch sleeping, Thatcher thought. And shivered.

All hardwood floors and old, wide windows, Papas's place; sensible bookshelves overstuffed with sensible paperbacks (one of the roommates'; Papas didn't read); CDs and tapes everywhere and the smell of incense. All good, but chilling cold in the joint. At the kitchen table for an hour with coffee and then a plate of eggs, Thatcher sat watching the two room-mates—friendly enough, *really nice to meet you, really*—circling and pre-paring then leaving for respective workplaces; he waited for someone to turn up the heat but no one did. Roommate One, a large male gay il-lustrator (described by King exactly, exactly, this way to Thatcher shortly before the fellow entered the room), wore a scarf thicker than Thatcher's coat. Roommate Two, a skinny female yoga therapist (identical descriptive technique), wore a sweater thicker than Roommate One's scarf. Maybe the cold was deeper than residual from porch sleeping, after all. Maybe it was just really cold.

King Papas—some things never change—wore jeans and nothing else, barefoot and bare chest, dark skin tight with cold but the guy sat unaffected. Between the departure of the roommates and the cooking of the eggs Thatcher had to ask: "Aren't you cold?" and King Papas just shrugged. "We all do what we can, man," he said, staring off into the distance. Thatcher had no idea what that meant and decided not to ask. It was possible King Papas was having a moment. A few minutes later came the hinge-squeak of a door opening followed by a redhead in a white bathrobe and furry slippers. She kissed King Papas on the top of his head then came around the table and kissed Thatcher's cheek. Papas's girlfriend, Claire; Thatcher met her once before almost a year ago, a beauty to be sure. The apartment had been hers, originally. She'd moved to Back Bay to be closer to work—she was a singer (isn't everyone?) but made money doing something related to dental hygiene—and King Papas had taken her room.

"I find his sensibilities refreshing," Papas said now of Larry, Roommate One, the gay illustrator. Papas drank his coffee black and took a big swig of it now. Thatcher stirred more sugar into his coffee and blinked, tired. Focusing was a challenge this morning.

"You find his what?"

"His sensibilities. Refreshing."

Thatcher didn't quite know what the King meant by that. Again, he chose not to pursue. He was reminded, though, of a younger King Papas, in a fervor only sixteen-year-old Pentecostals can achieve, railing in the high school cafeteria on the immorality and filth of homosexuality. Thatcher had seen the King's Christianity slip to almost nothing once out from under the roof of King Senior. It seemed all his views had liberalized. *Funny*, Thatcher thought. *Perhaps even ironic. If only I knew what* ironic *meant.* Thatcher felt his mind spinning off the way it did when he was exhausted. He said nothing and shivered cold and stirred his coffee.

Claire was neck-deep in the freezer, searching. "Who do you find refreshing, Pap?"

King Papas jutted his jaw, blinked hard the way he often did. "Larry," he said.

"You find Larry refreshing?"

"No—look, you can't walk into the middle of a conversation. Your contact is all off."

"Context," Thatcher said.

"You sure?"

"Yes."

"Context. Your context is all—you don't have any context."

Thatcher nodded. Claire emerged from the freezer empty-handed, closed the door.

"It's just funny for you to say you find Larry refreshing. In any context."

"I'm full of surprises," the King said.

"You referred to him as a goat-stinking hog the day after you first met him." Claire was drop-dead funny, she was. *Irony,* Thatcher thought. *I don't know what it is, but you can smell it from here.*

King Papas closed his eyes and explained—patiently, quietly—his drunken state on the day of the offensive goat-stinking description, as well as the lack of overall enlightenment he'd been living with at the time. "C'mon, I was only two days out of New Jersey," he said. "Make some more coffee, hon?" He held out his mug and Claire rolled her eyes, took the mug, went back to the freezer.

"I never left New Jersey," Thatcher said. "Not officially, anyway. Never changed my driver's license, even living in Virginia."

Papas did that thing with his eyebrows, then the jaw jut again.

Thatcher said, "I just mean to say, even *in* Jersey I never called anyone a goat-smelling anything. I don't think so, anyway."

"Yeah, but look at your mother, dude. You were born enlightened."

Thatcher was sipping from his mug as this got said and he came close to spitting his coffee across the table. He got it in, swallowed, thought about it, then said, "I think that's the nicest thing you've ever said to me."

"Yes, I'm sure it is," Papas said, then pushed himself up from the table and gathered their breakfast dishes. He was so tight that when he moved it seemed all parts of him moved in some way, in a symmetry. It was always impossible to tell with Papas if he was flexing or just simply moving.

"I really think gays are among God's chosen," Papas said. "Like the Jews, you know."

Both Claire and Thatcher were caught short by that. "You think who?" Thatcher said.

"No, really," Papas said. "I'm thinking maybe, just maybe, they're the caretakers of creativity. The guardians of it."

Thatcher put his chin in his hand. "Well," he said.

"I think you're off your rocker," Claire said.

Papas looked at her. "Half your friends are gay," he said.

"That doesn't mean they're God's chosen. I don't think any of them think they're God's chosen. And look at the Jews—I'm not sure there's a clear benefit to being God's chosen."

"This is all too visceral," Papas said. "I was just making a, you know—"

"Analogy," Thatcher said.

"Yes."

"Literal," Thatcher said. "Not visceral; literal."

"Whatever."

"I think you're attracted to men," Claire said. Both King Papas and Thatcher looked up to see who she meant, but she was in the cabinet, searching for filters, not looking at either of them. They both opened their mouth, but she spoke first. "I don't think you're gay, but I think you're attracted to men. I think all people are same-sex attracted, at some level. Especially artistic ones."

Thatcher waited for the King Papas explosion of denial, but it didn't come. The eyebrows moved, the jaw jutted, the blink blink blink. But no explosion. Instead, Papas sat back down at the table. *Maybe he is enlightened,* Thatcher thought. *Last stop for irony. All ashore going ashore.*

Claire had found the filters. She turned, eyed them both, then went back to her coffee prep.

"I could see that," Papas said. Thatcher wasn't quite sure who was speaking. This wasn't the Greek King he knew. Whoever that was across the table, it wasn't King Papas. "A body is a body, you know? If it's beautiful, well—" He looked at Thatcher. "You know?" Thatcher nodded. King Papas blinked. "Hey, you know David Moyer?" Thatcher nodded again. David Moyer was a theater critic for the *Times.* But he wrote on wooden music, too, and hung out at Geoff Mason's place in the Village. "Wouldn't you say David Moyer has a beautiful face? I mean, in an artistic way. Wouldn't you say?" David Moyer was slim, with black hair and soft, watchful blue eyes. He talked quietly, through thin lips, and his laugh was almost silent. He was one of those people who was so subtly attractive that he made people uncomfortable when he stood close by.

"Yes," Thatcher said. "No 'artistic way' about it. He's a beautiful person." *Again with the deepening irony,* Thatcher thought. All "artistic ways" aside, King Papas himself—like him or not or remain undecided—was one of the most beautiful human beings Thatcher had ever seen outside a magazine.

"So one night, late leaving Geoff's, and me and Moyer are talking, talking, I don't know what about. Something heavy."

"You were stoned," Thatcher said, and King Papas smiled and said, "Yeah, I was stoned.

"Anyway, he walks me to the PATH but we're all talking and he's like 'You want to just walk me home, you can crash on the couch?' So we're talking, we're talking, drinking at his kitchen table, two three hours. You know—I don't remember what all: Elvis Costello, Bruce Cockburn. You know, shit we both dig. All of a sudden I realize I'm staring at his face. Just staring at it. And I don't know if he knows or not, and he's still talking, but all of a sudden I realize I'm staring at his face and—dude, I'm not kidding"—Papas's hands went up in the air—"I wanted to kiss him. Just wanted to lean across the table and kiss him." He set his hands down flat. "So what do you think of that?"

"I think you were stoned," Claire said. "But you should have kissed him. David Moyer is gorgeous."

"Yuck," Papas said, and shuddered. "Yeah, I don't think so."

"But you might have, then," Thatcher said. "Kissed him."

Papas blink blink blinked. "I just wanted to *be* him," he said. "He was just so beautiful and so smart and I think I just wanted to be him." Papas looked at his hands, then looked back up at Thatcher. "So what do you think about that?" Thatcher opened his mouth to answer—he thought quite a lot about that—but King Papas suddenly noticed his watch and jumped up. "We're late," he said. "Get your coat."

Thatcher stood. "I never took it off," he said.

• • •

In King Papas's red Nissan, Thatcher rolled down the window, lit a cigarette, leaned his head back and closed his eyes. The King waited a moment, then said, "You could ask, you know. Before smoking." Thatcher looked over at him and said, "You've been in Boston too long."

The car was negotiating narrow, quiet residential streets, the sky gray and heavy with clouds and cold air. In Boston, full winter came earlier.

• • •

The gig that night was the twenty-fifth anniversary of The Nameless, the concert series that ran in a big church on a small street off Harvard Square. Pay was naught but prestige high for the anniversary show. A full house expected, much of the Boston singer-songwriter royalty confirmed, everyone aware this show was one of those things you were supposed to do. King Papas, who'd moved to Boston but never really conquered it, had no business on the bill for a night like tonight. Thatcher had even less—he could barely get a gig in New York, let alone Massachusetts. But Claire booked the series. King Papas and Thatcher would open the show (although not together—they didn't do that anymore). The gig wasn't until eight, but there was a full promotional schedule for the afternoon. It began at the University of Boston radio station. Thatcher and King Papas arrived first, almost an hour early (yet almost an hour late in the world of Papas). They found an empty studio with folding chairs and pulled out their guitars.

"What do you think of Claire?" Papas asked, strumming, tuning. He played a massive Taylor jumbo. Any other guitar looked small on him, and looks counted big with the King.

"Claire? She's smart," Thatcher said.

"Yeah, that, but isn't she hot?"

Thatcher nodded. "She's sweet, no doubt."

"She's red all over, you know," Papas said, and winked.

"Good to know."

"She likes it in the morning, Thatch. I gave her the business while you were in the shower. I'll bet you didn't know that."

Thatcher hadn't known that. He said, "What happened to the sensitive guy sitting at the table this morning?"

"Fuck you." Eyebrows up. Blink blink blink. "I think you're jealous."

"Of you?"

"Yeah. It's alright, dude." Papas said. "I'd be jealous, too."

"No, you got it all backward," Thatcher said. "I'm jealous of Claire. I wish you'd given me the business this morning. I just want to *be* you."

"Fuck off."

Papas dropped his low E string down to a D. Thatcher followed. "This is no kind of talk for folk music," Thatcher said.

"Fuck folk music."

They tuned, tried to. Papas shook his head. "Do you ever change your strings?"

"I changed them yesterday."

"You're sloppy, man. You know that? Sloppy."

Thatcher stopped and looked up. "Maybe I ought to go."

"What do you mean?"

"You know what I mean."

"Don't be so tender. Christ."

Thatcher spun a peg, trying again for tune.

"You won't see a gig like this again anytime soon."

"Probably not."

"So why don't you just move up here?"

"Are you leaving?"

"What do you mean?"

"We couldn't live in the same city."

"It's a big city." Papas reached over and began spinning Thatcher's pegs. "Just hit the strings, I'll get it."

This was bullshit, but Thatcher let him do it. He wasn't getting anywhere himself.

"What the fuck's in Hoboken anyway, Thatcher?"

"Place to live."

"New York is dead, man. Hoboken is the foyer to a death house."

"That's a pretty good line."

"You think so?"

"Yeah. For you."

"Dude," Papas said, face flush, then shut up. He was irritated, but he'd smacked first and knew it so couldn't say anything. Nothing got under his skin faster than a dig at his lyrics—especially from Thatcher—but he couldn't do anything about it now. Either escalate to fists, or just shut up. The new, enlightened King Papas just shut up. He spun pegs, listening to the drifting notes on Thatcher's guitar. After a few minutes he said, "She has the most amazing breasts, dude. I kid you not. Fucking outstanding."

The thing with King Papas was that he'd never really had a girlfriend before. Hard to believe, given the way he looked. But high school had been under the thumb of a vengeful, New Testament God and his trusty sidekick King Senior. Good Christians, the old King said, don't date. Papas slipped free after school, but slow out of the gate. Fear of hell is hard to overcome. Papas did overcome, finally, around the same time he realized what he looked like. Both were now minor obsessions with him—the women who wanted him and the way he looked to them—just a hair south of music success.

The studio door opened. A large man behind a gray beard said, "I'm Dave," and came at them with toothy smile and outstretched hand for shaking. "We'll be live in about fifteen minutes. Soon as the girls are ready." He turned, but no girls. He went back to the open door. "Girls? Come on in. You can tune up in here."

The girls walked through the door and Thatcher fell in love for the first time today.

"Hi," the first one said. "I'm Erin."

• • •

The real thing with the gig—the Boston subtext—was less about the anniversary, more about the fact that the duo Chapter Two had signed a contract with one of the majors this week. A subdivision of a subdivision of one of the majors—but still. This was Chapter Two's only Boston-area gig for the month, so would be the point of congratulations. Everyone loved Chapter Two. Erin and Eric; both female, never mind Eric's name.

• • •

The thing with Thatcher and King Papas was complicated. Their friendship had not been strong in high school, they barely knew each other, the formation of their trio purely through James. When James went off to college Thatcher and Papas had been left as de facto friends. That was okay for awhile. Then there was an issue with a girl: Papas celebrated his twenty-first birthday losing his virginity to a record-store clerk who Thatcher was seeing on and off. King Papas—always amazingly, harshly honest—had told Thatcher the next day. He'd pointed out the "on and off" part of Thatcher's tie to the record-store clerk, but the reminder of this information had not helped any. Thatcher joined the army around then, Papas went to Boston. They'd just recently started talking again; tentative, tentative.

• • •

Introductions all around, then the two were alone again in the dark studio. King Papas stood in the corner doing up-and-down-scale exercises, then turned and stood watching Thatcher tune for awhile.

"They're going to be big, man," he finally said. "Erin and Eric."

"You think?"

"Yeah. Have you heard them?"

Thatcher shook his head. "No."

"They sound amazing."

"They look amazing."

"They're beautiful, both of them. Even more beautiful when they sing."

"You think they'll be big?"

"I know it."

"It's possible."

"More than possible. It is for any of us, you know. Any of us who are left, anyway."

"Some of us," Thatcher said. "I'm sloppy, remember?"

King Papas looked at Thatcher for a moment, then said, "You, my dude, are a fucking star." Papas blink blink blinked, opened his mouth, then seemed to change his mind and didn't say anything else. When he opened his mouth again he said, "What is it with James?"

"What do you mean?"

"Why won't he talk to me?"

"How often do you call him?"

"Fuck that. He's an ass. Holier than thou." Papas blink blink blinked. "Hey, what's the deal with this rock band you joined?"

"Just trying something out. Good group of people, you know? Safety in numbers. Life boat."

"That guy Marsh, I know him. He books Maxwell's, right?"

"Yes."

"He seems mostly alright."

"He is alright."

"That chick, though, that friend of James."

"Lou?"

"Yeah. I've seen her around, at Geoff's. She's a big dyke, right?"

"The fuck?" Thatcher set his guitar down on the floor. "You can't talk that way, man."

"I can talk whatever way I want." Papas took a large step forward. Enlightenment gone; King Papas was back in the room.

"Bullshit. Why do you have to dig at everyone?"

"Hey, fuck you, army boy. I got you this gig."

The door opened, gray beard Dave again. "Time, gents," he said, and held the door open for them. Thatcher picked up his guitar and followed the steaming King Papas out of the room.

PARTICIPATE

In Hoboken, there was sun all afternoon, faces turned up to it the length of Washington Street. Lou and Mary Ann were walking slow, big bags in hand, back from mid-day sister shopping in the city. Lou had bought a shirt she thought would look good on stage, just a shade deeper than maroon, just a little fuzzy to the touch.

"It's all about having a good frock," Mary Ann said. "You can't rock without a frock."

Lou smiled but didn't say anything. She'd been fine in the city but her mood had dropped by degrees back in Hoboken, the closer she got to home. Mary Ann had said about all she was going to say on it; they walked the last two blocks in silence. At the door of Lou's building they cheek-kissed. "You'll be alright, kid," Mary Ann said.

"I know."

"Call me later if you want."

Lou kissed her again then turned to go inside. It was a three-story townhouse, carved into the three apartments, Lou had the top floor. There were cardboard boxes stacked at the bottom of the stairs, and another stack at the top outside her door. She held her shopping bag in her teeth, unlocked the door, pushed it open. Another stack of boxes at the opening to the small kitchen. Jaelene had a lot of stuff. Seeing the boxes, it occurred to Lou that when Jaelene was completely gone the place would be almost empty. Lou didn't have much beyond her futon, books, CDs, a framed picture of the five sisters—stair-dragging sister Helen with her arm tight around Lou, just a month before she died. Lou bit her lip. She set her bags down in the corner and started unwrapping the scarf from around her neck. She heard a noise in the bedroom and called out, "Hey."

"Hey, you're back." Jaelene stuck her head around the corner. "Sorry. I didn't know you'd be back this early."

"That's okay." Lou let the scarf drop to the floor. Jaelene stayed where she was, half leaning around the corner from the bedroom. She was half-Irish, half-Puerto Rican, with black hair and bright blue eyes.

"I really am sorry," she said. "I'd promised you I'd be gone by two."

Lou shrugged and said again, "That's okay." Jaelene gave a strained smile, then went back into the bedroom.

Jaelene worked for a record company. Not an indie, like Marsh; she worked for one of the majors. And she wasn't a musician, either. Like Marsh, though, she did radio promotion. On a much larger scale, with a much larger budget. Jaelene and Lou had lived together just over a year. Jaelene's parents lived on the Upper West Side, her father was a lawyer. Jaelene saw a lot of her family. Lou had never met them. It was an issue.

Lou ran her fingertip over the top of one of the boxes. She thought about how easy it would be to just walk in there, walk in the bedroom, put her arms around Jaelene. Put her arms around her and say *It's okay, it's okay, we're okay, it doesn't matter, we can live on your terms.* Put her arms around her and say all that and kiss and be done. Unpack the boxes. Go out for dinner, have a bottle of wine.

Instead, she picked up her scarf, wrapped it around her neck again, shoved her keys down in her pocket. "I'm going to Mary Ann's," she said, but didn't say it very loud and didn't know if Jaelene heard. Lou picked up her guitar case and went out the door.

TENS OF DOLLARS

In Boston, two of their own had just broke through, and everyone came out to see. There were more wooden-music artists in this one old church off Harvard Square than Thatcher had thought possible. The aging famous singer-songwriter from the Cape was there with her longtime companion and two adopted Korean children. The aging almost-famous folksinger from New Hampshire stalked the long hall just inside the church's front doors, flask of whiskey in hand. The aging almost-famous-younger-brother-of-very-famous-former-folksinger-turned-pop-star from Portland was there with his wife; he was the credited discoverer of Erin and Eric, making a phone call to someone who made a phone call to someone else who agreed to come hear them play after Chapter Two opened a show for him at Skidmore College.

King Papas blink blink blinked like tomorrow was in question, non-stop, partially kid in candy store, partially jealous voyeur peering through Gates of Pearl. "Damn," he said. "Damn, damn, damn." They were backstage, preshow, walking around the big room reserved for the big people. The movers, the shakers; the poohs, the bahs. "This is it," Papas said. "The place."

Thatcher shadowed the King for fifteen minutes but no one was really talking to them—friendly enough, smiles all around, *Hi nice to meet you*, but no real interaction—and finally he just slipped off to the farthest corner he could find, pulled out his guitar, and strummed and hummed quietly, warming up. Claire came over after a while to see what he was up to and Thatcher asked if she'd sing with him on a song.

"I like the one about the circus," she said. "I know that one, from your tape."

"Can you do the one about the Mexican sailor?"

"Yeah yeah," she said. "Let's do that."

Erin wandered over later. "I like what you did on the radio this afternoon, Thatcher," she said. She spoke in the manner of those who make it a point to use the names of people they've just met. It didn't come across annoying, though. Thatcher thanked her. She was short, lithe. Both of them, Erin and Eric, were built like dancers. "Good luck," she said, and stepped back into the sea of schmooze.

King Papas came up five minutes before the show began. His set was first. He'd wanted Thatcher to go first and that'd been fine with Thatcher but Claire had insisted on this order. "It's not about personalities it's about pacing, proper pacing" she said, "It will make for a better show." Papas allowed it, but Thatcher could tell he was not pleased.

"I'm nervous," the King said, jumbo guitar hanging from the white strap around his neck, pushing Thatcher back into the corner.

"You're never nervous."

"I know. But I'm nervous."

"Forget about it. You'll kill."

"I know I shouldn't care."

Thatcher shrugged. "It's a big night. Could be, anyway." He was nervous, too, but had found a good zone and was working it, working it. He was also sober, which helped.

King Papas turned and surveyed the room again. The place was clearing out, people going up front to take their reserved seats in the audience, schmooze suspended until the party after Chapter Two's set. Over by the cheese tray the almost-famous folksinger from New Hampshire had Claire trapped in conversation. She was nodding intently, but her eyes were darting around the room.

"Alright, it's time," the King said. He pulled down on his guitar strap, testing it. Thatcher was watching him carefully, mood and emotion moving across the King's face in waves. "You want me to sing one with you?" Thatcher asked.

"No, I've got my set down tight. I don't want to fuck with it."

"Just holler if you change your mind. I'll be backstage."

"You're going to watch my set?"

"Of course."

"Thanks, man." Papas ran an open hand down the front of his silk shirt than said it again: "Thanks, man."

Then he was gone, striding to the door and the stage beyond. Through it Thatcher could hear applause and the voice of bearded Dave, the public radio DJ who was hosting the gig, introducing the King. Thatcher slid his guitar so it hung down his back and went to watch the show. It did not go well. By the middle of his set Papas's veins were standing out on his neck. Claire came up from behind Thatcher and took one of his hands in hers. "Shit," she said, watching her boyfriend crash and burn. Thatcher said, "I had a night like this last week. Unbearable." Leaving the stage when he was done, King Papas didn't even stop, walked right past them, through the door and gone. "Shit," Claire said again. "I might miss singing with you," she said to Thatcher. "I have to go find him."

"I know."

Onstage, bearded Dave was wasting no time. "Once more for King Papas, ladies and gentlemen. Once more."

Claire turned and went to find King Papas. Through the curtain, Thatcher could see the famous folksinger from Cape Cod in the front row, her wife beside her, their children magically disappeared.

"Our next act is a new face to most of you. We had him on the radio program this afternoon and I think you're going to like what you hear. He's from Hoboken, New Jersey. That says something, doesn't it?"

The big introduction. Thatcher looked down, suddenly questioning his choice of attire, a black T-shirt, a pair of jeans; he hadn't really thought this through. Too late. Thatcher took the stage.

• • •

"Thanks so much. Like he said, my name's Thatcher. I'm going to play you some of this here folk music—the fancy, modern disco dance hall we're in might not be the place for this kind of music, but I'm going to sing it anyway."

A nice wave of laughter. Thatcher strummed down once. Way out of tune. *Fucking amazing*, he thought. *How does this happen?*

"Gonna start by demonstrating the ancient Chinese art of Tu Ning."

An even bigger laugh this time. Sweat beaded on Thatcher's forehead. He was no good at talking while he tuned, but he had to do it.

"I arrived tonight from a different path than most of the big stars you get passing through here," he said. The microphone smelled like a cigarette and Thatcher wished he had one right now. "Did a couple years in the army, you know." The B string was the root of all the evil. Thatcher twisted the peg gently, bending the note up. "Finally decided I needed to make a living, make something of myself. A career of some kind." Too far up. He tried to keep his face from wincing and twisted the peg again. "Read a book about Woody Guthrie somewhere in there, and said to myself, 'Self, that's what I want to do for a job.'" An audience chuckle. The famous songwriter from Cape Cod was watching the tuning with eyebrows raised. Thatcher looked up, caught her eye, and winked; she smiled. Thatcher struck a note then twisted the D string peg. "One thing I found out, though. A bit of a shock. Well, it was a shock to me. Maybe it'll be a shock to you, too." Thatcher rang the D and B strings; perfect. He leaned in to the microphone, *sotto voce*. "Believe it or not…there's not a lot of money to be made in folk music." Wave of laughter. The famous songwriter from Cape Cod threw her head back and guffawed. "Tens of dollars, friends. Literally tens of dollars to be made in folk music."

Straight strum, pitch perfect, and it was all smooth sailing from there.

• • •

In the wings, King Papas sat on a stool, far enough back so Thatcher couldn't see him. Claire was behind, arms around his neck.

"Why does he play the rube like that?" he said. "What is that about? Why does he talk that way up there? It's stupid."

Claire rubbed her hand on his chest but didn't say anything. Papas sat watching in the dark until the audience got to its feet at the end of Thatcher's set, then he stood quickly and eased out before he was seen. Claire walked with him.

"He better not take an encore," the King said. "We're already tight on time."

• • •

Thatcher floated off stage. *Finally*, he thought. *Finally*.

Erin and Eric were there in the wings, in their own zone already, barely nodding as he walked past. Didn't matter. Thatcher was floating. He looked around but no Papas. *For the best*, he thought. *I'm glad he didn't see that.*

Thatcher put his guitar away then went back to the wings to watch Chapter Two's first song. King Papas had been right: They were something to see. One guitar (Eric), two girls, moving and swaying as they sang. The harmonies were just this side of desperate; aching and pulled. *That's it*, Thatcher thought. *That's the real thing. Everyone else here is just pretending, next to that. Including me.*

The thought didn't bring him down. He'd killed and knew it. Thatcher stayed for another song, then went to find his smokes.

Outside the church the air had dropped a good ten degrees since they'd gone in, cold enough to snow. Thatcher watched his breath waft up. He lit a cigarette and made the cloud thicker. He walked down the steps, sat on the curb and smoked. He had to catch a late-night bus out of Boston tonight, work in the morning. The King had promised a ride to the bus depot but Thatcher thought he might not see the King again tonight. He'd get a cab.

Thatcher checked his watch; four hours to kill. Maybe he'd go over to Passim and see what was shaking. Pity the act on the bill tonight—Chapter Two at The Nameless had sucked all the available air out of Cambridge. He'd give it ten minutes, he decided, on the off chance Papas or Claire came out to find him. Ten minutes, then he'd go grab his guitar and head to Passim. Maybe find a drink somewhere, too. Thatcher sat on the curb and began whistling—the one about the Mexican sailor. He was floating.

Halfway through the second cigarette a body sat next to him. He looked over, expecting Claire. It wasn't Claire. He didn't know who she was. She was Asian, Japanese maybe, a delicate face under a red knit cap. Her black hair shot in tufts down over her ears and eyes. "Got a light?" she said, then, "Hey, you're that guy."

Thatcher held his lighter for her.

"I'm that guy," he said.

"I'm Alice," she said. "You were awesome."

"That's really nice of you to say. Thanks, Alice." She was something, Alice was. A tiny little mouth.

"You said you were from Hoboken?"

"Did I? Oh, onstage." Thatcher nodded. "Yes—now anyway. Not from there, but there. Now."

"I live in Queens. Astoria."

"No shit. Small world."

"No shit. I'm up visiting my old college roommate. She got strep. So I'm here."

"Nice to meet you, Alice. Hey, you want to go get a drink?"

She looked around. "Aren't you supposed to be back in there?" she said.

"My set's done. All eyes are elsewhere." He stubbed his cigarette on the curb. "Although you probably want to be in there for Erin and Eric."

Alice took a drag, gears turning in her head, then blew her smoke lightly in Thatcher's face. "No," she said. "Matter of fact, I think I'd love a drink."

THE CHRIST BENEATH YOU

Bruno always dressed in black; ten years of friendship, it was all Marsh had ever seen him in. But when Bruno unzipped his coat in the back of the cab a white sweater was revealed.

"Bruno, Bruno, Bruno," Marsh said, pulling at the sweater. "Branching out tonight. I am impressed."

Nonplussed, Bruno said, "I thought it appropriate for the evening."

They were in fact both branching out. The cab ride was transportation on a fact-finding mission, twenty-minute ride to a public high school deep in the Jersey burbs. The Land of White People, Bruno called it. The land of his fathers, home of his people.

"I'd just assumed you popped into existence in a poof of hip on a Soho street corner," Marsh said.

"No one is born in New York, oh ye rock-and-roll Ohio heathen" Bruno answered. "Those of us not from Ohio like you—which is most of us—are raised on white-people farms in Jersey and Long Island. The lucky ones discovered The Tubes and Hüsker Dü early on and then got to live urban when we grew up."

"But you live in Jersey right now."

Bruno didn't consider Hoboken to be part of New Jersey—or New York either, for that matter. "Hoboken is like the Statue of Liberty," he said. "An island of sanity, unto itself, floating alone."

"Hoboken, my friend, is neither an island nor particularly sane," Marsh said. "And my taxes go to the Great State of New Jersey."

All about nonplussed tonight, Bruno was. "It's an illusion," he said. "I can say no more about it now."

The cab took them deeper into Jersey, finally to their destination. The high school sprawled across a campus and looked more like the headquarters of a pharmaceuticals company. It's gym was the size of an airplane hangar and had been rented for the evening by an organization called Arise Productions.

"A ministry and outreach group," Marsh said, quoting the literature sent to him at the office. "Based in Cherry Hill."

"A South Jersey concert promoter cashing in on Jesus," Bruno translated.

"That's just so crass, young Bruno. Please, this is my new living."

Bruno shrugged. "I'm not young. And it's not crass. Everyone needs promotion. Even Jesus." He smoothed the front of his sweater. "Jesus knows I could use some promotion. Hey, Zippy Records is paying for this cab, right?"

Marsh waved the magical wave of junket and inclusion.

"Jesus is just all right with me," Bruno said. "Jesus was buff."

The gym was maybe a third full when they arrived, concert under way, the first of three acts on the stacked risers arranged under a raised basketball net. The kids in the audience were mostly all pressed close in, a few girls dancing tentatively. Bruno saw more boys than girls and didn't know what that meant. They seemed predominantly fifteen, sixteen, seventeen.

"It sounds like rock," Marsh yelled. "Loud like rock."

"Quacking like a duck, must be a duck."

They did a quick survey of the room then stepped back outside. Frosty out here, grass crunching under their feet.

"I'd hoped for a bigger draw," Marsh said. "Can't be more than fifty kids in there."

"Hard to sell Jesus in a predominantly Jewish neighborhood, no?"

They walked the length of the gym outside, went back in through a set of open double doors. The boys' locker room was the backstage, a few trays of food laid out across a line of sinks, some sandwiches and a few pizzas. Bruno helped himself to a piece of pizza. It was cold; he swallowed his bite and dropped the rest in a garbage can. An ice-filled tub under the trays was stocked with bottled water and juice boxes. He grabbed two bottles, stuffed them in his jacket pockets. The sound of the onstage band came muffled through the tile wall, the food trays vibrating with the bass. Bruno caught up with Marsh rounding a row of lockers and they both stopped short. What appeared to be one or maybe both of the next two bands were circled, everyone's eyes closed.

"Looks like they're about to play football," Bruno whispered. Marsh elbowed him lightly in the ribs.

One of the boys—none of the musicians, assuming these were the musicians, looked a day over eighteen—stepped into the middle of the circle. His eyes still closed, he raised both arms up in the air.

"Lord," he said, soft Dixie voice echoing through the locker room, "we just want to praise you tonight, and thank you, Lord, thank you for your presence here with us, thank you for being with us here in New Jersey." He was dressed in brown cords, black Docs, black T-shirt, flannel wrapped around his waist, knit cap almost to his eyes. *The singer?* Bruno guessed. *Must be.* The raised arms began swaying and the boy opened his eyes. "We need your light, Lord, to help us bring the glory to you, all the glory tonight goes to you, Lord."

"Hello, Cleveland," Bruno whispered, Brit accent, and Marsh elbowed him again, harder.

The kid was louder now. "Our worship is for you, Lord, and we just want to praise you right now." He'd started turning, waving his arms, a few more people coming into the circle from between the lockers—road crew, maybe, Bruno thought, although most of them looked suspiciously like parents. The kid made eye contact with Marsh and Bruno and waved vigorously, inviting them in. "We celebrate your presence, Lord!" the kid yelled, and kept waving.

"Yikes," Marsh said. He'd taken a small step forward but the kid turned then, and squeezed his eyes closed again, and Marsh switched direction and took a step back, instead. "Let's go check merch," he whispered, but Bruno was already gone.

• • •

The merch was just fine. A young woman sat behind a folding table set up in the back of the gym, piles of CDs arranged in front of her, and two stacks of books for sale. One was the Bible, with a bright purple cover and a subhead: *The Real Buzz!* The other book was thinner, *A Parent's Guide to What Your Kids Aren't Telling You.*

"What you don't know can't hurt you," Bruno said, flipping through the pages. He put his mouth close to Marsh's ear, trying to speak over the band. "I'll bet there's a whole world that Dash isn't telling you."

Marsh nodded. "I'm quite sure. He's a stud, Dash is. Big stud of first grade." He leaned across the table, introduced himself to the young woman. "How are CD sales tonight?" He had to yell it twice.

"Slower than normal," she said, and made a sad face. "We sold a hundred last night."

"Where were you last night?" Marsh asked.

"Coin Jock, North Carolina."

"Jesus has a better advance crew in Carolina," Bruno said.

"I'm sorry?" she said, cupping a hand to her ear. It was getting worse. Band number one—Fire Quest, they were named, which sounded to Bruno like a brand of smoke detectors—was wrapping up its set with a volume that would have made Metallica smile with pride. Marsh stepped in front of Bruno and said to her, "God bless Carolina." The woman smiled. Marsh pulled Bruno by the sleeve, out the door into the hallway.

"Play nice," he said.

Bruno grunted and stepped across the hall, admiring a glass-fronted trophy case. "Third in state, 100 meters, 1967. A point of honor."

Marsh had a notebook out and was scribbling something in it. Done, he stowed it in a pocket and turned round twice. "Let's see if we can't find a bathroom hereabouts," he said. "And I'd rather not go back into the locker room."

Bruno watched Marsh turn. He'd noticed a buried grimace on Marsh all night, and a deeper limp then he was used to seeing on the big man. "You okay, Marshall?" he said, his eyes on Marsh's leg.

"What?" Marsh said. "The leg? Yeah. You know. Acts up from time to time." He started down the hall on his bathroom quest. The limp was pronounced now, no hiding it.

"Looks bad, man," Bruno said, a step behind. "You been to the doctor?"

"I *am* the doctor," Marsh said. "They call me Doctor Love."

"Not here they don't."

There was applause from the gym, a few scattered whistles, and then a voice on the mike: "The Lord be with you!" and a loud shouted answer: "And also with you!"

• • •

They sat on a bench in front of the school, waiting for the cab they'd called. Marsh wrapped his scarf tighter, trying to bury his face from the cold. They sat silent awhile, watching their puffs of breath and listening to the ring in their ears. Jesus rock didn't mean quiet rock, that was for certain. Only a few CDs had moved tonight but it didn't matter. This was New Jersey. The tour was in Ohio tomorrow night—only fifteen miles from Marsh's home town as a matter of fact—and there would be sales aplenty. Marsh was sure of it. The parking lot next to the gym was emptying of vehicles, the crew and band members loading-out equipment to a big U-Haul pulled up to the gym doors. Marsh raised his head out of his scarf.

"You know a guy named King Papas?"

Bruno shook his head. "Never met him. Only by name. Is that his real name?"

"I think so."

"He's from Boston, right? I think I saw his name on a bill when I was up there with Dutch's band last year."

"He's from here, actually. Went to high school with James and Thatcher."

"Maybe that's where I heard his name. Why?"

"So you haven't heard his music at all?"

Bruno shook his head. "Why?"

"I know him only to talk to him," Marsh said. "He's been trying to get booked in Maxwell's back room for a couple years now. His tape didn't suck so I had him in once to the front room but he didn't draw."

"How was he?"

Marsh sighed. "I don't know. He didn't suck. All these solo kids these days. Not much that's different, most of them. But what do I know." Marsh ducked his mouth back under his scarf again for a second. A set of headlights rolled by; they looked up but it wasn't their cab.

"Anyway," Marsh said, "guy calls me again, few days ago. Says he heard I'm putting together a band, all songwriters yadda yadda—can he get in on it."

"You're kidding."

"No."

"That's a little bit forward."

"With a capital F."

"How did he even know?"

"Yeah, so I ask him that, and he tells me Thatcher mentioned something to him. Thatcher's going up there for some gig, they were talking on the phone, and he mentioned the band to him."

"Never mind for a minute all the other weirdness, but why did this guy call you? Did Thatcher tell him to call?"

"No, that's the thing. He didn't ask Thatcher at all. Two guys in the band he went to high school with but he calls me."

"What'd you tell him?"

"I killed him softly."

"Sorry, lifeboat's full."

"Yeah, nicer than that, though. They call me Doctor Love."

"Who phones out of the blue asking if they can join a band?"

"King Papas, apparently. Wonder if it will make things weird for Thatcher up there."

"I don't get people," Bruno said. "Especially musicians. I don't get them."

"You're one of them."

"Definitely. It's a problem in my life."

Headlights again, in the circle at the front of the school, their cab this time. Bruno stood. "I just want to praise you, Mister Cab Driver," he said. "I'm here to praise you tonight." He stepped toward the curb.

Marsh put his hand down on the bench to push himself up, pushed, and nothing happened. He grunted, pushed again, rose on his good leg but the polio leg had decided to shut down. Balance off, his push propelled him forward, his good leg sliding on a patch of ice, and then he went down, hard on his side—*whump*.

"Ah, Christ—"

Bruno turned, saw his friend, hurried back. "You okay? Marshall?"

Marsh had one arm under him but the other was free and he waved Bruno off with it. He was breathing hard.

"You okay?" Bruno was down on a knee now. Marsh breathed hard twice more then made himself stop, trying to catch his breath.

"Yeah, fine," he said and tried to laugh but it didn't come out right. "Just, uh, here, just give me a hand."

Bruno stood and took his hand and pulled as Marsh pushed up. He got halfway up and his leg slipped again and down he went, just about taking Bruno with him. "Mother *fuck*," Marsh whispered, fierce wince.

"It's okay, take a minute," Bruno said. He turned and yelled at the cabbie, "Hey, can you give us a hand here?" He turned back to Marsh, leaned down. "Does it hurt?" Marsh just winced.

The cabbie came around, shivering without his coat. "You need hospital?" he asked, arms wrapped around himself.

"No, I'm fine," Marsh said.

They got him up on the next try, and his rebellious leg seemed fine now, good enough, moving when he told it to. The rest of him hurt like hell, though. They stood there a minute, little trio in a circle, making sure Marsh could move. Then Marsh turned and started limping to the cab.

"Yeah, all good now," he said.

"You're bleeding," Bruno said, pointing to the polio leg. Marsh looked down. His jeans were ripped above the knee, blood stained around the fringes, skin dark through the hole.

"Yeah," he said, and opened the cab door. "Just a scratch."

It wasn't a scratch, it was a gash. Bruno helped Marsh in, then gently closed the door. "Damn," he whispered, walking behind the cab to the other side. "Damn."

Inside the cab Marsh had his eyes closed, trying to control his breathing, pressing a palm down on his bleeding leg. The cab pulled away. He said, "Find out who put that ice there, have them fired."

YOU HAVE TO GO SOMEWHERE

In Hoboken, the week ticked by, colder for two days, then not so cold, then kind of cold again. *What, are we playing games?* Flurries one day, rain the next, clear on the third. *Games, games, c'mon I ain't got all day.*

At Beginnings Behavioral Health, the week opened with the new records-room clerk receiving a second reprimand—this one official, he was told, on paper and filed in duplicate—for late arrival (*significant* late arrival, specifically) to a work day.

"You must understand, Thatcher," Herm said, scratching behind his ear with a pencil, "the whole shebang grinds to a halt without the charts getting pulled for the day."

"I do understand," Thatcher said, with what he hoped was an appropriate level of contriteness. He nodded, vigorously. "Won't happen again, Herm," he said. "You can count on it, and you can count on me."

Thatcher had to cross the in-patient unit to get back to his domain. In-patient was a sterile white circle of rooms, sterile white nurse station in the middle; bring us your manic, your violent, your hallucinating, your drunk—twenty beds, no waiting. Thatcher was fascinated by in-patient—those on it, those who worked it, the physical place itself. He always slowed when he passed through. Familiar faces, sometimes: Day Hospital patients, moved upstairs for awhile ("in for a tune-up," is how Orris explained it to Thatcher, an occasion when Thatcher asked why he hadn't seen a particular someone out smoking for a few days). Mostly not familiar faces, though. And more often then not, not the overtly organic mentally unstable. More of the covert. More than anything, in-patient at Beginnings was a quick-stop detox. The faces, when they sometimes peered out from the darkened patient rooms, were more gaunt than fleshy, more pale then dark. Tired eyes. Scared.

Thatcher had tried explaining the place to Lou, and the fear on the faces of the detoxers. "They need someone to love them," she'd said. Thatcher had replied, "I think sometimes love is not enough."

Today, in-patient stood calm. One woman, thin, in a white hospital gown, sitting by a window, smoking a cigarette. Rosealba the head nurse at her station, broad back and thick neck turned to Thatcher as he walked by, out of the unit, through the doors.

Down a flight of stairs then to Day Hospital, six group rooms, a large common room, a kitchen, a music room with upright piano. Day Hospital was many things to many people, but the majority of patients (or clients, Herm didn't like "patients," he encouraged the label "clients") were group-home residents. This is where they went weekdays. Orris's take was, "You have to go somewhere, right? There's worse places than here."

Thatcher returned five or six waves as he passed through Day Hospital. He hadn't made much in the way of inroads with the staff at Beginnings Behavioral Health, but the patients—*clients, we prefer to call them clients*—were a generally friendly bunch. Especially in Day Hospital. There were a few stand-offs, a few growlers, one or two decidedly lunatic scary, but mostly not. All the patients clearly on a continuum between just slightly off and absolute spinney-eyed insane—but even absolute spinney-eyed insane didn't preclude friendliness in most cases. Thatcher thought he'd learned how to read the faces, how to gauge anxiety, when to smile hello and when to keep head down and back away.

One of the few employees Thatcher had become friendly with was a guy named Thomas Barnes. Thomas Barnes's job title was Trenton Liaison, which meant he was responsible for committing the hopelessly insane from this corner of the county to Trenton State Psychiatric Hospital. When Thatcher told Thomas Barnes he'd figured out how to read the faces, Thomas laughed and said, "Yeah, okay. I saw a guy in Trenton last month with a big smile on his face walk up to his best friend and stab him in the eye with a pencil. He was still smiling when we strapped him down and hit him with the needle. Sweetest, most genuine smile I've ever seen." Thomas was only a year older than Thatcher, and it made Thatcher decidedly uncomfortable to know that someone his age carried the weight of commitment for Hoboken. Personally, Thatcher wasn't sure a twenty-five year old should be responsible for managing the swing shift at Burger King, let alone making decisions on committing the schizophrenics and bipolars of the world. Still, someone had to do it, and he liked Thomas Barnes.

At the door to the records room Thatcher changed his mind, turned and went up front to the main doors, out to the courtyard for a smoke. A reprimand, he decided, especially an official and duplicate-filed reprimand, merited a smoke. Orris was outside, on his bench. Thatcher sat beside him, on what was left of the bench. (The file theft was forgiven, done and buried, moved past. No one knew, and Orris assured Thatcher it wouldn't happen again. Thatcher believed him. To ensure compliance, he'd said, "If you want to see your file, just ask me. I'll make a photocopy, for Christ's sake." They'd sealed with a handshake, copasetic ever since.)

"I just got a reprimand," Thatcher said, lighting his cigarette.

"No kidding?" Orris looked over, fixing his good eye on Thatcher. The other eye jiggled. Thatcher barely noticed anymore. "What'd you do?"

"Late again." Thatcher ran a hand over his head. "Drunk again. Late again."

"Man," Orris said. "Man." He shook his head. "I could call you, you know. We got a payphone at the home. I could give you a ring, make sure you get up on time."

"Thanks, Orris." Thatcher put his hand out. Orris enveloped it in his sweaty palm and shook. "That's really nice of you. But I'll be alright." Thatcher looked across the courtyard. A group of pee-test failures were smoking, all of them looking away from each other. "Maybe I just need a new alarm clock."

"I never use an alarm," Orris said.

"How do you get up?"

Orris shrugged. "I just do. Don't know, really. I just do."

"That's admirable. An admirable trait."

"You think so?"

"Yes I do."

They both nodded, and smoked in silence for a minute. The pee-test smokers were an interesting bunch, over there with their directionless stares and group movements. There were a few of them always looked angry to Thatcher. He wondered what the anger was about—were they angry they got caught? Angry they were here? Angry with their lot in life, their hand of cards? Thatcher wondered if he took them upstairs, showed them detox, maybe they wouldn't be so angry.

Maybe, though, they'd be angrier.

Thatcher didn't get angry. He prided himself on this. The shrink he'd seen at his mother's insistence for like two minutes when he was sixteen had told him it wasn't healthy, never getting angry. Wasn't healthy at all. The shrink had said what Thatcher actually did *wasn't* not getting angry, it was not *allowing* anger, and *that* wasn't healthy—ahem, ahem, put that in your pipe and smoke it, Thatcher.

What the fuck did that guy know.

One of the pee-test smokers, a woman, pretty black hair and a ski jacket, looked over, met Thatcher's eye, then quick looked away. Better to look at nothing. *Better to look at nothing than to look at me*, Thatcher thought.

He coughed then said, "That was the reprimand, but I got yelled at for something else, too."

"What's that?"

"Too much hanging out with clients."

"Who said that? Mister Jeffries?"

Thatcher nodded. "He said interaction should only come from those trained and since I'm uneducated and untrained that means me. Any non-therapeutic interaction is socialization and ergo frowned on."

"Herm said all that?"

"Yep."

"He said 'ergo'?"

"Actually, no. He did say 'nontherapeutic interaction,' though."

"Isn't that something. What did you say?"

"Nothing."

Orris sat still a moment, contemplating the tactic. Then he said, "Good move." Thatcher nodded. Orris lit a new cigarette off the old. "I've never heard anyone say 'ergo' before, Thatcher. Not even the doctors."

"It's a good word."

"*Ergo*," Orris said, deepening his voice. "It *is* a good word." He looked up at the sky, put a hand to his head. "Dizzy," he said. "I gotta get some orange juice when I finish this smoke."

He looked awfully pale to Thatcher. Orris's skin generally didn't hold much in the way of color, but today Thatcher thought he seemed more of a sick pale. "You okay?"

"I got diabetes," Orris said.

"I know. You told me."

Orris pointed to his lame, jittery eye. "That's where this come from, you know."

"Diabetes."

"Yep. Blew my eye out." Orris hung his cigarette from his lips and clapped his hands together once, loud. "*Ka-blam!*" he said. Thatcher jumped; hangover nerves are no good with sudden noises. "Yep, ka-blam," Orris said softly. "Just like that."

"No warning?"

"Little bit. Things were dim, kind of. Shaky, I guess. Then she just went."

"What about the other eye?"

"Works fine."

Thatcher wondered if that might probably change but decided not to ask about it. Instead, he asked something else he'd been thinking about. "Did you learn anything from reading your file?"

"No," Orris said. "Not really."

"What did it say?"

"Said I'm paranoid. But I knew that already—that's why I took the file."

Thatcher laughed, quickly stopped short, saw Orris was smiling so let his own smile out again. "Do you feel any less paranoid now?"

"No."

Thatcher wasn't sure what to say to that, or to any of this, really. How to talk to the mentally ill about their own mental illness? How to talk about mental illness to the sanest-acting person in the building? Having said that, how to reconcile the fact that the sanest-acting person in the building wore the same set of gray sweat clothes every day and smelled like a fatty tobacco stew? Orris let him off the hook by not waiting for a question.

"I don't know what I thought I'd see in there," he said. "Tell you the truth, I don't feel paranoid. But I am, you know. I am. I'll say that, for sure. I know it." Cigarette between fingers, Orris tapped his knee with the palm of his hand. "I used to read a lot, you know," he said. "You always have your nose in a book, Thatcher. Or writing in one."

"Do I?"

"Yes. I see you in the lunch room. I liked to read, when I was a kid."

"Yeah?"

Orris nodded. "Can't read no more." Again he waved at his eyes.

"You see okay out of the other eye, right?"

"It's not that. I can see okay, but can't read. It all goes fuzzy."

"Is that the diabetes, too?"

"No, that's the meds for the schizophrenia."

Thatcher knew the diagnosis, of course—he'd read the file. All of Orris's files, back to when he was a teenager. But it was strange to have the word itself drop from a patient's mouth.

"Started with Lithium. That was the worst. I took Lithium for years, on and off, terrible stuff. Now it's—what is it—Haldol, I guess. Risperdal. You know. Whatever they're serving. It's better, I guess, but I still can't read. No matter what the med is, messes up my reading."

"That's rough."

"Yeah." Orris dropped his cigarette butt to the ground and toed it. "I think the doctors like it. Me not reading. This one doc told me that. I used to read a lot of Stephen King stuff, he said it took me bad places. Maybe it did, sometimes. But no reading at all…now I have nothing to do but think. That's not healthy, either." Orris looked around, sighed, said, "Time for group."

"What do you have now?"

"Current events."

"What's the latest in the world?"

"Thatcher got a reprimand."

Thatcher smiled. "Nice," he said.

Orris put a hand on the bench and pushed his bulk up and off and into a first step and was about halfway there when he stumbled, balance gone with a loose spin on one foot—bulky, fat dancer. Thatcher jumped up, grabbed his arm, kept him upright.

"Hey, hey," Thatcher said. Orris looked confused. Thatcher put his face right in Orris's. "Orris, you okay?" Orris's expression was blank for a second, then his good eye found Thatcher.

"Okay, okay," he said. "Need some orange juice I think."

"C'mon, I'll help you in."

"Yeah, good idea."

Thatcher held Orris's arm, inside and then across the lobby. He was walking but unstable, shuffling slow in his gray sweats. They were about to the Day Hospital doors when Herm came around the corner, stopping short, eyed Thatcher.

"Guy needs some orange juice," Thatcher said.

Herm nodded, standing there, until Orris turned his head and looked at him. Herm moved then, taking Orris's other arm, helping guide him to the kitchen in the back.

"Have to keep on top of the diabetes, Orris," Herm said. Then, "I've got it from here, Thatcher."

"I'll just—"

Herm looked over at Thatcher as the three walked. "No, really. I've got it from here. You can get back to work."

Thatcher looked at him, then let go Orris's arm. "You'll be okay," he said to him. Orris looked confused again and didn't hear. Herm pushed him along, and Thatcher turned and went back to the records room.

HEY, HEY, HEY

Lou thought she knew Hoboken all around and up and down but it took some strange turns and turning to find the mental health center. She'd never been back here, back by the rail yards. The neighborhood made her a little nervous. Last couple blocks, she looked behind her every few minutes. No one there, though.

It was funny that Thatcher worked there. He wasn't why she was going, but it was funny that he worked there. She'd have to stop by and see him, maybe. If there was time.

All I got, she thought, *is time*.

Maybe not all she got. But all she want.

What she didn't want: going to this mental health joint today. No, no, no.

"Nothing to be scared of," Thatcher had told her. "Not like they're locking you up, right? You're just visiting."

Ol' Thatcher. Good ol' Thatcher.

It was funny, having him around full time. There was a real yin and yang to Thatcher and James. Lou made buddies easy—she was a social cat—but not friends. Friends were few and often hard to grow into. And somehow both James and Thatcher had stepped into her bubble as if they'd always been there. James when she was still in college, at a worthless open mike in West Orange where they'd been the only two to show up—one of those opportunities where you make do with whatever or whoever falls in your lap. They'd ended up impressing the hell out of each other with ax skills, and—young and cocky—neither was easy to easily impress. They'd played together half the night—*wait wait wait, check it out, John Gorka wrote this*—talked through the other half, all fueled up on coffee and beer—ah, college—and ended up making out then passing out in Lou's Montclair dorm room. Awkward moment there, in the morning (morning, nothing; it was noon) as Lou began down the road of how it was with her and and and and. And nothing. James didn't blink. He yawned—*yo, lesbian, thespian, it's all good, where's the coffee*. She shut up and pulled out her guitar.

And Thatcher, she met him doing a favor for James, going to sing on a demo for this elusive friend of his, up from the army. A bad time, just shy of a year after her sister Helen died, Lou needed a new friend like she needed a third foot. The circumstances were all different, the vibe and end results the same, that jolt, then slipping in, like he'd always been there, Thatcher calling her every other day from Virginia—*whadja write this week, Louie? Sing it to me*. Him paging through his notebook, reading her lines and phrases. She'd shared a tent with Thatcher and James at Falcon Ridge Folk Festival this summer, then traveled as a trio to Georgia, to play Eddie's Attic. They split the driving and no one bitched or moaned.

"That's almost impossible," Lou had said in a truck stop parking lot on a sunny afternoon. Her two boys were laid out shirtless on the hood of her Mazda, one smoking, one pretending. "No one drives this far without complaining."

But here was the place now, Beginnings Behavioral Health, brick and long and low. She bit her lip at the front gate. Almost turned around and walked away. Then walked into an empty courtyard and through the door. She so did not want to be here. At the end of a tile hall she saw Jaelene, waving. They kissed, cheeks up, went in an office. A warm office, reds and browns, with a comfortable couch and easy chair.

"I'm Phyllis," said the woman in the easy chair, standing and offering her hand to Lou. "Thanks so much for coming."

Jaelene had been seeing Phyllis for years. "All lesbians need a therapist," she'd said to Lou on one of their first dates, horrified to discover Lou lacked one. "It's a law, right?" Today was the first time Lou had been invited along to Jaelene's session. "It would mean so much to me," Jaelene had said to her on the phone.

"But you've already moved out. I don't understand."

"It's not about moving out, it's about moving on. It's not a reconciliation, Louie," Jaelene had said. "I know we can't go back. I know you were right. You've been right all along."

"So—again, I don't understand."

"I need closure, Louie. I need closure."

So here was Lou, sitting down on the couch for an hour of closure. The hour was just fine, smooth enough, we're all adults here and these things do happen, sure enough. There were cheek kisses all around after, then Lou left the room, left Jaelene to her leaving, walked down the hall and asked for the records room. A stairs, two corners, a door. She found Thatcher alone in there, standing at a big table, putting patient files into stacks. He saw her in the doorway, pointed his hand at one of the stacks and said, "There but for the grace of God, Lou."

Lou nodded, smiled, said "Isn't that true," then broke down, crying out loud. Thatcher dropped the files from his hand, two steps across the room and his arms around her. She put her cheek to his chest and cried harder, unintelligible words from her mouth—sad, angry words and a bottled-up torrent of frustration and love and despair.

"Hey," Thatcher whispered, over and over, "hey, hey." He rocked as he held her, slowly, one foot back and forth, a slow, crying dance. "Hey," he whispered. "Hey, hey, hey."

SONGWRITERS ALWAYS GET THE LAST WORD

In Hoboken, Wednesday became the weekend then it passed and it was Wednesday again. You could mark the week passing in Hoboken by days of street cleaning on this block or that (requiring an early-morning run down in pajamas to move your car) and garbage collection on that street or the other. In Hoboken, the garbagemen took it all, within reason, so as garbage day progressed through the town block by block as the week passed, frugal apartment dwellers knew to rise early to look for the occasional not-too-bad couch or could-be-worse easy chair or put-a-magazine-on-the-scratches coffee table.

James moved his car on Wednesday morning, went to work, looked around, next thing he knows it's Wednesday again.

Gig night tonight. They'd rehearsed night before in Maxwell's back room until 3 A.M., a bottle of black rum circulating between songs. Thatcher called out sick and slept all morning. James went to work late, came home early. He got back to Hoboken around five, night shadows running long down the streets. Lou came around the corner from the other direction, met him at his building's door. They hadn't been able to talk the night before, Lou coming into rehearsal late and everyone drinking. They were good at the pause, though, James and Lou were. James called it the pause. If it was worth saying, it was worth saying with thought and reflection; if there was no time for thought and reflection, you pressed pause. He and Lou had pressed pause last night. Meeting now on his front step, he resumed play.

"I'm so sorry," James said, pulling her into him with his long arms. Her cheek to his chest she smiled and closed her eyes and said, "It's okay."

James whispered in her ear: "On the plus side, songwriters always get the last word."

"Three or four words, in this case," she said, "at least. And I plan on taking them."

They went upstairs to gather Thatcher. He was stretched on the couch with a notebook, pencil flying across the lines. He hadn't heard them come in.

"Beer?" James asked.

Thatcher shook out his writing wrist. "Oh, indeed."

"Share with the class?" Lou said, pointing at Thatcher's notebook.

"I'll sing it tonight," he said.

"Tonight?" Lou said. "*Cajones*, yo. Big fat ones."

Cold as it was tonight, the three took their beer outside. The roof would have been the place to go but James had seen the super's son go up there—a guaranteed twenty yards of pointless conversation no one needed. So they walked the six flights back to the ground and sat on the front steps with coats and hats and their bottles of beer.

"*Salud*, son," James said, and they clinked bottles. Thatcher took a long swill. The cold air made the beer taste sharper. He shivered, took another long swill. Lou lit one of her cloves and Thatcher bummed one and lit it off hers.

"Gimme one of those," James said. He took a cigarette from Lou's pack and hung it from the corner of his mouth, unlit. "Always strangely satisfying," he said.

"You're strangely satisfying," Lou said, and they toasted again.

A kid on a bike came slow down the sidewalk toward them from the direction of Willow, circling around trash cans and bumps. In the time it took Thatcher to think it was too cold for a kid to be riding around on a bike he realized it was a kid's bike but not a kid riding it exactly. Hard to tell; an old teenager or a young twenty, red wool cap pulled down tight over ears. He wore a brown corduroy coat. The bike was a kid's bike, though. And dated. A banana seat and high handlebars with all the trimmings, a thumb bell, a light, and an air freshener hanging from the cross bar. The kid made a big show of circling then stopping the bike in front of them. The air freshener was a picture of Mr. T, arms crossed and growling.

"Hi James," the kid said. He had a long nose, eyes close together and balanced on top.

"Hello, Jimmy."

The kid looked at Thatcher. James said, "Jimmy, these are my friends Lou and Thatcher."

"Hi, Lou. Hi, Thatcher. I've never heard that name before."

"Hello, Jimmy."

"James and I have the same name," Jimmy said. "Except I'm a Jimmy."

"It's a good name," Thatcher said.

"As good as they come," James said.

"Whatcha doing, James?" Jimmy asked. Thatcher noticed Jimmy didn't really look directly at you when he spoke, but just past you. His voice was an inch shy of monotone.

"Not much, Jimmy. Sitting here with Thatcher and Lou is all I'm doing."

"Do you live near here, Jimmy?" Lou asked, but Jimmy didn't answer. Instead, he reached into his coat pocket and drew out a cassette tape.

"I got a new tape, James." He held it up for them to see, but didn't offer it out to show.

"Chuck Berry?" James asked.

"*Greatest Hits*," Jimmy said.

"I thought you already had that one."

"No," Jimmy said, shaking his head. He put the tape back in his pocket. "It was called *Hot Hits*. This one is better. More songs."

"That's awesome."

Thatcher took a sip from his beer. "You like Chuck Berry a lot, Jimmy?" he asked, but Jimmy didn't answer him. The sort-of kid stared down the street, not saying anything. James leaned in toward Thatcher's ear. "Don't ask Jimmy stupid questions."

Jimmy said, "I don't answer stupid questions." James laughed and Jimmy laughed, too, staring off down the street and laughing a puffy sort of laugh. When they were done laughing Thatcher said, "Okay. So how old are you, Jimmy?"

"That's not stupid, but I'm not going to answer it anyway."

"How come?"

Jimmy shook his head.

Lou pointed at Mr. T hanging from the handlebars. "What's that, Jimmy?"

"Air freshener."

"Nice. Where'd you get it?"

Jimmy pointed in the general direction of his stare, vaguely down the street. "Over there," he said. Then added, "Found it."

"Nice find," Thatcher said.

"Yeah."

Then Jimmy moved on, air freshener swinging from the handlebars as he went. They watched him get smaller down Sixth, then two blocks down he turned and was gone. James raised his beer bottle.

"To Mr. T," he said.

They clinked bottles again.

. . .

Marsh had promised and sure enough the Shannon Lounge was theirs for the night. A good place for a first gig—much less pressure than the back room at Maxwell's. Shannon Lounge was a comfortable joint, a good gig, but if you bombed, your explosion (or implosion, as the case may be) would be relatively anonymous. If you bombed at Maxwell's, you bombed. Picking the Shannon for their first night was a strategic move on Marsh's part.

James, Thatcher, and Lou walked a quarter mile across Hoboken's early evening, three guitar bags on three backs, mostly single file against rush-hour sidewalks. Orange handwritten sign on the club's door:

9 p.m. Wednesday night—
NOT REALLY

first time anywhere

"They need to advertise incompetence and inexperience?" Thatcher asked.

"New Jersey's fair-warning laws," James said. "I still think we should have gone with Free Beer for the name."

And then they were in; warm inside, Irish and empty, early evening, two three overcoats at bar left and two three flannel coats bar right. Bald Dutch from the guitar shop plugging plugs and leveling levels on a big Mackie board, center room; Mary Ann feet up at a table next to him, chatting out her nerves; drums coming through in the arms of Slim Youngblood, house drummer for all of Hoboken, happily sitting in because they still didn't have a drummer, black-skinned with ivory hoop earrings; and alone onstage Marsh ruling in the biggest chair the bar had, sitting down but he was upright and he was here and his acoustic guitar was plugged in and he was playing. It hadn't been one hundred percent he'd be here—the leg more than a small thing for a guy like Marsh, and the fall he took, it turned out, not a cause but a symptom, although a blessing it turned out, revealing things otherwise unrevealed, two days in a hospital bed but onward now down the road to recovery, onward down the road to rock and roll.

Marsh strummed, Dutch at the board pushing the level then pushing too far, shade of feedback, a wince. Marsh leaned in to the mike in front of him: "A little more talent in the monitors please." He looked around, saw the arriving trio. "Damn kids these days," he said. "You should be ashamed," he said, "letting the cripple beat you to the gig."

"Where's Bruno?" James shouted across the room.

"Not my turn to watch him. Getting a coffee, I think. Hey, Woody Guthrie—what key is that thing of yours, the chick on a boat one?"

"E, capo 4," Thatcher yelled, shucking scarf and coat.

"Real men don't speak in capo, young Thatcher," Marsh said.

James—bent over and pulling guitar free from case—translated: "G sharp, Marsh. The blues in G sharp."

Marsh put a hand to his forehead. "The blues in G sharp, indeed," he said. "You're going to have to work that out between you and Jesus, Thatcher."

• • •

Bruno had strolled over to Carbone's for a coffee takeout, ready and willing to throw a played game right into Miguel's old face. But no Miguel. A kid behind the counter, Bruno thought he'd seen him at the dishwasher just a week before. No English, the kid, none at all, but you don't need much in the way of English for a coffee order. Bruno took the to-go cup, cracked the plastic lid, sipped. Right on. Out the door, time for work.

Coffee a must for Bruno, night like this. Hadn't had a drink in five years. No real worries on the backslide, but still—long night, crowded bar, James and Thatcher and the girls swilling like fish; you get that thing, that thing in your mouth. No real worries on the backslide, but that pull in the mouth, you needed a coffee or something to keep it all in its place. And bar coffee, as a rule, sucks monkey ass. Old Miguel made a good cup. Or the young dishwasher—whoever.

Bruno checked his watch, picked up the pace. Across the street, right up on City Hall, he saw something float, piece of paper or something, down then up on a draft then down. He sipped, stepped, looked again. There was another one. Wasn't paper. It was snow. Two then three then a handful then frozen faucet the sky opened and the snow fell—big fat flakes, slow and lazy falling down all around.

"Look at that," Bruno said. He'd barely made his peace with autumn, head down and working last few months, working on music and working on work. Hardly took time to look up. And now here, check this out—it was snowing. No wind, just fat and delicate silent snow.

Despite himself, Bruno smiled.

PART II

Spring

TIMMY T GOES OFF HIS MEDS
(and other true tales from the fax machine)

Late on a Friday afternoon, the first real warm Friday of the spring, deep in the bowels of Beginnings Behavioral Health's records room, a fax machine whirred to life, slick greasy fax paper creeping from its underside. With an internal phone system that was for shit, the organization relied on fax machines to send messages from the receptionist:

Dr Flint your wife 3pm call her car

Alison-----Timmy T off his meds, call Stu at Easter Seals

Dee: Kirk needs pens, staples, bandages...first floor

The faxes would drop into a metal basket. Thatcher would dutifully collect them and deliver the fax messages to the appropriate cubby. The records room fax machine also brought in faxes from the outside world:

All group MDs – Melissa Banko third attempt at Rx change, she is
barred
—10th Street Walgreens

And, a few times a day, messages of a less professional (but no less profound) nature:

Fucking beautiful today son...can you skip out now? –J

I wish, Thatcher thought, crinkling the message, tossing it in the trash basket. The afternoon files were delivered. Time for a smoke. He checked his watch—top of the hour, Orris would be out there. Thatcher definitely would take a break now. He hadn't seen Orris all day. The guy seemed a little out of it recently. Thatcher couldn't decide whether it was physical or mental. Orris looked generally exhausted, but it was unclear what kind of exhaustion. Anyway, Thatcher wanted to see him.

A few minutes after Thatcher left, the fax machine whirred to life again, spewing, spewing. A message hit the basket:

Thatch – can you leave or what? Tell your cocksucker boss Hermie Baby it's time to go home... Peace, -J

The fax paper hadn't even cooled when Herm stuck his head in.
"Thatcher?" he said. No answer. Herm sighed. The boy was never at his desk. Never. He crossed the floor, pulled the message from the basket. Read it. Crinkled it in a ball. Threw it in the basket. Pulled it back out of the basket, smoothed it flat. Sat down at Thatcher's desk and waited for Thatcher to come back. It was warm outside today, but in here the heat was still on—and would be until the first of May, when heat would

switch to air conditioning—sweat trickled from Herm's brow. He wiped it, shifted in the chair, his eyes on the door to the hall.

PASTIME IN PAST TENSE

In Hoboken, you don't speak of Abner Doubleday. Not if you're in Hoboken. Don't speak of Doubleday, and not of A.G. Spalding or old-man Amber Graves either. Don't speak the names. Hallowed, these men, in some circles of baseball. But not in Hoboken.

It was Amber Graves who trumpeted Doubleday and his fictitious Cooperstown debut. Granted, this wasn't Doubleday's fault; he was an alright kid, from most accounts. And something of a war hero, later on. That's not in dispute. But Amber Graves placed Doubleday in Cooperstown in 1839, said the young fella cooked up this new game right there and Graves saw him do it. With his own two eyes. Goddammit. Shook young Doubleday's hand with his own five fingers. Goddammit.

Except those same five fingers later murdered his wife and went up in irons at the crazy farm. And Doubleday, well he was at West Point in 1839, boning up on his war-heroing. Everyone knows it, everyone. There should be no question where the game started. Everyone knows. Everyone except that Goddamn Bud Selig and the know-nothings in Cooperstown.

If Doubleday rests in the Loving Arms, he too knows how it happened. In Hoboken, don't speak a word of Abner Doubleday.

In Hoboken, this is how they tell the story: It was June 19, 1846, and two gentlemen—fine gentlemen, Alexander Cartwright and Daniel "Doc" Adams—invited the fine gentlemen of the New York Nine athletic organization to come play their newly formed Hoboken Knickerbocker Base Ball Club at Elysian Fields. Cartwright had put together a set of rules to solidify the vague and unfocused cricket knock-off everyone seemed to be playing some version of—three strikes and you're out, for instance, was a Cartwright idea. And the thought that maybe you shouldn't peg the ball at a runner to literally knock him out. Maybe you could just tag him by hand.

Cartwright's rules were sent by messenger across the Hudson. The New Yorkers thought these rules sound and a schedule was set. On June 19 the New York Nine came out to Hoboken. Cartwright himself umpired. And perhaps his talent was missed on his own team, because the Knickerbockers lost that first-ever game of baseball, by a dismal 23 to 1, in only four innings.

Hoboken lost the game but won the war. Don't let anyone tell you differently. The first game was here, it all happened here, folks. It happened right here in Hoboken.

• • •

There is some speculation—among the dogged faithful, AM radio listeners, and smoke-break warriors—on precise location. No speculation among believers on Hoboken's status, but where precisely within the town limits…well.

Was it *here*, exactly? Or twenty feet over there? History says Elysian Fields and there sits Elysian Park but one does not necessarily follow the other, you know.

Marsh and Bruno—baseball fans both—have been known to share in some of this punditry whilst sitting in the sun at Elysian Park, especially this time of year, baseball's golden time, glorious spring.

"Sinatra was born at 415 Monroe," Marsh with a simple, sound logic. "No amount of anything is going to change that. For baseball, sign says it was *here*, so here it was."

"Sinatra was a skinny fuck with no sense until it got smacked into him—what's anything got to do with anything?" Bruno, the realist, placing it ever-so-gently into perspective.

Pundits abound at Hoboken's northern Little League field. Two views, two games going at once: ten-year-olds on field one, six-year-olds playing T-ball on field two. Half the stands parents of the athletes, other half pundits—old men, mostly, and various general Hoboken stragglers and hangers-on. Much squinting in the stands, squinting and hand blocking from the mid-day sun; new season, first days out, and in Hoboken it had been a long, cold winter.

Orris and Bill Pin had made it to just about every Saturday series of Little League games the year before, every Saturday it hadn't rained. Last year they'd sat top of the stands just about every time. Today, though, Orris only made it up three rows.

"Far enough, Bill," he said. "Have a seat."

Bill Pin glanced longingly up toward the top but followed Orris into the aisle.

Orris had a ball cap on for the occasion. Green and yellow, cursive script: North Hunterdon Lions. No idea where he'd picked it up. He had the plastic tab on the back adjusted out to the last snap. Orris carried a big head on his stump neck. He took the hat off now, wiped sweat from his forehead with the arm of his sweat shirt. *That's why they call it a sweatshirt*, he thought. Not hot by the thermometer, exactly, warm and sunny, but Orris winded easy these days it seemed. And he felt flush a lot.

The stands were about full. Nice day. First really nice day. Orris tapped his knees with both hands. Lots of people. He liked it better later in the summer, after most everyone lost interest, when dog days kept people inside just like it was winter. Come August out here, place just about empty. That was better. Less people.

"You got those sodas, Bill Pin?" he said. He didn't feel well. Didn't feel well at all.

Bill reached into his leather briefcase. Pulled out a can of Foodtown root beer.

"You want your sandwich, too, Orris?"

"No. Just the soda."

Bill Pin popped Orris's can for him, handed it to him.

"I'm going to wait on my soda," Bill said.

"That's your prerogative, Bill."

Bill Pin sat fairly straight and tended to stay that way through nine innings. Unlike Orris, he preferred the spring, much preferred this weather. With tie, jacket, vest, things got too hot later on. And then he'd sweat and couldn't keep his hair in place. This was nice, though. This was nice.

Bill didn't know much about baseball. He'd watch the game a little bit, but mostly he read his magazines. There was a lot of reading to get through each week: *People, Us, Star, Entertainment Weekly*. Bill didn't read fast, either—he liked to take his time, chew the details, think things over—so it was important he keep up with his reading schedule. He'd fallen behind once or twice and it always ended up throwing the whole month out of whack. The whole month.

He pulled this week's *People* out. He'd finished with the cover and got through the masthead this morning. He'd start at the table of contents here, see how far he could get during the game.

"Is that Matthew Broderick coming today, Orris?"

"I don't know, Bill. I don't think so."

Orris wiped his mouth with his wide open palm. Thatcher had made the first two games of the season, with a young bearded friend who didn't smoke. Decent enough fellow. Able, at least, to talk some baseball.

"Think he told me he's going to a wedding or something tonight, Bill Pin."

"He probably won't be here, then."

"No, I don't imagine."

"Big star like Matthew Broderick, he'll need all afternoon to prepare. Hair, clothes. All that stuff. I don't envy him, that's for sure. I don't envy him."

"Yeah. Hey, you know, I will take that sandwich."

"And with that nose—well, he must be something with the ladies."

"Look at that kid, Bill." Orris half-stood then, yelled "Good one!" Clapping his hands. Most of the crowd turned to look at him. He didn't notice. "That's how you swing it! Yeah!" Orris's legs let go and he sat hard, winded again. His face wasn't so pale now, but still not healthy. Kind of splotchy, purple. "That's some kid, Bill Pin. Some swing for such a little guy."

"I'm going to drink my soda now, Orris."

"That's good, Bill. That's a solid decision."

Bill Pin had trouble with decisions; so said the Day Hospital counselors. Orris tried making it a point to notice when Bill pulled through with one, and provide praise and reinforcement.

• • •

The swing in question *was* a good swing. It was off a T, the little guy who nailed it with more hair than any other boy on the team or on the field, probably. Nailed it, right between second and third where the shortstop was watching a Continental jet rising over Hoboken from a Newark take-off and that puppy went all the way out into the field. The batter ran as fast as he could, made it to first base no problem. This was his first season, third game, first good hit. He was ecstatic. He waved to his folks, on the bottom of the stands. His mom was waving, his dad swinging a cane up in the air. The boy stood on first and gloated.

"You show 'em, Dash!" Marsh yelled. Carla poked him in the ribs with her elbow.

"It's not the second coming, you know," she said.

"Yes it is."

She put her arm around her husband as far as it would go. Marsh waved with the cane again, waved at his boy. The cane had been in use on and off since he went down on the ice, early in the winter, then ended up back in the hospital for almost two weeks with a septic infection. Lately the cane usage had been more off than on, but things felt weak this morning so he'd grabbed it. He'd like to leave it forever, but imagined reality was he'd started down a road you don't really walk back from without a cane.

There are worse things than canes, Marsh thought.

YOU HANDLED THAT WELL

"Thatcher?"

"Oh boy," Thatcher said, pressing palm to the phone's mouthpiece. He rolled his eyes at James. They were sitting at the apartment's kitchen table, stacks of yellow postcards piled, rolls of stamps. James raised his eyebrows. The window was half open, ambulance or cop siren wailing by, a warm breeze if you stuck your arm out the window but the air still in here; still and smelling of Chinese takeout—Kung Po. Thatcher moved his hand, said, "Suzanne?"

"Hi, Thatcher."

"You found me."

"We found you." There was a laugh on the other end of the phone, what Thatcher thought of as a sorority laugh. Which was funny in itself, because Suzanne was about as far from sorority as you could get. Wesleyan vegan house, her pedigree; a completely different laugh. But here was Suzanne, sounding all sorority. She was nervous. Clearly.

"Well, I guess I'm not hard to find," Thatcher said.

Suzanne was his mother's current assistant. Mona hired her first assistant when Thatcher was six; she'd been through more than ten since. Thatcher was now, for one brief moment in time, parallel to the average age of the average assistant. He hadn't thought of it until just now, on the phone. Across the table, James was ripping, licking, stamping. They'd been stamping almost an hour, gig cards for the band's mailing list. Both their tongues gummy with it. James mouthed, "Who?" grimacing around stamp glue. Thatcher just shook his head.

The phone spoke to him. "Mona has a new book coming, Thatcher."

"The evils of pornography—I read it."

"No, a newer one. She's just finishing work on it. We have the galleys here now. And the last book wasn't about the evils of porn, it was about the power of true eroticism and the difficulty achieving it in a world of commercial sex and—"

"I know, Suzanne. I was making a joke."

No one ever got his jokes. Especially college girls. He couldn't figure.

The sorority laugh again. Well, she was trying. Although it was weird and just a little creepy. The sorority laugh didn't suit the Suzanne he'd met.

"Anyway," she said, "this book, Thatcher, the new one, Mona wants to—oh, wait." Silence on the phone, then, "Can you hold a second, Thatcher? Mona's getting off the other line. I'll switch her over."

Thatcher didn't have time to answer. Hold music—WBGO, Thatcher knew—flooded his ear. Not everyone had hold music from their home. Mona did. Thatcher shouldered the phone receiver, picked up a roll of stamps and began ripping again. "Holding for Mona," he said.

"Good song title," James said.

Thatcher pursed his lips. "Write that down, will ya?"

There was a Sharpie marker on a string ducktaped from the top of one of the table legs. James grabbed it, scrawled across a corner of the table. All good lines uttered in the apartment went on the wooden table top and were then open for picking and choosing by any who came by. Marsh had three songs wrapped around lines found on the table. Lou and James were tied with two songs each. Neither Bruno nor Thatcher had yet written table songs although both claimed contributing more than half the table's contents. On the phone, the DJ ran down the set list—two by Monk moving into two by Mingus.

"What do you know about Mingus?" Thatcher asked.

James looked at the ceiling, moving tongue around in mouth. The stamp glue seemed particularly harsh today. "Mingus," he said.

"Yeah, Mingus."

"Mingus, well," James said. "Mingus died in Mexico."

"I didn't know that."

"Yep."

Thatcher thought about this. He said, "Write that down, too." Then he said, "Have you met Suzanne?"

"Who's Suzanne?"

"Mona's assistant. Current assistant."

"No, I don't think so. Not this one."

"You know we're about the same age as the assistant now? Maybe even a little older?"

"Really?"

"Really."

"That means that very shortly we'll be significantly older than the assistant."

"That's what it means."

"Doesn't seem right."

As a kid, James had spent more time with the assistants to Thatcher's mom than he had with Thatcher's mom. Which was okay with James; nothing against Mona, just that the assistants—always female, generally between twenty-one and twenty-five years old—were much more intriguing to a boy. Mona didn't have much in the way of money, mostly just what came in from the books and book income isn't nearly what people might think it is. But she never had trouble finding an assistant. Some had volunteered, some had been low-paid interns. All of them beside themselves to move into the back bedroom in Mona Smith's house for a year—a real bedroom, mind you, not the basement—open and answer her fan mail, keep her calendar, type her notes, and drive her son and his best friend to their little league games, guitar lessons, and, later, as teenagers, on at least three occasions, provide transportation for double dates.

"This one's been on for a year or more now," Thatcher said. "Never met her?"

"Don't think so."

There was a crink hardening in Thatcher's neck. He switched ears, went back to ripping stamps.

Through all this the noise of the shower hummed soft behind the bathroom door. It stopped now, rattle of shower curtain and rod, then silence. James sighed, put down the stack of postcards he'd picked up, said, "You still on hold?"

"Holding for Mona."

The bathroom door opened, steam billowing out, Alice wrapped in a big red towel, her black hair shaggy and damp.

"James," she said, "your bathroom, well—"

"Leaves something to be desired," Thatcher said.

"Yes."

"You're both welcome to bathe elsewhere," James said.

Alice crossed the kitchen, kissed his cheek. "I think your bathroom is just lovely, James," she said. She stepped around the table, kissed Thatcher's cheek. "Who are you talking to?" she silent-mouthed.

"Holding for Mona," James said.

"My mom," Thatcher said.

"Your mom put you on hold?"

"No—her assistant, actually. Mona doesn't usually place calls herself. She's kind of afraid of the phone."

Alice tilted her head, a subtle *What the fuck?*

Thatcher reached his free hand out, put it on the toweled small of her back.

"Mona's busy," he said. "I don't mind." Alice's expression did not change. *WTF?*

What had changed, Thatcher thought, over time, was Alice's general attitude toward his mother—a woman she had never actually met, even though she'd been dating the woman's son four months now, and only fifteen miles separated Hoboken from Gary Ridge. Thatcher hadn't seen Mona in that time, either.

Anyway, introduced or not, Alice had an opinion of Mona, an attitude, and Thatcher thought it had changed. Shifted. He thought so, anyway. Maybe. Or maybe not, he thought. Who knows. Maybe he was just sensitive on it, overanalyzing.

Alice and Thatcher's first date together—spontaneous date, rounds of post-gig whiskies in Harvard Square and a 3 A.M. lift to the Boston bus depot for the last bus that would get Thatcher to Hoboken and work on time—that night had seen a breadth of conversation but not a word of Thatcher's parentage. That came not long, though, after. Enraptured, Thatcher made it to Alice's studio apartment in Queens just a few days later; the walls of the tiny room breathed books, and one shelf was devoted to the thoughts and words of Mona Smith. This wasn't rare for Thatcher but it had been a while, a four-year army break from such surroundings. Corporal Parker Calton, for instance, had never heard of Mona Smith before she met Thatcher. But the army was over now and Thatcher could see that the world was returning to—well, maybe normal wasn't the word, but something like it. When his maternal lineage came up with Alice, Thatcher shrugged for days, not a big thing you know. But within a month, as their romance settled down for the winter, Thatcher took Alice through the books, showing what a college course couldn't show, pointing out the parallels, puns, nuggets that even many critics missed.

"You know you told me one of those first nights you hadn't read her books, Thatcher," she said once.

"I said that?"

"You did."

"Well," he said, and didn't say more. He had, in fact, read Mona's books. All of them, numerous times. The ones written when he was young he'd read at a very young age.

"Is it weird?" Alice asked once.

"Having a famous mother?"

"No, being the son of a woman who has so much to say about men."

"If you look at it statistically, Mona has written much more about women than she has about men."

"You know what I mean."

"Whatever," he said. "And no, it's not weird. It's made me a better man."

"You think so?" She wasn't sure if he was joking or not.

But he nodded. "Sure it has. How could it not?"

"I think it affects you, too," she said.

"In what way?"

"I'm not sure yet."

Alice had a lot to say about everything, Alice did. Not shy on the personal opinion, was Alice. It was one of the things Thatcher really liked about her. Except when it was not.

Back in the real world, phone to ear, Mingus went away with a click. A voice on the line, but not Mona. A male voice. "Thatcher?" From the depths of Castle Stanley, the voice of Stanley himself. It was a deep voice, and had deepened further with age. Thatcher identified the voice with short-sleeved plaid shirts and hairy forearms.

"Holding for Mona," Thatcher said.

"I didn't know that was you on the phone until Suzanne told me. I don't think your mother knew. She just left—a car came for her." *Ah, Suzanne*, Thatcher thought, *you wimped out on me.*

"That's alright," he said. "Tell her—"

"She's worried about you, Thatcher. Come by one night."

"Why would she be worried? I can come on Tuesday."

"Tuesday—no, no good. We're in Montreal, Tuesday. Actually, all week we're gone. I have a convention. But give her a call sometime."

"Yeah, okay. Listen, I'm not sure why she would be worr—"

"No idea where she's off to today, somewhere in the city, some museum opening, something. I have to get back to my shop." Stanley was a woodworker, his shop laid out across the two garage bays of the house in Gary Ridge. Corporate attorney by day, woodworker by night. Night and beyond, now, Thatcher supposed. Stanley had retired the year before.

"Okay, Stanley," Thatcher said. "You take care." Stanley was already gone. Thatcher hung up the phone.

"Holding for Mona," James said, "but delivered unto Stanley."

"He invited me for dinner, then said they'd be out of town. Carpentry convention—*yee-ha*."

"Why is it they only ever go where he wants to go?" Alice said.

"That's not true." Thatcher stood and went to the window. He lit a cigarette, took a puff, held it out the window. "What, are you kidding?" he said. "She's Mona Smith. She's nationwide."

Alice had her brush now, working it through her wet hair. "I'm just saying," she said. "Only my impression."

Thatcher said nothing to that, just smoked. James had nothing to say. He'd grown up around Mona and Stanley; there wasn't much to say about it. He pulled a cigarette from Thatcher's pack, hung it from his lips unlit. Finally he said, "How is that evils of porn book? Melissa's reading it now."

Thatcher smiled. "Melissa's reading it? Melissa-from-the-shore is reading Mona Smith?"

"What of it?" James pulled the cigarette from his mouth.

Thatcher put his hands together, all apologies. "Nothing. I'm sorry."

James picked up a stack of postcards. "We have to finish this sometime today, jackass. Let's go." They had a wedding, up north Jersey. Not a gig, as guests.

Thatcher flicked ash out the window then said, "You know what it is about that book, Mona's porn book?"

"What?"

Thatcher scrunched up his face. "Well, Mona's on the cover of *Time* magazine for this non-right-wing, non-Christian attack on the porn industry—smack on the cover, where she always wanted to be." Thatcher sat down again. "And it's, you know, take it or leave it, whatever—maybe she's got a point, maybe not, whatever."

"She's got a point," Alice said, firmly back in Mona's camp for the moment. "A big point."

"Yeah, okay. I'll give you that." He picked up a roll of stamps and began ripping again. "But *you* know"—he pointed at James—"and *I* know what was in Stanley's top drawer my whole childhood, so you just have to ask, 'If it's okay for her husband….'"

James nodded, smiling.

"What was in Stanley's drawer?" Alice said.

James whispered: "Dirty stuff."

"Porn," Thatcher said. "And not *Playboy*."

"Not by a long shot," James said.

Alice laughed. "What was it?"

"A lot," Thatcher said. "Wouldn't you say?"

"Oh, I would say," James said. "I would say."

"*Goat Fuckers Galore*?" Alice said, laughing.

"Not far off," James said. "And better alliteration. *Always Anal Amy*."

Thatcher laughed. "Oh my God, you remember that one?"

"Remember? Christ, I had a wet dream about it just last night."

Alice put her brush down. "How old were you guys when you found this stuff?"

James said, "I don't know when hombre found it. He showed it to me, what, son—twelve? Thirteen?"

"I was like ten, I guess, when I found the stuff," Thatcher said. "The collection expanded over the years."

"*Always Anal Amy*?" she said. "What is that, a novel?"

"A magazine. That was a good one—a nurse and a doctor and two or three patients. Amy always wanted—well, you know."

"Everything in the drawer was anal," James said.

"Not all, actually," Thatcher said. "But most."

"Holy shit," Alice said.

"Indeed."

"Ten years old—that can be a little warping, no?"

"I don't know," Thatcher said. "It's all natural I guess."

"Did she know?"

"Who? Mona?"

"Yeah."

"Of course she knew."

"How do you know? Maybe she—"

"Mona knew. I have first-hand information on that, trust me."

"Thatcher got busted," James said. "Many more times than once, but once in a particularly memorable way."

"And that's all we'll say about that," Thatcher said.

"More than once?" Alice said.

"Well—" Thatcher said, but James cut him off.

"Let me just say, at *my* house, I swiped the ol' *Penthouse Forum* from my Pop's closet once. My mom found it in my room, screamed at the old man for days. For *days*."

Thatcher was smiling. "Oh man, your mom can yell, too."

"That poor guy didn't have another dirty thought for ten years, I'd bet."

But Alice was still staring at Thatcher. "I'm not getting this whole 'caught multiple times' thing," she said.

Thatcher shrugged. "You know, I'd get caught—some magazine or book missing from the stack in his drawer or whatever. I'd get what was coming my way from Stanley because of it. He'd lock the drawer up, I'd pick the lock, I'd get caught again—on and on."

"He just kept confronting you with the stuff? That is so amazingly embarrassing," she said. "He never moved it? Or threw it out?"

Thatcher shook his head. "No—it was his stuff. After I found the stash, he just started locking it up."

"And you just kept going back?"

"Well, yeah—I'm pretty tenacious." Thatcher said. "And that was some hot shit he had in there." James laughed.

Alice said, "You were ten?" She thought about things a minute. Then said, "That's entrapment, you know?"

"How so?"

"What, are you kidding? You have an adult say 'Here's this candy bar, kid, I'm going to put it right here—but you can't touch it.'"

Thatcher smiled, then stopped smiling. "Well," he said. "You know. What horrible lesson would I have been shown had he thrown it all out? That wouldn't have sent the right signal, now would it?"

"Oh, you got a strong signal, all right," Alice said. "So listen, how can you be sure Mona knew about all this?"

James jumped up, said, "Hey, look at the time!" and made for the bathroom.

"Well," Thatcher said, "Mona had a drawer, too."

"No!" Alice said. "Porn?"

Thatcher shook his head. "Course not. Mona's anti-porn, you know." He smiled. "No, Mona's drawer had toys."

"Oh, Christ. You didn't."

"Sure I did. I took 'em."

"You didn't."

"Sure I did."

"Oh my God, what did she say?"

"Who, Mona?"

"Yeah."

"Nothing."

"She said nothing?"

"Of course she didn't say anything." Thatcher put his thumb and pinky to his ear and mouth, telephone style. "Holding for Mona," he said.

"She just let it go?"

"Not let it go—Stanley handled it. Mona's job was to be Mona. Stanley handled everything else."

"What did he do?"

"He said I was a sneak and a thief, and that the *items* had to be returned."

"You returned them to him?"

"No—he made me return them to *her*."

"I can't even listen to this."

Thatcher remained stock still, staring at the table.

"So Stanley had his drawer of porn, and you returned the toys to your mother…how? You handed them to her?"

Thatcher nodded once. "It was long and drawn out and a little more complicated than that. But essentially, yes. I handed them to her."

"Jesus. And then what? They finally threw everything out?"

"Well, you'd think," Thatcher said. "And I thought so at first. I went back into my mother's drawer the next week—of course—and her stuff wasn't there."

"But—?"

"It wasn't thrown out. Stanley had just put it in with his stash. Locked up in his drawer."

"He kept it all."

"Far as I know, it's still there. Otherwise there would be no lesson taught."

"It's all about the lesson?"

"It's all about the lesson."

Alice tried her best to make a joke. "And what have you learned here today, Thatcher?"

"Not sure," Thatcher said, answering seriously. The sarcasm had melted from his face, replaced with nerves and discomfort. "Guess I'm still holding for Mona."

• • •

James reappeared with beers all around. Alice took hers and went to change for the wedding. James shuffled the gig cards, stacked them, rubberbanded the stacks. They'd addressed and stamped a few hundred cards over the afternoon, all the names and addresses gathered at Not Really's gigs over the winter. The winter gigs had been good, each generally better than the one before it, each generally better attended than the one before it. A song Thatcher wrote with James and Bruno (the one about the Hoboken cab driver, Thatcher did the initial verses and chorus, Bruno rewired the progression for the chorus, then James carved a middle eight) was getting a daily spin on WFUV. Lou sang the lead.

"Good stuff," James said. "That's a fat mailing."

Thatcher leaned back to the cabinet, pulled an Arlo cassette from the deck. "I don't want a pickle," Thatcher said. He pawed the stack of tapes, stuck in Stills. Stills II. Thatcher opened his mouth ridiculously wide and sang falsetto as the leader ran:

All of the ladies attending the ball
are requested to gaze in the faces found on the dance card.

"Sweet Jesus," James said. "Have you no testicles, son?"

"'Fraid not," Thatcher chirped. He was always threatening to bust falsetto on stage. So far he'd been good, but he kept threatening. He leaned forward again, pushing his matches around on the table. "I don't want a pickle and I don't want to go to this wedding tonight."

"I know. You have to."

"You sure?"

"Yep." James stood, stretched. "What have you told Alice?"

Thatcher squinted. "Not much."

"Meaning nothing."

Thatcher nodded. "Meaning nothing."

"Good luck with that."

"Thanks."

Thatcher leaned back to the tape deck again. He'd changed his mind. He pushed stop on Stills, eject, traded it out with Guns N Roses, turned it way up. Alice yelled, from the other room: "That isn't folk music!"

Completely unheard under the weight of Axl Rose, Thatcher said quietly, "Sure it is."

• • •

Safe in the knowledge this wedding would be the longest night of his life, Thatcher did his level best to speed it along by getting as drunk as possible as early as possible. James was at the same table, sitting across from them with Melissa the girlfriend. He was matching Thatcher drink for drink just to keep him company.

"Thatcher," Alice said, "we're not going to be able to enjoy our hotel room if you keep going at this pace." Neither of them made enough to afford the hotel hosting the wedding reception; they'd pooled resources and sprung for the room anyway.

Thatcher waited until she looked away then downed his glass in a swallow. He found himself doing a lot of that lately. She hadn't come out and said as much, but Thatcher suspected Alice thought he drank too much. Actually, she had come out and said it—Thatcher chose to interpret the message in his own way.

Alice, he thought, was gorgeous tonight, some kind of gray satiny thing open at the throat. Somehow this made it worse and he couldn't concentrate on her, couldn't seem to concentrate on anything. He chewed a piece of bread and ordered another glass of wine.

They'd skipped the church—nobody needs that—so Thatcher hadn't actually seen Joanne yet. Almost two hours after they arrived at the reception the DJ finally announced the entrance and she came in the room on the arm of a tall, thick-around-the-chest tuxedoed fellow. Thatcher had never met the guy before, just seen his face in the pictures on Jo's nightstand. He was handsome, Thatcher supposed. Jo swirled on his arm, beaming, a bright wide smile, tan skin glowing off the silk of the wedding dress.

"She's beautiful," Alice said.

"You think so?"

"Absolutely. Don't you?"

"I went to school with her."

"I know. What does that mean?"

Thatcher blinked.

"That's so odd," Alice said. She sipped from her glass of water. "She's really stunning. Anyone would think so."

Thatcher blinked again. Alice tilted her head to the side the slightest bit; *WTF*. She looked at Jo, looked back at Thatcher.

"Did you two date?"

"Who?"

"You two. You and her." She hooked her thumb at Jo.

"No! That's crazy." He smiled, drunk and weak. "Why would you think that? I would have told you or something. You don't think I'd take you to the wedding of someone I dated without telling you, do you?"

"I don't know, Thatcher. You're acting very strange."

"I'm not strange."

Alice didn't say anything. She took another sip of her water and said, "I'm going to the bathroom."

James leaned over as she crossed the room. "You handled that well."

"You think so?"

"No."

Dinner was served and the new bride and groom circulated. Everyone stood when Jo came over. She said a few words to the others at the table— Thatcher had no idea who they were and had been too busy drinking to introduce himself—then circled and kissed first James then Thatcher on the cheek.

"In suits," Jo said, looking them over. "Who would ever believe." She was standing between him and James, holding their hands. "Introduce me," she said, and squeezed hard on Thatcher's hand.

"Jo," James said, "my friend Melissa."

"Meetcha," Melissa said, and stuck out her hand. She wobbled a little and giggled. She was possibly drunker than Thatcher.

"Jo was our class vice president in high school," James said, putting an arm around Melissa to help hold her up.

"Treasurer," Jo said, and winked. "I was the treasurer."

Thatcher cleared his throat and said, "This is my girlfriend, Alice. I've told you about her."

Jo took Alice's hand and said, "What a beautiful dress."

"Thank you. You look lovely. So happy."

Jo smiled. "That's sweet, thanks. I've heard so much about you."

Thatcher reached for his cigarettes. Jo opened her mouth to say something else but then the photographer was there and they all posed in place and smiled and then she was gone. When the groom—*Barry*, Thatcher reminded himself, *the guy's name is Barry*—came by ten minutes later Thatcher was at the bar getting fresh drinks; he'd seen him coming.

Thatcher kept his eye on the main table and when he saw Jo get up and head for the bathroom (he in fact saw two of her getting up, until he tightened his vision and brought her back into focus) he excused himself and followed her out of the ballroom and down the hall.

The hallway was empty. Thatcher stood around until Jo came out of the ladies' a few minutes later. He took her arm and pushed her toward the glass door to the balcony and they went outside. The day's warm was gone, chilly night, Route 46 through New Jersey speeding under the balcony. Jo turned and put her hands on his chest, flattening his tie.

"My little Thatcher all dressed up. If I'd thought it was possible—who knows?"

"That's not funny."

"Sure it is, sweetie." Jo leaned forward and whispered. "It's funny as long as we think it's funny."

"You're really beautiful, Joanne," he said. "I mean it."

"Thank you," she said, then leaned forward and kissed him on the cheek.

• • •

Thatcher and Alice were given a room on the eighth floor of the hotel. James et al were in the next room. The et al was Melissa, and Melissa, it turned out, was a screamer. Thatcher, blind drunk and miserable, dropped his clothes and pretended to pass out when he crawled into bed. But after ten minutes of Melissa through the wall he pushed himself up from the mattress. "I don't believe this," he said.

In the other room Melissa let out a yelp, then let fly a long series of top-volume pants. "I don't know how she keeps it up," Thatcher whispered.

"I don't know how *he* keeps it up," Alice said.

"Whiskey," Thatcher said. "They could go on all night."

Alice pushed her fingers through his hair. It was longer now, thickening out from the barbarity that had been his army high and tight. Alice liked it and pushed her fingers around in it. She was naked; he hadn't noticed before. He put his arm around her. The hell with Jo anyway. And this whole situation. It was ridiculous. He'd been with Alice a few months now, and it was just crazy. He didn't love Jo. That's not what it was all about. It was just about wanting what he couldn't have. For ten years, wanting what he couldn't have. He knew it.

Unfortunately, knowing didn't solve anything.

"You smell good," he whispered. She did, too. She always did. Alice smelled dark, spicy. He'd fallen hard for her, he had. She was different, Alice was. Different than any other girl he'd been with. She pushed back, Alice did. Pushed hard. There was nothing easy about Alice. He fought it, of course. Thatcher didn't one bit like being pushed back, held back, questioned, or interpreted. And yet he was also sure it was why he was still with her, the root of the attraction.

He tightened his wrap on her, said it again: "You smell good."

"You smell like a barroom floor," Alice whispered, and rolled over, her back to him. "I think you were into her, Thatcher," she said. "Maybe even in love with her."

"With who?"

"Joanne."

Thatcher opened his mouth, closed it, opened it again. "We've just known each other a long time," he said. "James has known her just as long."

"I think you were in love with her," she said. Then, "I think you fall in love with everyone you meet, Thatcher."

Thatcher stared between her shoulder blades. What to say to that. He didn't know, so he said the first thing that came to mind: "Is that a bad thing, Alice? If you think about it, is that such a bad thing?"

Alice said nothing.

WELCOME, THE BIG BANANAS

Important to know: no one had a record contract. No one. All these musicians in all these places—Hoboken, Manhattan, Philly, Asheville, Halifax, Boston, Austin, Kerrville, Bloomington, Denver, Mendocino, Seattle, Vancouver—all working, all out on the road when they could, but no one had a contract. It wasn't on the radar screen, really; not in any but the most far-fetched way. You just didn't get record contracts with any *real* kind of music, these days—and it just wasn't expected.

Instead, you did it old school—the way old school was the new school. Geoff Mason showed how in the early 1980s, doing it up like the old blues artists down South; head on with reality and just bypassing the man, having his own LPs manufactured, selling them from the stage. Sketch a logo, slap it on the cover—presto change-o, got yourself a record company. With CDs it went from acceptable alternative to actually the better way of doing business. Even if a record company wanted you (which they didn't), the bottom line was hard to argue: LPs cost six bucks to make and sold for ten; CDs only cost a buck or two to make, they sold for fifteen. It was the difference between a grilled cheese or a cheeseburger, out on the road; the difference between coffee and toast or go ahead, Sally, and bring me one of those Sunday Night Trucker's Specials. With an extra pickle.

So no one had a record contract. Oh, there were albums made with entities that looked like record companies—Zippy, in Hoboken, an obvious example; Marsh's employer. Up in New England, your Rounder, your Eastern Front, your Green Linnet. Windham Hill, pre-whoredom. Signature. Red House. But even those who walked into records with these folks; well, it wasn't a contract. Not a big label contract like it's understood. Nice, no doubt. Nice to have. It got you in the stores; some stores, anyway, for a few weeks, anyway. But not a sign-on-the-dotted-line-have-a-cigar-with-the-bald-suit record contract.

No one had a record contract. No one, that is, until Chapter Two up in Boston jumped the fence. And until a few months later, when King Papas topped Chapter Two, jumped an even higher fence, and scrawled his signature on the back of thirty-seven cramped pages and cashed an advance check for the big bananas.

MARCONI AND CHEESE

Orris had been buzzing all morning and it wasn't good and it was getting worse. Not buzzing like some people meant by buzzing, beer and such. Orris didn't drink beer; never had, really. Didn't know much about that. This buzzing was a different thing altogether. The buzz wasn't because of anything he did. He didn't think so, anyway.

Orris forgot about the buzz sometimes. Like if you hit your hand with a hammer. That hurts, for certain. It hurts, and when it happens, well, it's all you can think about. You hit yourself in the hand with a hammer and mister there ain't a whole lot else to talk about. But, you know, next day, it doesn't feel that bad anymore. And second, third day: well, you could easily forget you'd hit yourself in the hand with a hammer earlier in the week.

But let me tell you: a year later, two years later, whatever, whenever—next time you hit yourself in the hand with a hammer, it all comes back, like it never went away.

This was how Orris explained it to Dr. Flint the last time the buzzing hit. Dr. Flint had listened and said "Mmmhmmm" and said something abut childbirth and scribbled something and admitted Orris that afternoon up on the floor. Sent him in for a tune-up.

Beds weren't that good, up on the floor. The sheets were real starchy, the mattresses hard as concrete blocks. Better than a trip to Trenton, mind you, not a doubt about it—he'd been there once, for a complete overhaul. But still. The in-patient floor just wasn't good. And in Orris's experience there wasn't anything they could do in the hospital for the buzzing better than he could do for himself.

It snuck on him, this time. Come up from behind when he wasn't paying attention. Orris just woke up in the morning and realized it was there and then realized it had been there maybe a few days but so low and underneath everything that he really hadn't heard it.

"Would you say it's like bees?" Bill Pin asked. They were sitting in two plastic folding chairs out behind the group house, watching a yard dog load up a semi in the lot next door. Bill Pin was eating orange cheese cubes from a blue plastic bag. It was late morning, getting warm. Orris was already warm and actually wondered if he might have a fever. He wiped sweat off his forehead, rubbed it on his sleeve.

"Well, Bill," he said. "No, it's not like bees."

Bill swallowed a cheese cube, cleared his throat. "Would you say it's like an air conditioner, maybe?" he said. "You know, humming in the window?"

"No, Bill, that ain't it, and you know it's not like that or anything, really."

"Kind of like—"

"No, Bill, it's just buzzing. That's all. Not like anything else. Just plain old buzzing. All my own."

"Well," Bill said.

Orris stood up. "Hey," he said, then caught his balance. A little unsteady, he was. He took a moment, then felt okay. Okay, except for the buzzing. The dizzy had passed, though. He was pretty sure he had a fever, but the dizzy passed. "Listen, Bill Pin," he said. "I'm going for a walk."

"Should I go with you, Orris?"

Maybe Orris hadn't heard Bill's question, because he turned and walked away, walking around the house and toward the street. Bill watched him go. He held the bag of cheese cubes in his lap, nervous. He wanted to eat another but was unsure if appropriate.

• • •

In his gray sweats and old sneakers Orris walked east until he came to Willow then turned right and walked south, downtown. He'd thought of walking to the ballpark but when he got to the turn he'd moved on, in his head, moved on without remembering about the ballpark. So he went south, and thought maybe he'd walk all the way to Church Square Park. He had a friend down there.

The buzz was in his head but more in the little nubble on the top of his spine. That's where he felt it most. It bothered him. Interfered. Walking helped.

"Hey, Marconi," he said, and shuffled along. Off a curb, cross a street, up the curb, down the next block. "Hello, Marconi," he whispered.

Liked that name, Orris did. Liked it a lot. Good ring to it. Marconi. Distinguished. Liked the name, and liked the man behind the name.

"Read a book on him, Thatcher. Back when I could still read."

Yeah?

"Sure. They make you learn about Marconi, growing up in Hoboken. But they make you do a lot of things—doesn't mean you like it. But this book, good stuff."

Marconi. Sounds like macaroni.

"That's not funny, Bill Pin. Making fun of a guy's name."

It's just, if you're a celebrity—well, you should have a better name.

"Don't get me mad, Bill Pin."

Off a curb, cross the street, up the curb, down the next block.

"He was half Irish, you know that, Thatcher? Did you know?"

Doesn't sound very Irish, Orris.

"No, but he was. Marconi."

Okay.

"Hey, Marconi."

In Church Square Park the biggest thing is the Four Chaplain Monument. The nuns would bring them all down in the springtime, sit under it for lunch. Right around this time of year, maybe.

"I'd be scared of dying, Sister."

Don't mumble when you talk, young man. Speak up!

"They were brave men, Sister. The Four Chaplains."

Yes, and you remember that, young man.

"I read that book, too, Thatcher. It was the USS Somethingoranother—torpedoed. And these four made sure everyone was good to go before they died and tried to keep it all straight I'm just trying to keep it all straight, Marconi, just trying to keep the buzz down low and keep it all low and transmission's low down to zero low down low low low—"

Orris stopped in his tracks, middle of the street, turned around slow. Took a minute to remember it all, then he was okay.

"I'm okay," he said. "Going to the park."

Finished crossing the street, up a curb, down the block, into the park.

The Four Chaplain Monument was big, but Orris skipped it. Went to the pedestal engraved to his friend.

"Hey, Marconi," he said. "Hey, how you doing."

It helped, sometimes, being here. If you hit it at the right time of day, Marconi's transmission was stronger, stronger than anything, it pushed down the buzz, pushed it right down and clear.

"Hey, Marconi," Orris said. There was a bench there and he sat on it, very winded, very hot. "Let's see," he said. "Let's see." Orris lit a cigarette and closed his eyes and when that didn't help he opened them again and just stared at the little pedestal. "Hey, Marconi," he said. "Let's see."

Late Sunday afternoon, Thatcher and Marsh found an empty sidewalk table at Salt Girl's Café on Washington Street. Two espressos, then two again. Four blocks and a world away from Marconi. The sun low but pleasant still, warm in the air, heads tilted up all around. Early on enough in spring for that—heads tilted like flowers, following the sun. Folks strolling past on the wide sidewalk of Washington, moving along, moving along. Thatcher and Marsh sat outside and tilted toward the sun. Marsh ordered up a plate of Salt Girl's bruschetta—goat cheese, sun-dried cherry tomato, drop or two of pesto. Thatcher said he wasn't hungry then ate more than half the plate, popping the crusty bread slices whole into his mouth.

"You look peaked, my boy."

"Wedding last night, me and James."

"Hurt yourself?"

"I'll say."

Thatcher and Alice had slept until noon, crawled from the hotel, gone to their respective homes and back to bed. Thatcher felt a little better now, but weak, not quite solid. If he could grab a hair of the dog in the next hour or so he thought he'd probably be alright.

"Weddings," Thatcher said. "You know."

"Sure."

"Did you have a big wedding, Marshall?"

"No, we eloped."

"Vegas?"

Marsh laughed. "Poughkeepsie."

"That's beautiful."

"We're both from Ohio, you know. Carla's from Ohio, too."

"I thought you met at CBGB."

Marsh nodded. "Yep. Met at CBGB, found out we were both from Ohio. Married six months later."

"In Poughkeepsie."

"In Poughkeepsie. Her sister was up there."

"Did you get in trouble? Back in Ohio?"

"You know it. Kind of, anyway. My family, well, we came right home and it was all good. Took a little more work with the in-laws—Carla's dad, especially. Said he'd beat me like a redheaded step-child. They're from Toledo, though. You'll have that."

"How long had you been out here when you guys met?"

Marsh wrinkled his nose, thought about it. "Couple years, at least. Five years, I guess."

"When did you first leave Ohio?"

"As soon as I found out we were free to go."

Thatcher laughs. Marsh cracks a smile, too. "Right after college, first time. I was back six months later, then left for good a year after that."

"And this was…?"

"Long freakin' time ago, youngster."

One of Marsh's early bands had a video that made MTV. This alone wasn't particularly impressive in Hoboken—everyone makes MTV sooner or later. The fact they'd been on in MTV's first year—first six weeks, actually—*that* was impressive, if only for historical reasons.

Thatcher drained his espresso and laid a few bills carefully on the table. Marsh blew a kiss at the waitress and they started walking up Washington, headed north, strolling slow. *Boulevardiers, baby,* Thatcher thought. *Marsh was born to be a boulevardier.* They passed a church rec center, three boys throwing a tennis ball off the brick wall. There was a sign stenciled on the wall: NO BALL PLAYING.

"I'll tell you a story about Ohio," Marsh says. "From the dawn of time. This is about the day I decided my sanity required an Ohio exodus."

"You made a snap decision?"

"Sure. It was Biblical, kind of. Anyway, early summer, word gets out— big rock show coming. First one ever in the county."

"This is like 1942?"

"Fuck you, youngster. So, promoter rents the old movie theater downtown. Big show. Daryl Hall. John Oates."

Thatcher smiles around his cigarette smoke.

"Don't laugh," Marsh says. "Big names at the time."

"I'm not laughing. Solid band, too. T-Bone Wolk, right?"

"Exactly."

Thatcher nods.

"So," Marsh says. "Big show. All the kids are excited. Hell, I'm excited. First thing I do, I—"

"Score a gig with security, so you get in free."

Marsh reaches over and clasps Thatcher's shoulder.

"Exactly. Perfect. Right. But not security. Local sound crew. Front of the house. They've hired old Tommy Mack for front of the house. Tommy Mack sold me my first set of guitar strings."

"Of course he did."

"Of course." Marsh stops in the middle of the sidewalk, a little winded.

"You okay?"

Marsh waves a hand. "Of course." He starts walking again, favoring his healthy leg now, the limp heavy.

"So, here it is, week before the show, and I have to go downtown. I don't remember why. Pharmacy, maybe."

"Rubbers?"

"Well, that'd be a good story, I'll consider it for future tellings—but no. Probably like a truss or something."

"Ouch."

"Anyway, I'm cruising down Main Street, arm out the window, loving life and my little Ohio town. They've impressed me. They're bringing in Hall and Oates."

"And T-Bone Wolk."

"Exactly. So I go through the intersection past the post office, and up ahead I can see the marquee for the old theater. Big as day. I squint, blink, squint again. And decide right there and then I have to leave Ohio and never come back."

"What's it say?"

Marsh just shakes his head. "You wouldn't even believe it, Thatch."

"Sure, try me."

Marsh stops again, facing Thatcher. He enunciates carefully. "The marquee said, 'Friday Night: Haulin' Oats.'"

"No."

"Yes."

"Haulin' Oats. Well, it's a good country name."

"I left that week, young Thatcher. I shit you not."

"I bet. Did you go to the show?"

"Of course."

"How were they?"

"They rocked."

Up out of the retail district now, high up on Washington, they passed Maxwell's then turned right off onto 11th Street, two blocks over to Elysian Park. Past the playground there was a gazebo, small group of people gathering around the lawn on beach chairs and a few blankets spread out. Thatcher spied Dutch hanging off the side of the gazebo, hanging something, a speaker.

"Is there any sound to be had in Hoboken that isn't Dutch-produced?" Thatcher said.

"If you can hear it, Dutch juiced it."

There was James then, standing at the back of the gazebo, head down to his guitar, tuning. Thatcher and Marsh stepped around blankets, made for a bench on the far side. A girl on a blanket in front of them was pulling on a sweater and Thatcher wished he'd brought a thicker jacket; the spring warm was waning in the late afternoon.

"Smoke a cigarette, will you?" Marsh said. "I always like a smoke after an espresso."

Thatcher obliged, lighting a Marlboro, Marsh next to him on the bench breathing in the second-hand with satisfaction.

"So what do you think of your boy?" Marsh said. "He sure stepped in it." Marsh read the trades. He knew just how much Papas had been paid.

"Stepped in it?" Thatcher said. "Yeah."

"So what do you think?"

"I don't know. That's a complicated question."

"He's back in the city, yes?"

Thatcher nodded. "Got a place in Chelsea or something."

"I hear he's recording at Record Plant," Marsh said. "I hear he's calling everyone, bringing in everyone in town." Marsh held out two fingers. "Two ways to record your first big record, you know: Stripped down to three of you doing all the work, or the other extreme—you call everyone in town."

"Papas, I think he'd do it alone."

"I hear he's calling everyone, though."

"How'd you hear that?"

"He called me."

Thatcher flicked the ash on his cigarette. It was about full dark now, and Dutch turned on the gazebo lights. James up there was drinking from a bottle of Rolling Rock, some guy from the Town Park Commission monotoning into the microphone a schedule of upcoming events.

"He called you?"

Marsh nodded. "Said he had a song he wanted me and Mary Ann for backups on. To sing."

"I didn't know he'd ever heard you guys sing."

Marsh shrugged. "I didn't say it made sense, Thatcher. I just said he called me."

Thatcher didn't ask if Marsh had agreed to come in. Who doesn't agree to come in? Thatcher felt an arm around him, a kiss on the cheek then one on the other, Lou and Alice, Lou squeezing between Thatcher and Marsh, Alice hugging up to Thatcher's left side.

"Ladies!" Marsh said, over the crowd applause as James began to play.

Up on the gazebo platform, Dutch lit a handful of incense sticks and jammed them into a hole in one of the posts. The smoke wafted in the still evening air, James smelling it as he sang, the incense smelling good. He saw Thatcher and Marsh out on a bench, Lou and Alice. He'd call them all up later, of course, to sing, but for now he wanted to be alone and was, smiling as he sang, eyes closed, fingers moving across the strings like a spider on her web, you don't even think now, you don't even have to think, just let your fingers do the walking and sing.

VOTE EARLY, VOTE OFTEN

In the two weeks that followed James's evening gazebo concert the weather warmed considerably, spring stretching limbs and digging in, the season rolling slow and steady, like the Hudson itself, warming around the edges then, over weeks, penetrating to the core.

In Hoboken, years ago, you could measure the passage of springtime by flowerboxes—how they changed, when they changed. Mrs. Quatrone's place on the second floor of the building at Sixth and Clinton was on a corner of the building, three of the apartment's windows over the alley but three facing Sixth Street below. These windows—two from the parlor, one from her son's studio—had the flowerboxes. When her husband was alive, before they owned the building, every window on two sides, on each floor, overlooking Sixth or Clinton, had flowerboxes. Every one. And this just one of every building in Hoboken. In May, oh beautiful—*bellissimi fiori ovunque*. Across the city you could smell the flowers, strolling the sidewalk. On a warm day, with a small breeze, you could smell them all.

Then—not so much. She remembered around the time her son was in college, the years around there. No one cared for the flowerboxes anymore.

You could still see them, in many cases, the boxes empty, hanging where they'd hung for years, doing nothing now but filtering rainwater, collecting spiders. Broke her heart. Her boy came home from college for a weekend and he noticed—"Ma, you got the only flowers on the building."

It was the times. Dark times, the 1970s, Mrs. Quatrone remembered. In less than ten years, all the good jobs left Hoboken. It only got worse in the 1980s.

Bad things happen, but staying that way—well, that's someone's fault, Mrs. Quatrone thought. Someone asleep at the switch. Those years in the 80s, Mrs. Quatrone had blamed the president. That old man president, he came through Hoboken once, had a big lunch at the Italian-American Society. Mrs. Quatrone remembered everyone went out, all in a fever they were, to sit and eat overcooked pasta with that wax dummy and his scarecrow wife. Mrs. Quatrone found out later—not to any surprise—that the old witch spent the whole time talking about Frances Sinatra: "my Frankie," she'd called him. "To think he rose from such humble roots." The woman didn't eat a bite, Mrs. Quatrone heard. Not a bite.

Her Frankie—Jesus, Mary, and Joseph give me strength. No wonder all the flowers in town died. That woman put a ten-year curse on the place, just by visiting.

Everyone came out to the Italian-American Club to sit and have their picture took, though. Most everyone. Not Mrs. Quatrone. "That's not my president," she'd said. She didn't go. Jimmy DiBasi, he didn't go either. That young man was just a few years out of high school then, didn't seem long past being in Mrs. Quatrone's first-grade classroom, one of her last. She must have done something right, because Jimmy DiBasi kept all his boys home that day, the whole crew, ordered them home. Said the same thing Mrs. Quatrone had: "That's not my president." Jimmy DiBasi's name was on the ballot in the fall. Mrs. Quatrone voted for him. He became the youngest mayor in Hoboken's history. Next day the Newark *Star-Ledger* ran a subhead under the victory headline: RUMORS OF DIBASI WIN TAINTED BY OLD HOBOKEN ADAGE—VOTE EARLY, VOTE OFTEN. Mrs. Quatrone didn't know anything about that. Jimmy DiBasi had always been a good boy; she was sure he'd be a fine mayor.

Here was the funny thing, the thing itself: a few years after that old robot president left office, the flowerboxes began coming back. Mrs. Quatrone had no illusions they'd ever be back like they were—those days were as dead and buried as Mr. Quatrone, may he rest in peace, the days of the streets filled with flowers everywhere you could look. But Mrs. Quatrone never failed to be surprised by people surprising her. And this surprise was that it was some of the young people planting flowers now. In her own building, on the fourth floor, a young couple, the Cotters. Not Italian, but a nice couple anyway, the young man always in a suit and off for the bus every morning at 5:45. His wife had been the same when they moved in but then they'd had a baby—a little scrapper, too, that boy—and one morning here's Mrs. Cotter at the door with a nice basket of fruit, asking the whys and wherefores to jumpstart the empty flowerboxes outside her windows. Mrs. Quatrone made coffee and put some seeds into an old egg carton: Johnny Jump-Ups, marigolds.

Marigolds—you can sprinkle marigold petals on top of a salad. Mrs. Quatrone's son liked that. Said it was brain food for his painting.

One thing that does not go on a salad—and how it is that most Americans seem to think it does was a mystery to Mrs. Quatrone—is a tomato. A little grated Pecorino Romano, some pine nuts, a splash of balsamic and vinegar—okay. Not a tomato. Tomatoes are for sauce, for the gravy.

Out the side window of the kitchen you could look down and see some the ground from which grew some of the finest tomatoes in Hoboken. Mr. Izzo kept a trim, fenced garden sandwiched between Mrs. Quatrone's building, Victor's Autobody, and the back of Mr. Izzo's own brownstone. Mr. Izzo was older even than Mrs. Quatrone. He'd been old when her husband had still been alive. He'd always been old, Mr. Izzo. He grew tomatoes and he grew Sangiovese grapes, from plants he'd brought back from Sicily thirty years before when he'd gone for the funeral of his brother. The tomatoes he divided up between the more sensible women in the neighborhood (Mrs. Quatrone received, by special arrangement, a disproportionate amount) who in turn supplied him with gravy for the sausages he cooked for his dinner four nights out of seven. The grapes Mr. Izzo smashed for his own vintage. Mrs. Quatrone's boy helped every year, had since he *was* a boy, still went down for the yearly chore, coming back up now his hands, wrists, and forearms purple, grape pulp in his mustache.

It made for an okay bottle, though.

From that little plot of land, right out the back window.

Mrs. Quatrone opened the kitchen window now, the spring air warm and fragrant as the tomatoes Mr. Izzo would be harvesting come August.

Flowerboxes out front, the side windows more utilitarian. The clothing line, running on a wheeled system across the alley, directly over Mr. Izzo's garden. He used to yell about it, on summer days, if she put her laundry out to dry, yelling she was blocking the sun. Mrs. Quatrone would remind him who made his sauce and that would shut him up.

He was a good old man, for the most part, Mr. Izzo was. But like all old men, he grumbled.

The trick to life, Mrs. Quatrone thought, was not letting a little bit of grumbling from old men get in the way. Whether they're your neighbor or the president—don't let the grumbling old men get in the way.

• • •

In his studio, Quatrone's window had been open all morning. Work done, he was thinking of lunch. Used to be, he would eat as he worked, his mother bringing him plates of whatever. He'd eat without thinking, stepping back from the easel every few minutes, mouthing a forkful while he looked at what he had, stepping back in with the brush as he swallowed.

In his forties now, he was coming to realize this might be the road to fat land.

New plan, implemented this week: no eating while working.

It made Quatrone a very hungry painter.

Coming out of his paint zone, he looked around: his brushes needed cleaning.

They could wait. He was hungry.

Quatrone pulled a brown sweater on over his head, made for the door.

"Going out, Ma!" he yelled. He could hear the squeak of the clothesline wheel as he stepped out of the apartment.

Down on the sidewalk he stopped, checked his watch, considered his options. Lunch was an important meal, and he was particularly hungry. Louise and Jerry's was only a short walk. But Quatrone didn't like to eat alone. The painting studio isolated—emerging, he craved engagement. Quatrone checked his watch. Almost noon. He knew one other human being headed onto his lunch right now who might just have an appetite to match his own. He could be at Marsh's office in less than five minutes, if he walked fast.

Quatrone headed east and walked fast.

"Lunch?" Marsh said, and slammed his desk drawer closed. "Christ, yes." Quatrone smiled. Marsh always said the right things. He came around the desk, offering his strong arm.

"Here," Quatrone said. "Let me give you a hand."

Marsh allowed himself to be pulled up from his desk chair, reached for his cane, got his balance and bearings. "Let's eat," he said. "Somewhere not far."

At Carbone's, Miguel himself served their booth; a rarity—Miguel seldom ventured from behind the counter.

Tap tap tap. "Let's go, let's go…we playing games?"

"Not a game in sight, Miguel," Quatrone said. "Reuben, please. Onion rings."

Marsh closed his own menu. "Pencils down," he said. "Reubens and rings all around."

"The diet is killing me," Quatrone said, sipping his black coffee. "And really, I'm not getting any work done. Half the time I can't concentrate. When I do paint, I'm painting apples and cheese rounds."

"Cheese rounds. It's no way to go through life, son," Marsh said.

"We're not getting any younger, Marshall."

"That's for sure. I'm reminded too often, hanging out with these kids." He meant Not Really.

"That's going good, though, right?"

"Yes," Marsh said. Then did a *mezza metz* with his hand. "Mostly yes. The bloom might be fading from the rose. People getting on each other's nerves just a little bit."

Quatrone waved it off. "You're all great friends," he said. "It's to be expected, right? It'll pass."

"I'm sure. No, it's all good. It's fun while it lasts."

"Lasts? You guys are going all the way."

Marsh smiled. "I'm just happy when I get to go all the way with my wife," he said. "Bands are even trickier than wives."

"How'd that thing go," Quatrone said. "In the city." He meant Marsh and Mary Ann going to sing on King Papas's record.

"It was something, alright," Marsh said.

"Good?"

Marsh thought about it a minute. Then he said, "It's kind of like getting called up from the minors by a team you're not sure you want to play for." He rolled his fingers on the table. "Nice to be asked to the party, but it's not your party and you can't help but be reminded of that, and at the end of the day you have to go home."

This was about the most cynical Quatrone had ever heard Marsh. The big man was staring off into the distance a little. But he smiled then. "Still," he said, "who doesn't like a party?"

Miguel brought their Reubens, plates dripping with grease and onion rings. They ate big then Quatrone walked Marsh back to the Zippy Records office, up the stairs and to his desk. Marsh was panting out loud by the time they got there. Quatrone's mother raised him to pretend not to notice these things. Instead, he put his eyes on Marsh's desk, stacks of CDs. He pulled one off the top—Fire Quest, the Jesus band with the smoke-detector name. Quatrone turned it around in his hands while Marsh got himself situated in his chair, caught his breath, cracked a bottle of water and drank from it. Quatrone put the CD case back and tapped his finger on the cover.

"Do you believe in God, Marshall?"

Marsh sat back, looked up at his friend. He said, "Well, I grew up in Ohio. Which, on *this* subject, is not much different than growing up in Hoboken."

Quatrone raised his eyebrows.

"Lots of churches," Marsh said. "And an expectation that you should be in a pew on Sunday." He took another sip of water. "Very different pedigree, of course," he said. "None of your pope nonsense in Ohio." He waved his hand at the stacks of CDs. "No pope in Jesus rock, either."

Quatrone smiled.

"But believing in God—it's a funny thing, Quatrone. I had two relatives who were doctors, when I was a kid," Marsh said. "My one uncle on one side, and an older cousin on the other side." Marsh held his hands apart. "These two guys, they didn't even know each other. My uncle, one day he says to me and my sister, 'Watching the beauty of a child being born—that's how I *know* there's a God.'"

Quatrone nodded. He could see it.

Marsh nodded, too, then he said, "Couple of years later, I'm with my mom at my cousin's house, and he says, 'Watching the beauty of a child being born—that's how I *know* there is no God.'"

Quatrone laughed. He clapped his friend on the shoulder. "But what about you?" he said. "What do you believe?"

"I believe I ate too much lunch," Marsh said.

FAME, FORTUNE, AND FOR THE LOVE OF LEONARD COHEN

Bruno met Thatcher and Lou for dinner at Chairman Tao's on Bloom-field, all spring rolls and dumplings. Lou ordered a Tibetan yak-butter beer and almost spit out the first sip. She passed it to Thatcher who was able to choke it down. There had been no shortage of things Tibetan-yak in the shadows of Mona Smith's academic lecture tours; likewise back-stage on his own folk journeys.

A parallel, he thought.

Holding for Mona.

The three bandmates were talking fame. Comparing notes. Between them they knew some famous people. Mid-conversation Lou let the Ran-dolph secret out of the bag.

"Oh, shit," she said, hand to mouth. "I'm so sorry, Thatcher...I was just talking."

Thatcher waved her off. "Hardly matters," he said, meaning it. The Tibetan yak-butter beer, he noticed, got easier with each sip.

Bruno was nodding his head. "You know, it makes sense," he said. "Randolph's kid. Somehow it makes sense."

"What does that mean?"

"I don't know. Mostly, it just seems like the thing to say."

They laughed at that, and it was okay.

"Mona's son—I always thought was a stretch," Bruno said. "Randolph, though—this is much more comfortable to me."

"I'm awfully glad you think so."

The waitress brought Lou a replacement drink, a plum iced-tea. Bruno recommended it. He ate here a lot and swore by the plum iced-teas.

"What will we be like, famous?" Lou said.

"Sonsabitches," Thatcher said. "Pure-D motherfuckers."

"I'm afraid he's right, Lou. You're destined to bitchdom." Bruno was smiling. Thatcher didn't see Bruno smile that often. He didn't seem like an unhappy person per se, but he didn't smile much. Maybe it was just all that black he wore. Maybe it absorbed all the emotion from the face. Perhaps. Bruno was smiling now.

"I'll tell you one thing," Bruno said. "Marsh is way too nice to ever be famous."

"You think?" Lou asked.

"I hate to say it but it's true."

They thought on that a moment. "I think you might have a point there," Thatcher said. "No one famous is really nice. Even the nice ones."

"He's niced himself out of the market."

"Damn," Lou said. "Well, don't tell him."

Thatcher pointed at Bruno. "You, my friend, you'll go all recluse on us, when we're famous. Holed up in a hermetically sealed penthouse, sanitizing *The New York Times* in the oven."

"No fucking hippy communist folksingers allowed in, either," Bruno said. "That means you, you freak."

Thatcher waved him off again. "Oh, that's a given anyway. As band-mates, if we're not sleeping together, we should never be seen together. Matter of fact, I don't even want my guitar traveling in the same truck as your bass."

"What if you guys just start sleeping together?" Lou said.

"Bass players don't sleep with guitar players," Bruno said. "Only cross-pollination is allowed in intraband sexual outings. Guitar to drums, drums to keyboards."

Lou poofed at her hair bob and said, "Who gets to sleep with the chick?"

"Everybody," Thatcher and Bruno said together. "Unless, of course," Bruno added, "the chick is a lesbian. In which case she's the sole prop-erty of the redheaded road manager with the big boobs and the flannel shirts."

"Is there a redheaded road manager with big boobs and flannel shirts?" Lou said.

"If you want one," Thatcher said.

"Absolutely."

"Then she's all yours, Louie."

"Of course, you actually lived it," Bruno said, his chopsticks leveled at Thatcher's chest.

"Lived what?"

"Famous."

"I haven't lived it," Thatcher said. "I've only seen it. From an extreme distance. And that's a much different kind of famous, anyway, than rock star. I'm not sure what Mona is. But people don't want to know Mona as much as they want to be Mona."

"Really?" Lou said.

"Really."

"That's creepy."

Thatcher nodded and said nothing.

Bruno sat back in his chair. "Think about it, though," he said. "I don't know if that's so unique to Mona. I think maybe that *is* what it is to be famous. You say you want to know the famous person, but deep down what you're really after is *being* the famous person."

"What's that like," Lou said, "having people want to be your mom?"

"Wanting to be the person who is his mother," Bruno clarified. "Not actually wanting to be his mother."

"No," Thatcher said. "You're wrong there." He held up a finger to the waiter, threshold crossed, Tibetan yak-butter beer number two, please. Fuck it.

"What they—" Bruno said, but Thatcher cut him off.

"Okay, check it out," he said. "Let's say there's a category. This category is 'women who picked up the slack taking care of Thatcher backstage at a lecture or in the kitchen of a party or whatever.' In that category, we've got fifty percent who are just nice. Maybe somewhere deep inside they *do* want to be Mona because, let's face it, we all want to be Mona, but at the moment they've found themselves with this kid and they're being nice to him just to be nice to him. Most of this fifty percent was younger, college girls and around there." The same demographic as Mona's assistants through the years, and in fact the majority of Mona's assistants had fallen into this category. "The other fifty percent is a different story. Some of them, I was worried they might take me home."

Lou laughed then stopped. "You're kidding."

Thatcher shook his head. "No, not kidding."

Bruno said, "Ten minutes alone with you meant they got to be Mona for ten minutes."

"Bingo."

The waiter brought Tibetan yak-butter beer number two. Lou grimaced. "You have to be certifiable to drink that, Thatcher."

"Remember where it is I spend my working days," he said, and took the first sip. The first sip of this one was not as good as the last sip of the last one.

Lou—who had read all of Mona Smith's books by the time she was eighteen, but avoided mentioning that to Thatcher—drummed her fingers on the table and said, "Maybe ten minutes alone with you didn't mean that for ten minutes they got to be Mona. Maybe they were hoping Mona would walk in and see them being nice to you—brownie points. Not like that's any better, but—"

"No—I mean, definitely there was that, too. A lot of that. But no kidding, Lou, there were women who scared me." Thatcher took a drink from his beer, thought about it a moment, then said, "When I was six, my mother walked in on a woman who was punishing me because I wouldn't call her mom. She was supposed to be my babysitter, at one of Mona's lectures."

"Dude," Lou said. "That's sick."

"Kind of."

"No kind of about it."

Thatcher shrugged. Bruno tapped his chopsticks, thought about it a moment. He said, "Well, at least she wasn't trying to breastfeed you. Although, I'm pretty sure my own mother didn't breastfeed me at all."

"Explains a lot."

"I think you're right." Bruno chewed a dumpling, thought things over. He pointed a chopstick at Thatcher. "But the babysitter gone bad, my friend. You know when they write about you in the *Rolling Stone*, that'll be the lede."

"It is my destiny," Thatcher said.

• • •

Thatcher and Lou were off to Geoff Mason's after dinner. Guitar cases a-shoulder they walked to the PATH, slipped under the river, came up in the Village. Christopher Street alive, warm and loud, the corners all strutters and watchers. Lou grabbed Thatcher's hand, holding it as they walked.

"Madam," he said.

"Sir."

"Your new mama is a cutie."

"You think so?"

"I wouldn't kick her out of bed for eating crackers," he said.

"You wouldn't kick anything out of bed, buddy."

"I resent that."

She squeezed his hand, smiling. "She *is* a cutie, isn't she?" Lou had brought her around the week before to Maxwell's. She was a graduate student in anthropology, and a soccer player.

"I'm a sucker for a soccer player," Lou said. She let Thatcher's hand go to light a cigarette.

"I'll bet the soccer player doesn't like that," he said, pointing at her pack.

"The soccer player knows where her bread is buttered."

"Where her pasta is sauced."

"Where her crumbs are crumbled."

Lou took Thatcher's hand again and they walked slow, letting it all flow around them, taking the long way around to Sixth Avenue then down to Houston Street and Geoff's place.

The little flat was packed with people and guitars, everyone out of their shell with spring. Anna was at the stove, stirring olives into a big bowl of pasta. They both leaned up to kiss her cheeks.

"My favorite freaks," she said. "My Jersey freaks."

Thatcher had been buoyant all night and stayed that way for the next ten minutes—*hey, howyadoin* here and *longtimenosee* there and *lemmegetyouglassofwine*—hanging by the door because he couldn't get any farther in, talking to David Moyer and three people he didn't know, watching a roaring conversation in the far corner where he assumed Mason was buried. Then, two quick glasses of red down, he realized the roaring conversation was about King Papas and the making of the Papas album.

"He was just here," Anna said, coming up behind him. "Didn't you guys see him on the way out? He left literally a few minutes before you got here. He's getting everyone in town to play on this thing. It's pretty cool."

"Is that right," Thatcher said, and suddenly it all wasn't so fun anymore. He refilled his glass, stood back against the wall.

"Where's my boy? Where'd you go?" Lou whispered in his ear a few minutes later. Thatcher pretended he hadn't heard her.

Across the room the crowd parted as Mason stood from his chair. He spied the new entrants, crying out with arms raised: "Woody Guthrie!"

"Motherfuck," Thatcher whispered.

"Be nice," Lou said.

But it was alright. Thatcher couldn't be mad at Mason, not for more than a few seconds. He took Mason's greeting as the okay to literally walk over people to cross the room, giving the old man a hug and back patting. Thatcher hadn't been around since his long afternoon here the autumn before; he'd been out to dinner with Mason and Anna once or twice, and been to some gigs, but hadn't been to the apartment.

"I heard your band's drivel on the radio," Mason growled. "Good choice, making the chick sing it." He waved at Lou, still across the room.

"I never hear your drivel on the radio, Geoff," Thatcher said. "Maybe you should consider letting a chick sing it."

Mason hugged him again and someone offered Thatcher a chair. He took it. Mason raised a glass: "To public radio and the tens of dollars we make there!"

The plates were passed, time to eat, then the notebook went around. Geoff had been making his visitors sign in for twenty years now. The book was choked with songwriter signatures, most obscure and never-to-be-heard-from, more than a few of the now rich and infamous. Most of the signatures were under a line or two of wit. It was a lot of pressure—that was twenty years of wit to differentiate from with little or no notice as the notebook was passed to you. Thatcher held it in his lap for two minutes, then passed it on, unsigned.

The guitars came out, room quieted down. Thatcher felt cocky. *Fuck y'all*, he thought. *I'm going first.* No one ever wanted to go first—it was a room full of performers, who wants to volunteer to open? Thatcher felt cocky. *Gonna mow you down.* He waved Lou to come sit near him.

"Lou's gonna sing this with me," he said. "Wrote it middle of last week." A lie. He'd written it three weeks before. Still, it was new.

Lou's harmony was wavering and fragile wrapped around his voice, hanging in the air over him as he sang. Thatcher sometimes got sloppy when he drank, but his fingers moved dead-on tonight, hammering down point to point, fret to fret, string to string.

A beat of silence when they finished, then applause. You weren't supposed to applaud; the neighbors got bothered, you were supposed to make like a beat poet and snap your fingers. But sometimes people clapped, and when Thatcher and Lou finished they clapped.

"Well," Mason said, "you're no King Papas, but I guess it didn't suck." Everyone laughed. Later, finding themselves in a corner together, Lou said, "Why's he mad at the King?"

"No one's supposed to be successful, especially someone from his circle. Success takes all the fun out of it."

"Takes the fun out of it for who?"

"For whom, Louie dear," Thatcher said, five sheets by this point. "For whom. And the fun, as you say, is taken from Mason."

Across the room an argument was growing, something about Leonard Cohen. Geoff Mason on his feet again, pointing at a young, smirking pale boy sitting on the old sofa. Thatcher recognized him from the old days, couldn't place his name. He was Argentinean, he thought, some kind of weird rich Argentina Euro-trash crossover, stranded in New York lo these many years. The smirking pale boy never played a guitar, but ended up in Mason's apartment on a regular basis. He called himself a connoisseur. Mason was shaking a long finger at him.

"What was that?" he sputtered. "Say that again?"

The smirking boy was clearly drunk, as drunk as Mason. In a loud voice he repeated himself, accented and calm: "What I said, Geoff Mason—my observation, if you will—was very simply that Leonard Cohen never wrote a political song."

Mason stood still a moment, taking it in, then turned and picked up his half-full wine glass from the floor. He turned back around, raised the glass in a toast, then threw it across the room at the smirking boy. The glass flew over his shoulder and exploded on the wall, a dripping flower of red cabernet on the wall, glass and wine drops falling all over the couch and the desecrater of Cohen.

This cheered Thatcher immediately. "Oh, that's beautiful," he said, and put his arm around Lou. "What a beautiful thing."

• • •

In Hoboken, at dinner, Thatcher had said he'd only seen fame from a distance, but this wasn't entirely true. Thatcher had stood in the path of fame—someone else's fame—feeling it like the tropical wind running before a hurricane, ruffling his hair while he held Mona's hand as tight as he could.

When Thatcher was six they went to Chicago for the weekend. Mona was speaking in a packed college auditorium. Thatcher was deposited backstage with a woman in jeans and a bright yellow sweater, a large woman with long brown hair halfway down her back who remained mute as Mona introduced herself and handed off Thatcher. When the entourage cleared, the woman paced the room and stared at Thatcher. He'd brought Chutes and Ladders with him but she didn't really play, she wasn't playing right, and in the end Thatcher just moved the pieces around on the board by himself, building lives and stories around the good kids and the bad, letting some of the bad kids climb a ladder and sending that smirking girl and her perfect homework down a chute. Every few minutes the woman would walk behind Thatcher and stroke his hair. Each time he would swat her hand away. He didn't like to be mean so tried to make it seem like he had an itch but it wasn't working and she kept doing it and she didn't like him swatting her hand away.

She said nothing.

What Thatcher really wanted to do was leave but he knew he was supposed to stay in here and would get in serious trouble if his mother came back and he was gone. He'd be in trouble if she had to go look for him. She'd tell Stanley about it, when they got home.

He already knew this room was called the green room, and from where he sat on a red cloth couch in the not-green green room he could see both of them in a big mirror—himself, and the silent woman. Every few minutes she would light another cigarette and stare out the window and pace and then look at him. Every few minutes she'd come back and touch his hair again. He would swat her hand away. She didn't like that.

Later, when Mona came in, the woman wasn't silent anymore, but speaking—at him, loud—and Mona heard it as she walked in and she yanked Thatcher away so hard it hurt his arm, his face pressed into his mother's neck as she lifted him and he could smell her powder and soft sweater and as Mona ran down a dark hallway calling for her assistant Thatcher pressed himself into her as hard as he could so no one would see that he'd peed.

THAT ONE TINY THING

Back in Hoboken, Lou and Thatcher stumbled from the PATH, stumbled the five blocks to Lou's apartment. They were singing, both of them, top of their lungs, Geoff Mason's drinking song.

"He's my hero," Lou said, breathless, as they stopped at her building.

"Mason?"

"Yeah—he's my hero."

"You're my hero," Thatcher said, and threw his arms around her, lifting and spinning her. Lou screamed and when her feet hit earth again she squeezed him hard, their arms around each other there on the sidewalk. She looked up into his face.

"You're okay, young Thatcher," she said, aware she was slurring her words. She leaned up and gave him a kiss. Thatcher held her tighter and she squeezed him again and then pulled away.

"Louie, Louie," Thatcher sang, and did a little dance on the sidewalk. Lou lit a cigarette, watching, applauded when he finished. He bowed and said, "You going home now to your hot-assed soccer player?"

"I'm just going home," she said. "I suggest you do the same, little boy."

"Ms. Alice is in Boston for the weekend," Thatcher said. "I'm going to Maxwell's."

"You be careful. I like that Ms. Alice. She's a keeper."

"She is, isn't she?"

Lou nodded.

· · ·

Thatcher was at the bar, making the decision it was time to walk home—one more drink and his capacity to walk might disappear—when Jo came up from behind him. She grabbed him, spun his stool around.

"Holy shit, you look great," he said. Tan from her two weeks in the Bahamas, she was wearing a white silk blouse and khaki shorts. She kissed him, hard, pulling his body close to hers.

"Madam," he said, "you're a married woman."

"Exactly."

"Exactly what."

Jo smiled and played her fingers on his chest. "You don't know?"

"I don't think I do."

"That one tiny thing," she said, "that smallest of small things. That has always been a problem. Is not a problem anymore."

He raised his eyebrows.

She leaned in and whispered in his ear, "Assuming, of course, you're still interested."

Ten years he'd been waiting. Ten years.

"I mean, if you're not interested…"

He grabbed around her waist and pulled her back in. She reached into her front pocket, pulled out a little tightly rolled plastic baggie. Thatcher almost fell off his stool. "You are such a Jersey girl," he said. "Is that coke?"

She leaned back in, whispered in his ear. "Remember when we were seventeen?" she said. The only other time he'd ever done coke with Joanne, a winter Sunday when Mona and Stanley had been out of town.

"Barry's in Connecticut," Jo said now, "and I just thought maybe we could go to my place and have a little party."

"I have to work tomorrow," he whispered.

"Fuck that," she said, and Thatcher couldn't have agreed more.

I DO WHAT I DO

The World Trade Center, James thought, was like a tuning fork, these
two silver towers set down on the bottom of Manhattan, humming in the
wind, holding the vibration. He could lean back in his chair, eyes closed,
fingertips to his desktop, and feel it there, humming, humming. He took
it with him, James thought, when he left work every day, there in his
fingertips.

Today James took his guitar with him, over his shoulder; he'd brought
his guitar to work. He didn't bring it every day. Thatcher said he brought
it every day—*it's fucking glued to you, dude*—but fuck Thatcher anyway.
James didn't, as a matter of fact, bring his guitar every day or everywhere
or every anything.

But he'd brought it today. He grabbed his guitar and left the building. Early. Swoosh down the elevators, down down, across the wide lobby
and cut through the tourists, across the great plaza. Loved leaving early,
James did. Loved it. The presence of all those others behind your back, all
of them sitting there, glued there, and you were gone. All you were now
is gone.

James was leaving early but he was also late. It goes like that sometimes. He hailed a cab. Not an everyday occurrence. Another Thatcher point of annoyance—*dude, just get a fucking cab*. Thatcher took cabs everywhere. It was the Mona in him. The boy had no money, none to speak of, ever, but if there was an excuse to take a cab, the cab was getting took. It had occurred to James more than once that Thatcher's love of cabs was what kept the kid in slow orbit around Jo. Like Thatcher, Jo adored a cab. Unlike Thatcher, she had Daddy's money or a good job or both and could afford her adored cabs. In the autumn, before Alice, it seemed Thatcher and Jo were falling out of cabs all up and down the opposite shores of the Hudson. Since Alice, no cabs. Alice couldn't afford cabs.

No one can afford a cab, James thought, begrudging this one already. Lou never took a cab anywhere. Even when she could afford it. James dug that about her. Alice was the same way. It was tough.

Not that Thatcher wasn't tough. He was tough. Except when he wasn't.

Thatcher hadn't been home yesterday. Yesterday was a Monday. Today was Tuesday. For that matter, he hadn't been home this morning, either. James guessed the boy hadn't been to work. Messages from Herm stacked on the machine, ominous, grim. There was a Not Really gig tonight. Thatcher never missed a gig. There were a few gigs James wished Thatcher had missed, but he'd never actually missed one.

The cab pulled to the sidewalk. James made the hated payment, counted his change, slammed the door behind him. A beautiful afternoon it was, a beautiful afternoon to leave work early. James took his time crossing the sidewalk to the doors.

He was, he had to admit, curious. He'd hated to admit it, but no getting around it. He was curious. Papas had called and it was weird and then it wasn't and then he'd said sure, I'll come by. Well, not quite true that suddenly it had not been weird. The whole phone call was weird, the whole situation was weird. There had been a time King Papas and James had listened to LPs together, gone to concerts together, talked music until dawn; but that time was a long time ago, relatively.

And now, well.

Well, this was all unexpected.

Lou had put her arm around him at the bar one night, the night they'd found out. "Ah, James," she said, but hadn't known what to add to that. Finally she'd said, "It's a hard pill for you guys, I think. For you especially, maybe."

"What is?"

"You know, for you and Thatcher. Maybe more for you, right? I mean, you and Papas don't really like each other anymore, right? So, it's—"

"What? I don't even know what Papas is doing. He doesn't do what I do. It's a different thing altogether. It's—" he waved his arms. "It's whatever Papas does. I don't know." He drank his beer. "It's not what I do. I do what I do. He does something different."

But he could admit it was hard, yeah, it was hard. More weird than anything, though. Really, they didn't do the same thing. Really.

And then Papas called.

"Yeah, listen, man," he'd said, and he had that way of talking that drove James absolutely batshit. That was almost a hang-up right there. But he'd hung on. "Hey, you know, I was thinking, we used to share a lot, James," he said. "I'm just thinking, if you could put your fingers on the strings for a tune, it would mean a lot."

"What do you mean?"

"You know. Play."

"Me? On your thing?"

"Yeah."

"That's—"

"Just come over, sit in, see what happens."

James took the elevator to the eighteenth floor. Potted plants every-where, and blond wood. Blond wood, blond receptionist. Blond, smiling receptionist.

And then King Papas, striding long legs across the floor, arm ex-tended.

"Yeah, man," Papas said.

YOU SING LIKE AN ANGEL

They were back at the Shannon Lounge, where they'd played their first gig, night of winter's first snow. It was all different now. That night, they'd played to twenty people, maybe; all friends. Tonight the room stood full, a hundred or more. They'd played Maxwell's the week before—same sized crowd.

Marsh and Bruno walked in together, stopped still and looked around. It was hard not to be impressed. *Maybe*, Marsh thought. *Maybe this band is it after all.*

Most of the room behind the stage at Shannon was filled with an old brown couch. Thatcher sat on one end, working through his second gin and lime and something in a plastic cup, talking to a serious kid in a flannel shirt writing in a notebook.

"That's the *Village Voice*," Mary Ann whispered to Lou, pointing at the serious flannel.

"Listen," Thatcher was saying, using his free hand to emphasize, "it's not a direct line on the heels of this or that, per se. It's a new thing, man, altogether new." He took a slug of his drink, waiting for the serious flannel to catch up with his notes. "Having said that, let's be clear: there's tradition, and our embrace is real. But it's varied, man. You got your straight-up Johnny Cash and your Jerry Lee Lewis boogie-woogie shuffle beat over here"—he held his hand out and wiggled his fingers—"and your Pretenders and The Clash and whathaveyou over here"—the hand moved, fingers wiggling; serious flannel licked his lips—"but down here, man, from out of nowhere, down here it's The Weavers, baby, standing straight across the stage and singing the truth, man, singing the truth." Thatcher took a drag on his cigarette. "And we're all of that, man."

"Good God in the morning, he's excellent slinging the bullshit," Mary Ann whispered. Then, even softer, "Who are The Weavers?"

Thatcher leaned closer to the kid. "You seen how we line up straight across the stage? That's The Weavers, man, coming at ya." Flannel nodded his head—good shit.

James stuck his head in, pointed at Thatcher. "Let's go, son. We have to clear the room and warm up."

Thatcher shrugged. "We'll talk more after the show," he said and shook serious flannel's hand.

With the kid gone James squeezed himself and guitar in.

"You just kicked the *Village Voice* out of the room," Thatcher said.

"Nothing for him to write about if we suck," James said. It had gone well in the studio with Papas this afternoon—it had gone well and now he was irritable and he didn't know why he was irritable and that made him even more irritable. He turned to say something to Lou but Lou and Mary Ann were gone, off in search of Bruno. James looked back at Thatcher, who hadn't made a move. Thatcher was playing with the ice in his cup, one foot underneath himself on the couch. "Hey, where you been for two days?" James said.

"Something came up."

"You don't look good."

"You should have seen me yesterday," Thatcher said. James pushed a smile but it wasn't very effective. "What?" Thatcher said. "Had a little party with Jo, Monday, down in New Brunswick. Slept most of today." He patted his cheek. "I think I look pretty good, actually."

"Work called for you. Couple of messages on the machine. Alice, too."

Thatcher crunched a piece of ice. "Yeah," he said. "My whereabouts—we don't need to mention that to Alice."

"Whatever."

Thatcher looked up, pissed. "Whatever?" he said. "I could mention a few times I've covered for you, Mister Jimmy."

"I said whatever, dude. I'm not going to say anything. And don't fucking call me Jimmy."

Bruno was suddenly there, but maybe not so suddenly. They hadn't seen him.

"Let's all stop pissing in the punch, boys," he said.

Marsh was already on stage, seated, a palm slap to each of them as the rest walked to their microphones. They had an opening and they did it now: "Who?" James said into his mike, with the answer from Thatcher into his mike: "Not Really." And he thought *Okay?*

Marsh counted it off, Slim Youngblood hit the snare hard, and they started the thing, opening with one of his like they almost always did, Marsh and Mary Ann singing, Thatcher strumming by the numbers, stepping forward to add a voice on top at the chorus. Not for the first time, he stared wistfully at the drum set and wished to be behind it. *That*, he thought, *looks like fun*. Slim crashed a cymbal and winked. They still didn't officially have a drummer, but only because Slim was too drama to sign on to something for real. He made every gig, though.

Second verse, Marsh singing alone. He sounded strong, although he'd told Thatcher it was hard for him to sing sitting down. "Can't get my lungs stretched," he'd said. But he just wasn't able to stand for a show anymore. Or stand at all, really, for more than five minutes. "It's not very rock and roll to sit down for a gig," he'd said. "Nonsense," Bruno told him. "It's not very Yankee, but it's deep Delta. You'll just have to change your name, is all." Thatcher offered up a name: Slow Gin Fizz. And Ol' Gin Fizz was tearing it up now, seated or not. Eyes closed, he'd actually stopped playing, his big hand hovering over the strings of his guitar (a beautiful luxury afforded by having four guitar players on stage). It was a good tune, a good opening number. From the other side of Marsh, Mary Ann winked at Thatcher then blew him a kiss. Thatcher stepped forward to sing on top the chorus. James was looking at him as he sang, a look like he was trying to communicate something. Thatcher couldn't figure it, though. He kept singing.

Wild applause, after the song. Marsh told a joke, more applause. Thatcher leaned down to grab a swig off his beer bottle. As he did so, James stepped to the mic. Talking to Dutch out at the board he said, "Gotta take Thatch's mike down, okay?"

Thatcher looked up, looked around. Dutch cupped his ear and James said it again. "Thatcher's mike, gotta take it down."

Thatcher stood straight, glancing at the audience, then at James. James looked over, smiled, and said—into the microphone—"My brother, you sing like an angel, but the levels are too high."

Thatcher stared at him, strummed down. His face was red. "Yeah," he said. "Whatever."

• • •

At the break, Thatcher pounced, finding James in the can, standing before a urinal.

"The fuck, man?" Thatcher said. "What the fuck was that?"

"What?" James said, and shrugged, zipping his fly.

"My levels are too high? I'm singing too loud for you, or too bad for you, and you need to share this with the audience? You need to do this in public?"

"Dude," James said, even. "I don't know what the hell you're talking about. All I said was Dutch had your levels too high. You were drowning everyone out."

"How the hell do you have the nerve to talk about someone's singing right in front of the audience?"

"Dude, it wasn't you—it was the levels."

"Yeah, right. You don't like me busting in on that song or you don't like my harmonies or maybe you just don't fucking much like me—but you don't announce it in front of the audience."

They were in the hallway now, and Lou was there, not catching the substance but clearly catching the drift. "Hey!" she said, stepping between them. "Enough."

• • •

Marsh never left the stage. He made a move to stand at the break but felt it wasn't going to work out and just stayed put.

"A Diet Coke, my man," he said to Bruno, and waved him off to the bar. Carla came up on stage and crouched down beside him. "I'm fine," he said. "Just having an audience with my adoring public."

And he did, friends coming up and saying hi and a few music people from the city he hadn't seen in a few years. After ten minutes Mary Ann walked back out and sat next to him opposite of Carla, and the three stayed there for twenty minutes, chatting and laughing and having a drink. Lately, the second set had been started by Marsh alone and in this case it just worked out perfectly. Carla pecked him on the cheek, Mary Ann squeezed his arm, they both walked off, the lights went down, and Marsh situated his guitar in his lap.

"It's all about comfort," he said into the mike. He strummed down a few times, adjusted the tuning. Then he looked out into the audience. "Thanks," he said. "From all of us. Thanks for being here, kids."

And then he sang.

I used to live for the moment, and man, that's a great way to live.
I was born reckless, a pusher and a shover, something just had to give.

He liked this song, Marsh did. It was new, just a few weeks old, and it fit nice, he thought.

And then a misunderstanding, and I wound up here.
A guest of the governor, his guest for ninety-nine years.

Mary Ann had walked out onto the stage next to Marsh, and as he hit the chorus she opened her mouth and laid a harmony above his melody. Eyes closed, Marsh felt her voice in his ear, in his bones. *There is nothing finer*, he thought. *There is nothing finer than this.*

• • •

Ten feet from Marshall, James and Thatcher stood watching. At the second chorus, Thatcher put his hands in his pockets.

"Yo, man," he whispered. "I shouldn't have yelled."

James nodded. "No, you were right," he said.

"Fuck you, is all I mean."

"Yeah."

"Fucking Marsh," Thatcher said, looking again at the big man in the chair. "He's a rock and roll Buddha."

James smiled at that. They had two more songs before they'd be on-stage again. "Let me steal you a warm beer," he said, and they both walked back to the couch room.

• • •

"So what was it like?" Thatcher said.

"What?"

"You know—in the house of the King."

"Oh." James took a deep pull off his beer. Then he shrugged. "Being there was cool, I guess. Cool place. It's what we always wanted, right?"

Thatcher was peeling the label off his wet bottle. "Yeah," he said. "It is." He took a swallow. "For us."

"What do you mean?"

"I don't know. Record Plant. It's cool, but I wanted to walk through the door for me," Thatcher said. "Or at the worst, you." He flipped James the finger. "But not for—you know, someone else." He stood up, stretching. "Maybe that's just stupid."

James finished his beer, reached for his guitar. "I guess what I'm surprised at is the way he's going about it. I figured, if that guy ever lucks into making it big, he's blowing everyone off and we'll never see him again. So this is—I don't know, a surprise."

"You can't show how big you are by blowing everyone off," Thatcher said. "No one can see how superior your house is unless you invite them in."

"Hadn't thought of it that way."

"I learned that one from Mona," Thatcher said.

"Those are Mona words?"

"Nope. That's Mona's life."

• • •

Between songs, Marsh didn't say anything. This was unlike him. He was a master of banter and patter. But the last chord rang and he found he had nothing to say. He looked around the room, looked over the heads of the audience, and found himself not unhappy but absolutely at a loss for words.

DINNER TIME

On the other side of town, in the little group home near the warehouses, Bill Pin hovered at the kitchen counter, white apron tied tight in place to protect his suit. Orris sat at the plastic table in a blue bathrobe, crouched over. Hair whispy and messed, breathing hard, the big man's face was blotched purple and sick, his loose eye vibrating. He'd been sitting there for almost an hour and hadn't said a word when Bill Pin offered to cook him a meal.

The microwave beeped. Bill put on oven mitts and lifted a TV dinner out. Bill Pin set the meal tray down on the table and Orris gripped the table edge and flipped it up, standing suddenly as he turned the table over with a roar, the meal flying across the room and splashing on the back door with a gelatinous *thup*. There was a moment of silence as Orris's yell echoed. Bill Pin had jumped back, and looked over his shoulder now at Orris and the mess. Bill's heart rate accelerated, his mouth moving but no words formed. Finally his mouth stopped moving and the two just stood there, on opposite sides of the mess and flipped table. Then Orris turned, said "I have to go to bed now, Bill Pin," and left the room. Bill listened to the sound of the big man's steps on the stairs then silence again. He didn't want to turn around and look at the mess. That would be very upsetting, so he thought he'd just stand here a moment or two longer, not moving, and just look at the kitchen wall.

HERMINATION

The machine spit a fax at 4:30—

Almost there, baby

Herm came at 4:45. "Thatcher," he said, "you need to clean out your desk."

Thatcher was shoulder deep in *The Heart is a Lonely Hunter*, hiding the paperback in an open patient folder. He closed the folder as smooth as possible. "My desk, uh—" he said, trying to figure. His desk was clean. Thatcher's desk was always clean. Four years in the army will do that to you. "My desk is pretty clean, I think."

"Not clean, Thatcher," Herm said. "Clean out."

Thatcher not getting it. Still in his novel, at the lunch counter at midnight with John Singer.

Clean out? Mr. Scapaletti the day guard walked into the records room behind Herm. The old man had a limp. Herm pulled at an earlobe and looked around the room.

"Unfortunately, Thatcher, we have to terminate your employment."

Old Scapaletti had a cardboard box in his hands. He put it on Thatcher's desk. It was empty.

"You'll need to clean your desk out now, Thatcher," Herm said, checking his watch.

Thatcher stood up.

"You're firing me?"

"I'm afraid, Thatcher, the only option open to the organization at the moment is termination."

"You're firing me?" Thatcher walked around the desk. "I don't believe this," he said.

"Hey now," Old Scapaletti said. "None of that."

Herm crossed his arms, took a step back.

"It can hardly be a surprise to you, Thatcher."

Old Scapaletti tapped the box. "Let's get your stuff in here, kid."

Thatcher looked at Old Scapaletti, looked at Herm. "And you brought a security guard?"

"It's standard protocol, Thatcher. Nothing personal."

"To escort me out?"

"Let's just get your stuff here, kid," Old Scapaletti said, but Thatcher ignored him. He grabbed his cigarettes from the desktop, shoved them in his pocket, and walked out the door.

"Thatcher!" Herm yelled, but Thatcher was gone, down the hall and gone. *Escort, my ass*, he thought. He was halfway down the stairs before he remembered his book.

"Shit," he said, stopping short on the stairway. He'd immediately written off his desk contents—not sure really what he had in there anyway, but damned if he was going to stand there in front of them and pack it. Kind of reminded him of being ten and getting into a fight over something in James's front yard, James yelling at Thatcher to get his damn bike and get off his damn grass and Thatcher yelling back, "You can't make me take my bike anywhere," and stalking off without his ten speed. This was a fine repeat of that—but he couldn't leave the novel behind. He was only halfway through. He turned around, then turned around again. Nothing he could do. "Shit," he said again. "Fucknuts." Strut removed from his step, he sighed and walked slow toward the building's entrance and his surprise freedom.

• • •

The firing moved with such speed (the firing was not, on reflection, unexpected, but nonetheless speedy in the moment) that when Thatcher hit the sidewalk he stopped short, breathless, not even sure where he was going, only partially clear on why he'd just left the building. He hovered a moment, almost tip-toe, considered going home, back to the apartment. Is that what you do when you're fired? Just go home? Just go and do what you would do on any other normal day if you weren't working? Weren't working a job you hadn't been fired from?

Somehow, simply going home didn't seem right. It had become an extraordinary day. This was not normal. Thatcher turned around on the sidewalk, not knowing at all what to do. He patted his pockets, realizing now what he'd left behind besides his novel: he'd had a spare capo, in a drawer. Couple of cassettes. Pair of sunglasses. Couldn't go back now, though. He'd call someone. Maybe Thomas Barnes. Thomas was one of the few staff members he'd connected well with. Thomas Barnes could go in the records room tonight or tomorrow, get Thatcher's shit.

Thatcher turned around on the sidewalk again. Took two steps toward home. But again, it didn't feel right. How do you just do what you always do? He pulled out his wallet. Twenty dollars in there. There was a bar, small joint, neighborhood room, two blocks into the railroad-yard section. Thatcher had never been in, but knew it was there. Going home didn't seem right, so he went to the bar.

Twenty bucks buys plenty at a dollar-drafts joint. Red plastic bar stool, glass of beer. Thatcher drained it, held up a finger.

Terminated, Herman Jeffries said. *We have to terminate your employment.* Good ol' Herm.

What a fuckhead. *Terminate.*

Whatever happened to *fired*?

The bartender filled Thatcher's glass. Thatcher slipped a dollar over, said, "Whatever happened to fired?"

"How's that?"

"Fired. You know, fired. They say 'terminate' now. Or 'sever our relationship.' Whatever happened to just getting fired?"

The bartender rubbed an open palm over his bald head, tugged at the collar of his white shirt. "Search me," he said. "You just get fired?"

"No, I just got terminated."

The bartender nodded, pushed Thatcher's dollar back across the bar. "On the house, this round." Thatcher drained the glass, ordered another.

You can drink a lot on twenty, when the drafts are a buck. Down in Virginia, there'd been a joint off-post that did fifty-cent drafts every Sunday morning from ten until two. Fifty-cent drafts and seventy-five cent cheeseburgers. Now that's living. You could pull yourself from the barracks around ten on a Sunday, head on over, lay your change out on the bar and consume. You almost *had* to, really. Deal like that. Like going to the grocery store and seeing four-for-one on pickle jars. Maybe you love pickles and maybe you don't—probably you like them okay but could take them or leave them. But when it's four-for-one, well, what can you do. You can say you don't want a pickle, but at four-for-one you're going to buy some pickles. You'd be a fool not to. So when beer is dollar-a-draft and you've got twenty in your wallet—well.

You don't turn your back on that.

Thatcher made a mental note to allow James in on the existence of this place. James was nothing if not mindful of a bargain. Mental note made, Thatcher ordered another, slipped a dollar across the bar.

This was going to be hard on Orris. The firing. The termination. It would be hard on him. Then Thatcher wondered if it would be hard on him at all. Maybe it would be hard on Orris. Maybe Orris could care less. Maybe Thatcher just thought it would be hard on Orris.

And where was Orris, anyway? Thatcher hadn't seen him in a few days. Hadn't seen him in a few days, and in the days, weeks, beforehand they hadn't talked much. Orris seemed…strange.

Thatcher snorted beer out of his nose on that one. Strange. The guy was a patient—*client!*—in a fucking lunatic asylum. Of course he seemed strange.

Thatcher wiped his face, lit a cigarette.

Not that it was really a lunatic asylum. And not that Orris was a lunatic. Neither of those things, really. So. There you are.

The poor guy had seemed strange lately, though. And hadn't come to Day Hospital in a few days.

Maybe he was sick.

Come to think, Thatcher hadn't seen old Bill Pin, either. Could be they were both sick.

Well. Couldn't have himself fired—*Herminated, motherfucker, you ain't been fired, you been Herminated*—and then just be gone without talking to Orris. Let's face it, Orris was the only friend he'd really made at the place.

Thatcher thought about that one over a beer or three.

JULIE NEWMAR VS. EARTHA KITT

Melissa-from-the-shore was no more. *A drifting,* James thought. *That's a nice way of putting it.*

James always liked to find a nice way of putting it. Whatever *it* was.

"It was a drifting, that's all," he said now.

He was on the roof with Loopy Lenora Lupisella. She took a swig of her beer, said, "Ships in the night, baby."

"Ships in the night." James raised his bottle in toast. They clinked. He said, "Ships in the night that passed and then circled back and then tied together for awhile and had a little underway party but then someone got worried about all that rubrail friction and pulled the line and then—you know—the ships drifted."

"Fuck me," Lenora said. "That's a helluva metaphor."

"I'm a songwriter," James said. "Don't try this at home."

Loopy Lenora was easily in James's top-ten Hobokenites. But they hadn't seen much of each other lately. Lenora had gone a little down after Larry Ritzi's suicide in the fall. She'd hibernated most of the winter, coming out just for soup and work, really. Not much else. Then the spring. James had pulled her out for a few Not Really gigs. She had a hard time at the first one—all those people having fun. But she was getting better.

"Can I ask you a question?" James said.

"Of course."

"I don't want to be insulting."

Lenora put her arm around James's shoulder. "Sweetie," she said, "I don't think that's possible for you."

"So—isn't it just deadly boring in that tollbooth all day?"

Lenora laughed. "That's it? That's all you wanted to ask?"

"Well, you know—I just wondered."

"No, dude," she said. "It's the greatest job in the world."

"No shit."

She nodded. "No shit." Lenora reached around, found her cigarettes. "Do you mind?" she asked, and lit one.

"You know what I do all day, James?" she said.

He shook his head.

"Nothing."

He thought about that.

"Hmmm," he said.

"I can tell you're not sold," she said. "But check it out: what do you do all day?"

"Nothing," he said.

"Exactly. And don't you pretty much spend your entire day trying to cover the fact that you're doing nothing?"

"Pretty much."

"Not me," she said. "It's not like I'm just doing nothing. It's not like I'm doing nothing and have to look like I'm doing something. I get *paid* to do absolutely nothing."

"You have to give change," James said.

"That's me, man," she said. "I'm just giving a little bit of change to the world. And don't you think the world could use a little more change?"

"Damn right."

"So there you go."

"So there you are."

They toasted.

"Lenora," James said.

"Yeah?"

"I don't know if I said this last year or what I said, but—I'm really sorry about Larry."

"Yeah," she said. "Thanks." Then she said, "Man, there just seemed to be a lot of death in Hoboken last year."

"You think?"

"Sure. Helen, for one." Lou and Mary Ann's sister. Helen the librarian. "Helen alone would do it. God, that's the most awful thing ever. I mean, I loved Larry and all, don't get me wrong. But Larry—you know." She drank from her beer. "Well, you know."

James nodded. He knew.

"But Helen," Lenora said. "Jesus. I don't know how Lou and Mary Ann get out of bed most mornings."

"Lou…" James said. "I think sometimes she doesn't."

"That chick split on her too, right?"

James nodded.

"Fucked up," Jennie said.

"Yeah."

"She's damn good, James. In your band."

"I know it," he said. "She makes it."

"Y'all make it," Lenora said. "But Lou sure is sweet up there. Your boy, too."

"Woody Guthrie?"

"Yeah. You two are funny, you know," she said.

"How's that?"

"You guys are friends from, what, childhood?"

"Yes."

"You're just so different from each other. Like worlds apart in some ways. Almost hard to believe you could be friends. But when I hang out with both of you, you can see—a lot of common water," Lenora said.

James put his hands out, said, "It's kind of like coming at the same problem from different approaches."

"How so?"

He thought about it a minute. Then he laughed out loud. "Okay," he said. "True story. And this doesn't leave the roof."

"Scout's honor, baby."

"My first wet dream—it was about Catwoman."

"Catwoman? From Batman?"

"Yep."

"Okay. That's funny."

"Thatcher's first wet dream? Also Catwoman."

"No shit. You guys are a couple of freaks."

"No, it gets better. Did you watch the old Batman show?"

"Of course. Every day after school on Channel 9. *Ka-Blam!*"

"Yeah, so—you know there were two actresses playing Catwoman. My Catwoman dream was Julie Newmar. Thatcher's Catwoman was Eartha Kitt."

Loopy Lenora spit her beer out in laughter.

"Common problem," she said. "Different approaches. Damn, that's good."

THE NIÑA, THE PINTA, AND THE SANTA MARIA

Heavy dusk when Thatcher made it to the house, purple shadows low and heavy across the vacant lot beside the group home. Bill Pin sat on the porch, level straight atop a plastic beach chair. He wasn't reading. His leather briefcase stood closed under the chair. Bill's hands were on his knees. He reached to adjust his glasses as Thatcher came up the steps, then rested his palms on his knees again.

"What do you say, Bill," Thatcher said. "Mighty warm for that suit, isn't it?" Bill didn't say anything. He wore a suit every day. Three piece. Thatcher knew it. What do you say when someone says something so obvious. What do you say. Bill Pin hated predicaments like this. He laughed a little laugh and said nothing. Socially awkward, this was. What do you say.

Thatcher swayed on the top step. He grabbed tight the rail, steadied himself. Stood a moment, acclimating.

"Haven't seen you fellas in a few days."

Bill Pin adjusted his glasses again. Instead of answering he said, "Oh, the ladies must just go wild over that hair of yours, Mr. Broderick. Just wild."

"Sure they do, Bill. They go nuts." Thatcher stood silent a moment, looked around the empty neighborhood. Then said, "I was worried you were sick or something. Hadn't seen you at Day Hospital in a few days."

"I don't think—" Bill said, then paused, then said, "I don't think Orris feels very good. He's in bed. Been in bed all yesterday, all today."

"Flu or something?"

"Yes. No." Bill Pin shook his head. "Yes, I don't know, really. Poor Orris. He doesn't feel very good, Mr. Broderick. He just doesn't feel very good."

"Maybe I should go in and see him."

"Well. He's in bed, you know," Bill said, pointing inside. "Hasn't been out. I haven't been able to go to the store and get my magazines. Not in a few days."

"Are you sick, Bill? You feel okay?"

"No. But Orris isn't feeling right, I think. He's in bed."

Thatcher took a step onto the porch, swayed a little. Christ, he was drunker than he'd thought. Big time. Wicked. Felt a little sick with it, too. A little sick in the belly all of a sudden.

"He's in bed," Bill said again, and Thatcher said, "Okay, Bill." He opened the screen door and walked inside. He remembered from meeting the boys here to go see baseball that there was a toilet right off the living room. He moved toward it, stumbled, pivoted, then sailed through the door, hit his knees, jammed his fingers down his throat and vomited into the bowl. Stayed there a few minutes, repeating, until his stomach was empty.

That'll help, he thought. *I hope.*

• • •

Thatcher found Orris's bedroom down the second-floor hallway. Dark in here, but a clear mountain of human visible under the blankets on the bed, clear smell of human crisis—a heavy odor, socks and sweat and sick.

"Orris, hey Orris."

"Marconi?" His voice was high, questioning. A kid's voice.

"What's that?" Thatcher stepped into the room. The odor was worse. *There are things,* Thatcher thought, *you don't want to know about your friends.*

"Hey, Orris." Thatcher was whispering. He couldn't make out if Orris's eyes were open or even what direction his head was pointing. He seemed to be laying full down, though. Thatcher moved his palm around on the wall, looking for a light switch. Found it, clicked it, nothing happened.

"Marconi?" Orris said again. Thatcher figured it, now—Orris was on his side, facing away, toward the far wall. Thatcher swayed. He had to sit down. He took a step and sat on the edge of the bed. Orris was saying something else now, but Thatcher couldn't make it out. Repetitive, almost like a song.

"How you feeling, buddy?" Thatcher said, and Orris stopped his song. He stayed silent a moment. Then he said something, deeper now, from the back of his throat, sounded like: "I'm electrified."

"You're—"

"Electrified. I'm electrified. And dehumanized."

Thatcher closed his eyes. Even in the dark everything was spinning. He gripped the edge of the bed with his right hand and said, "I guess I'm not sure what you mean, Orris."

No immediate response. After another moment, Orris began his almost-chant again. Thatcher strained his ears but couldn't make out what Orris was saying. Something in a rhyme that sounded like it ended with "Maria."

Thatcher reached out his hand to grip Orris's shoulder, than changed his mind halfway, his hand hanging in the air. He looked around, his eyes adjusting; the room was small, a single four-drawer dresser, a New York Yankees poster. Orris, with his chant: *ba-ba baba ba baba ba baba ba.*

"I'm not sure what you mean, Orris."

Ba-ba baba ba baba ba baba ba.

This was hard. Thatcher couldn't think any more straight than he could walk. He should probably be worried, he thought. The guy seemed pretty sick.

"You think I should call an ambulance, Orris?" he said.

Ba-ba baba ba baba ba baba ba.

Thatcher rubbed his forehead. Suddenly, Orris stopped his chant. The silence hung in the air, as thick and visceral to Thatcher's drunken head as sound. Then Orris started again, this time louder, and Thatcher finally figured out what he was saying over and over and over again:

"*The Niña, the Pinta, the Santa Maria. The Niña, the Pinta, the Santa Maria. The Niña, the Pinta…*"

"Oh, boy," Thatcher said softly.

Thatcher stood up. He stepped to the end of the bed, gripped the footboard, stepped to the other side. He'd have to come around, to see Orris directly, to let Orris see him, to see if he could help.

"*The Niña, the Pinta, the Santa Maria. The Niña, the Pinta, the Santa Maria. The Niña, the Pinta, the Santa Maria. The Niña, the Pinta, the…*"

Thatcher stood still, gripping the footboard, not moving forward.

He'd have to get into Orris's face.

He didn't want to see Orris's face.

"*The Niña, the Pinta, the Santa Maria. The Niña…*"

Thatcher did not want to see Orris's face.

Standing still, he whispered: "Hey, Orris."

"*The Niña, the Pinta…*"

"Hey, you think I should call an ambulance?"

"*…the Santa Maria.*"

Thatcher slid straight down, butt to floor, leaning against the footboard. *He's electrified,* Thatcher thought, *and dehumanized.*

What does that mean?

"The Niña, the Pinta, the Santa Maria."

What does it mean?

Thatcher closed his eyes. He didn't know what it meant. He did know he hoped Orris stayed put. Because if he didn't stay put, if the big guy got up out of bed, then Thatcher would have to see his face. And Thatcher was really very quite sure he didn't want to see Orris's face tonight.

"The Nina, the Pinta, the Santa Maria."

A little bit later the chant stopped, and shortly after that Orris broke the silence with three syllables of barking: "MARCONI!"

Thatcher didn't stir; his back to the footboard, he was asleep. Sometime later—drenched in sweat, feverish and his muscles twitching—Orris, too, passed into sleep.

• • •

Downstairs, Bill Pin had moved inside shortly after Mr. Broderick had entered the house. Bill wasn't sure where to go, and finally settled on the couch; that way he'd be seen if anyone came downstairs and perhaps he could be of assistance. There was a star in the house, after all.

Bill Pin sat down on the right side of the couch, changed his mind, shifted to the left side of the couch. He placed his hands on his knees and waited without moving. When, an hour later, a loud yell ripped through from upstairs—*MARCONI!*—Bill blinked uncomfortably, and began rocking, very gently, rocking; hands on knees and waiting to help, rocking just enough to keep his blood moving.

TERRIFIC

In restless sleep, drunken sleep—eyeballs twittering under thin lids—Quatrone is in Thatcher's head. Quatrone painting in his studio, shirtless, poking the canvas with his brush, poke poke poke little dots of orange, while Thatcher sits on the cold radiator and drinks the big man's beer.

De Kooning, Quatrone said. And explained how the great artist stowed away for New York as a young man but stopped—for a year—in Hoboken.

In Hoboken, Quatrone said; de Kooning in Hoboken.

There's a black and white photo of de Kooning in a book on Quatrone's dresser and Thatcher stares at the slick hair, the sharp face.

He bunked in the Dutch Seaman's Home in Hoboken, Thatcher—you know where that was? Quatrone tells him, explains.

The words under the picture say de Kooning said everything was "terrific." It was his only English word for a long time, and even forty years later remained his favorite. Everything was terrific with de Kooning. Even when it wasn't.

Terrific, he would say, and clap. Terrific.

Thatcher can see him, in the spare, scrubbed Dutch Seaman's Home, drinking nickel coffee and eyeballing Manhattan across the river. Wondering, preparing.

Here's the thing, Thatcher, back then, he didn't even know an artist was something you could be. He could paint, alright—but he just wanted to be a sign painter.

Is that right?

That's right.

Terrific.

Yeah.

Hey Quatrone, you know Woody Guthrie was a sign painter too?

No he was not.

Yeah man. Painted every sign in Okemah, Oklahoma. Made a living at it.

Guthrie and de Kooning. That's a beautiful thing.

Quatrone told him then how the man painted, and Thatcher didn't understand, so Quatrone said, Look it's the materials that are important. Because he used what he did, the stuff won't last. See that there?

A postcard reproduction, tacked to the wall.

That's *Woman I*. It's a different painting now than it was in the 1950s.

How so?

It's aged. The materials he used, it's aged. Decayed. It's a different painting.

Is it bad?

No. Just different.

Like it's not his anymore.

Kind of. He painted it. But then it—

Changed.

Yeah.

That's like a song, Quatrone. Just like a song. Literally. You paint it and it's yours. And then immediately it's not.

Materials decay, that's a fact.

Quatrone was looking at his own brush now. Thatcher stared at the calluses on the tips of his fingers.

. . .

Woody died in an institution, Quatrone. Waylaid by the family curse. Huntington's Chorea. A jittery jumpity Parkinson's that jitters your mind and then your body and finally jitters you to stone. But all that bopitty bop in the brain—is that bad for a songwriter? Is that so bad? Maybe boppity bop isn't a bad place for a lyricist.

Course it is, killed him.

Yeah, but everything decays. What happens in the process, though? Is it so bad? Maybe it's what it takes.

De Kooning painted through Alzheimer's. Didn't even know who he was anymore. Incontinent. But still painting. It was de Kooning's hand, though. It was art.

Boppity bop.

Materials decay, but it's still art.

Terrific.

WE DO WHAT WE DO

Thatcher stopped at the apartment to grab his guitar and James's gig bag and the JBL speaker, swallowed four aspirin with a slug of orange juice, then back out the door. Thomas Barnes was waiting for Thatcher in a booth at Carbone's Diner, remains of breakfast laid waste before him. Thatcher pushed his guitar and gear down the empty bench, slid in beside.

"I know you got fired and all yesterday, Thatcher. But I have to say. You look like shit," Thomas Barnes said. "If you don't mind me saying."

"I've been getting a lot of that."

Thomas reached into the pocket of his jacket, spread a capo, picks, a deck of cards, address book across the table. "From your desk."

"Thanks."

Thatcher picked up the items one by one, examined each as if he'd never seen it before, stowed them one by one into the pocket on the front of his guitar case.

"Sorry you got Herminated," Thomas Barnes said. "What'd you do?"

"The list is endless."

"That's tough."

"Yeah. Hey, there's this guy in Day Hospital, big guy, blind in one eye—"

"Orris Mack."

"You know him—Orris?"

"Of course I know Orris."

"I think he's kind of sick. I don't know if anyone should do something, or what. But he doesn't seem well."

"Sick like the flu?"

Thatcher shook his head, tapped his forehead. "He's kind of—gone."

"You been hanging out with Orris?"

"Slept on his floor last night."

Thomas set his coffee cup down on the saucer. "You're kidding."

"No. He doesn't seem well. Hasn't seemed right for a few months, really."

"You're friends with a client?"

Thatcher shrugged.

Thomas Barnes sat back, took a sip of his coffee. He said, "He's de-compensating."

"He's what?"

Thomas waved his hands in the air. "You know. In the professional—he's losing it."

Thatcher pursed his lips. "Losing it?" he said. "He's a Day Hospital patient. Isn't whatever 'it' is kind of already lost?"

"Well, to a degree. But there's losing it and then there's losing it." Thomas reached over, took a cigarette from Thatcher's pack. "Schizophre-nia and related maladies—works in cycles, most times." He held his hand out like a plane, level. "Maintenance, maintenance—" he dipped his hand. "Then crash. Crash and burn."

"No stopping the crash?"

"Depends. Depends on the meds, depends on the patient. Depends on fate and the variance of the wind, half the time. Who can tell."

"You ever seen Orris go down before?"

Thomas nodded. "Two three years ago, maybe, he did a run at TPH." Trenton. The state hospital. Thatcher knew the initials well. The place had a very distinctive stamp they used on their discharge paperwork. "This was right about when I started here," Thomas said. "First time I met Orris he was maybe fifty pounds lighter."

"That's hard to imagine."

"Trenton always takes it out of you, seems like. You come out of Trenton with your name sewn to your clothes and a need for a tighter belt."

"So you go up, you go down—what, forever?"

"Most times, older you get the valleys aren't so deep." Thomas lit the cigarette he'd borrowed. "The highs aren't so high, either, though."

"They kind of mellow out as they get older?"

"They kind of dull out. Exceptions, mind you. All kinds of exceptions. But, you know, in general." Thomas took a drag, held it, exhaled. "The hardest break is almost always the first one, of course. They might hit one or two more pretty hard. Then the curves—"

"Flatten?"

"No, they don't flatten. Round, is more the word, I guess."

Thatcher thought about that for a moment, watching Thomas smoke. Then he said, "What was that word you used before?"

"Which?"

"De-something."

"Decompensate."

Thatcher turned that one around in his head. "Decompensate," he said. "That's a good word."

"A good word?"

"Not a good thing—just a good word. A precise word."

"Hadn't thought of it that way." Thomas said. "Guess so."

Thatcher had grown a fascinated attachment to the dry parlance of the professional mental-health world, these precise stones that filled the patient records he'd spent the winter reading. Much like the army world—and completely unlike the real world—everything meant exactly what it meant. Which made everything not nearly as bad as it sounded to a lay person, or in fact extraordinarily worse.

Decompensate. Significant. Appropriate. Remarkable.

"Decompensate," Thatcher said again. "That's some word."

Thomas Barnes raised his eyebrows. He took a drag from the cigarette then said, "So what are you going to do now?"

"Now?"

"You know, since you were—"

"Fired?"

"Yes."

"This morning I'm going to play some guitar."

"No, you know—I mean, for money."

"Yes, that's what I mean."

• • •

Down, down son—go on down. Glide and slide from the city and rise home to Hoboken in the evening, but the mornings, baby, in the mornings you know you go down to the subway. Hot in the city this morning, hot already, but cool down below, cool in the underground.

And good thing, what with the carried load. Guitar and knapsack on shoulder, JBL speaker in right hand, milk crate of cords in left.

Time to go to work. Time to go. Time to do what we do.

We do what we do, man. We do what we do.

• • •

Click, the plug into the speaker. *Click* the plug into the bottom of his guitar. His shoulder pressed back until *crack*. The train pulled out, Thatcher strummed down. The speaker put a nice ring on it—a warm, round ring. The echo of the station, the warm ring of the speaker. A man could play some gui*tar* down here.

Strum up, strum down.

What to play.

Two teen girls on the way out the platform, giggling and pointing— "Hey, you do some Janet?"

Thatcher smiled. *We do what we do.*

So what to do?

A mom with a boy, down the end, the boy with an Elmo, Elmo dancing.

Young man in a suit. Not such a great suit. Not such a great job this one heading off to. Real estate? Not even. Car-rental assistant manager.

Thatcher dropped the pick in his open case, turned the knob up on the JBL. He'd fingerpick it.

What to do.

Another young man, younger than him; this guy in shades. White suit, shades. Cool. California cool.

That's it.

Thatcher lay his fingers on the strings and began to pick, fast, the strings ringing out beautifully the way they only can in a subway station or certain churches. He leaned forward and put his lips on the microphone.

> *Lot's of folks back East say*
> *they're leaving home every day*

Do Re Mi, Woody's song about the troubles with going West. California Cool took a glance over at Thatcher, smirked. Thatcher smirked back. Yo, man—we do what we do. California Cool moved on, bored. Move on, my man, move on.

The po-lice at the port of entry say
you're number fourteen thousand for today

Elmo was dancing, in the kid's arms. Dance Elmo, dance. Thatcher was smiling now, wide out smiling. Young man in the car rental suit was smiling too, tapping his foot. He do what he do.

Believe it or not, you won't find it so hot
if you ain't got the Do Re Mi

Train pulling in, drowning the wooden sound in a cacophony of steel and screech, rattle and moan. Everyone on their feet. California Cool without a backward glance, in the train, Mr. Cool Breeze, in the train. Elmo gone, but with a floppy wave. Car-rental suit with a dollar to the open guitar case.

Thank you, my man—Thatcher with a mid-verse wink. *Of such are fortunes begun.*

And with that he slowed tempo, slid key, switched gears. From the late, great Woodrow Wilson Guthrie to the late, great Dr. Winston O'Boogie.

Thoughts are floating out like endless rain into a paper cup
They slither as they pass, they make their way across the universe...

• • •

Thatcher made $40 in three hours. On packing his gear felt much better about this new unplanned unemployment than he had this morning. He'd like to stay longer down here in the subway, make more, but had an appointment.

King Papas met him in the lobby of the studio. He had a good shirt on, Papas did; purple with white stripes. It accentuated his length. His black hair looked oiled. *He's having it done,* Thatcher thought. *How much money did they pay him?*

He do what he do.

"Yo, man," Papas said, looking for all the world like he wanted to lay a big show biz hug on Thatcher, but Thatcher was loaded down with guitar and subway gig gear. "Hey, what's with the *eh-cushtonauts?*"

"The who?"

"You know, *eh-cushtonauts?*"

"*Accoutrements,*" Thatcher said.

Papas blinked. "Dude," he said. "Whatever."

He put an arm out and took the JBL speaker from Thatcher, began walking toward a long hallway and down it. "You have a gig tonight?"

"Did. Today. Subway time."

King Papas looked over his shoulder. "You did the subway today?"

Thatcher nodded. "Not as lucrative as the T up in Boston, but not bad."

"I don't know, man. I never played the T."

"We do what we do."

"What's that?"

"You lived in Boston two years—you never played the T?"

"I never played the T." Papas was moving fast, past a row of framed gold records.

"Nice joint," Thatcher said.

"Yeah." Papas led him into an orange-lit lounge, couches and a long black table with candles. "You can throw your shit here."

"How's Claire?" Thatcher said, leaning his guitar case in the corner. "Did she come down to stay with you?"

Papas ran a finger across his neck. "We're done, dude—I thought you knew." He gave a big stinking grin then. "I'm chasing Eric, dude—Eric and Erin, Chapter Two?"

Thatcher whistled. "She's alright," he said.

"She's more than alright. I'm staying in her spare room—she moved down from Boston, too. Got a third-floor on Washington Street."

"Washington Square?"

"Washington *Street*, dude. Hoboken."

"You're living in Hoboken?"

"It's a beautiful thing, no?"

Thatcher pulled a smoke, lit it, enjoying the sneer on Papas's face as smoke filled the room. He inhaled long, blew out a ring. "I though Hoboken was the foyer to a death house."

"The what?"

He forgot the best line he ever wrote, Thatcher thought. *Guess I'm free to steal it now.*

Thatcher sat back, looked around. Thatcher had made the counter-argument, but James had pretty much nailed it: this is where they'd always wanted to be. And yeah, it was alright. He'd sing on Papas's shit. And why the hell not.

Papas was up. He pulled a guitar—a sweet-looking Larivee—off the wall and strummed it in place. "I saw your mom the other night," he said.

"Fuck you."

"No, really—like, I *saw* your mom. At the 92nd Street Y."

"You hang out at the 92nd Street Y?"

"Fuck you back. No, Eric wanted to go see her. Mona was doing a talk, a book-signing something."

"Really?"

"Yeah—is her new book good?"

Thatcher shrugged. "I dunno. Haven't read it."

"Me neither. Eric bought it. She's a big reader. Pretty jammed, though, with the schedule. They're recording now, too. Out in Brooklyn."

"Did you talk to Mona?"

"Yeah, of course." He winked. "Chick points, dude. Chick points."

"Of course."

"I told her I'd probably see you soon. She was pretty wrapped up in her thing there. When did she get so big time? Going in, there was pa-papitzzi and everything."

"Paparazzi."

"What?"

"Paparazzi."

"Whatever." Papas tilted his head. Something was off. He reached up and adjusted one of the tuning pegs.

Thatcher leaned forward. "So what do you have me doing, Pap? Let's take a look."

"What's that?" Papas turned the peg again, got it this time, strummed down. Sweet guitar, no question.

"What you want me to do. Today." Thatcher waved in where he thought the general vicinity of the main studio was.

Papas stopped playing, looked over. "Oh, hey, listen—I just—I mean, I just thought it's be cool if you wanted to hang or something, Thatch. You know."

Thatcher inhaled off his cigarette. Looked at Papas. The King said, "I mean, I don't have anything now, if that's what—you know. I just thought you'd think it was cool to hang out for awhile. That's why I called."

"Just come down and hang out."

Papas smiled. "Yeah, just hang out."

Thatcher nodded. "We do what we do," he said.

King Papas blinked. "How's that?"

Thatcher shrugged. "We do what we do," he said.

"I'm not following you."

"That's alright. You don't have to follow. This is your story. You're in the lead."

. . .

Thatcher went back to the subway later. He didn't set up the gear, but he did sit down, and he pulled out his guitar. *There's an answer here somewhere,* he thought. *By god, by god, there's an answer here somewhere.*

SLIM SOLACE ON COLD PORCELAIN

In the great, sprawling Borough of Queens, Alice lived alone. Rare to live alone, in any part of metro New York, at her age. Out of college, most of her friends had made for the Village, Brooklyn, Hoboken, cutting rents in halves or thirds or quarters to afford the lofty prices levied for the lowliest lofts. Alice couldn't stand the company, though. She'd rather alone in Queens than civilization in the company of others.

She had, though, recently, asked Thatcher to move in.

Alice liked that boy. Oh, she liked him plenty.

She'd broken a year-long celibacy for Thatcher. She'd told him half the general story the night they'd met, the drunken night on the sidewalk in Boston, and she'd told him the second half of the story a few nights later, back in Hoboken, a night they ended on James's couch. Thatcher traveled to Queens that weekend and they spent two days with the shades pulled down.

In Queens, Alice woke up alone, thinking over these things, turning them around in her head. The morning light sneaking under the blind played tricks against the far wall. Alice thought about these things, stretched out in bed, Alice watched the tricks of light against the wall and thought about that.

• • •

Thatcher had not yet told Alice about his Hermination. A ripe moment for this precise conversation hadn't presented itself. Awkward, with Alice's invitation—and his immediate acceptance—to move in with her. Awkward. She wasn't hurting for rent money and he knew he'd replace the job in due course, but still. Awkward. He was sure a ripe moment would indeed present itself shortly, and he'd divulge all then. But for now, though, every time he thought about telling her he just felt stupid.

What he told her instead this afternoon, back in Hoboken, holding her hand as they walked across Washington Street and back toward Sixth and Clinton, was about the phone call he'd received the day before. It was a reporter, young-sounding female, name of Meadows.

"Stacy Meadows," Thatcher said. "Heard of her?"

"No."

"From *Time*."

"*Time* magazine?"

"That's right."

Alice squeezed his hand hard.

"That is so cool! First the *Village Voice*, now *Time*? Holy sh—"

"She wasn't calling about music," Thatcher said. "Well, not my music, anyway."

"I don't get it."

• • •

The woman on the phone had introduced herself then said, "Just want to make sure I'm right here, on this: you're Mona Smith's son?"

"Sure."

"Sure?"

"Yes. I'm Mona Smith's son."

"Great—you don't mind talking?"

Thatcher said, "No, Stacy Meadows, I don't mind talking. What should we talk about?"

"Mostly I guess I'm looking for reaction, if that's okay. I just finished reading the galleys of your mother's new memoir."

"I didn't know the book was that close to publication. It's another memoir?"

"Yes, well, I'm hoping if you could give us a quote, then—"

"Sure, Stacy, but I haven't read the book. I guess I could make something up, but—"

"Oh, I don't think you'd have to read it, right? Just a quote about the revelation, and Mona's reasons for keeping it under wraps and how you feel about it all."

That shut him up. Then he said, "I'm not sure I'm—"

"You know," the reporter said, from somewhere far down the phone line. "Randolph."

• • •

Now, passing City Hall, Mona said, "Mona wrote about Randolph being your father."

"Yes."

"But she didn't talk to you about this before she published it?"

"No."

"How could she tell your story without asking how you felt?"

"It's not my story," Thatcher said. "It's Mona's story."

Alice looked over at him. Thatcher's face was as straight as she'd ever seen it. They walked in silence for a few minutes and then Alice asked, "Why exactly did Mona decide to keep the whole thing a secret in the first place?"

Thatcher shrugged. "I don't know. We'll have to read the book."

Alice was still looking at him. His face hadn't changed.

"Why don't you ever get mad about anything, Thatcher?"

"What?"

"Aren't you mad about this?"

He shrugged again.

"You should be. Mad."

"I had a shrink when I was a kid tell me the same thing. Well, he didn't say I *should* be mad. He said I never seemed to get mad."

"It's not healthy."

"I don't know."

"Really."

"Look, you know—it gets boring after awhile. What, I'll be mad all my life? It's old, gets old. Numb is old hat, Alice. I can't go through life pissed off."

Alice was biting her lip. "It's not healthy."

James's apartment was empty when they got there. Thatcher retrieved the portable phone so Alice could call the movie theater for show times. Then he went into the bathroom. He latched the door behind him, dropped his pants, sat. Thirty seconds later the phone rang.

"Should I get it?" Alice yelled.

"I don't want to talk to anyone. Let the machine get it."

It rang four more times then they heard James's voice on the speaker—"Yo, yo, yo, ain't no one home,"—a click, then a woman.

"Sweetie," the voice said. It was Jo.

"Oh, fuck," Thatcher said aloud, yanking toilet paper off the roll as fast as his wrist would move.

"You outdid yourself, lover," the Jo voice said, slow and sighing and over the top.

"Fuckfuckfuckfuckfuck," Thatcher whispered, having a very difficult time with the toilet paper. Almost the whole roll was now on the floor and he couldn't quite get it to rip.

"Anyway..." and then the Jo voice sighed again. "Listen, Barry is out of town again for two days next week. You know the number."

Thatcher froze his frenetic roll attack on one clear, vivid thought: *She didn't say my name.*

"Thatcher, honey—tell me the wait wasn't worth it."

Pants around ankles, lost in a sea of toilet paper, Thatcher hung his head.

The phone clicked off. The apartment was very quiet.

And then something sounding suspiciously like an answering machine slammed into the bathroom door.

"You asshole!" Alice yelled, and the bathroom door shook with her efforts. The flimsy lock bent but held.

"It's not like—" Thatcher mumbled, attempting to work toilet paper, flush lever, and pull pants all at once. "It's—"

"How long?" The door knob rattled again.

"Listen, Alice—"

"And she's *married*!" There was a pause then the answering machine slammed into the door again, followed by a barrage of fists. "And we were at the *wedding*!"

Thatcher imagined Alice was quite beautiful on the other side of the door, all that Asian blood pushing fast through dark, angry skin. He gave up and just sat there, slim solace on cold porcelain.

"You two deserve each other," Alice said, and it was a growl.

There was another slam of answering machine carcass against the door, then a pause, then the slamming of the apartment door. Then silence.

"Oh, boy," Thatcher said. He reached over and tried rerolling the unrolled toilet paper, slowly, one turn of the tube at a time. "Oh, boy," he said again.

• • •

How do I drink thee? Oh let me count the ways. So many ways to drunk, so many happy roads. All roads lead to drunk, you could say. You could say it. You had to say something, Thatcher figured; you might as well say that.

Loneliness, a lame guardian at the gates of sobriety. Nowhere to go, nothing to do; a bad set of circumstances. Black rum in James's cabinet, down she goes, yep.

"Gawd," Thatcher grimaced, shaking his head, then hit another slug. He paced, paced, the apartment in paces, steps, up and back, across and over. He lit a cigarette, hit another slug, "Gawd."

There might have been time, reason, hope to run after Alice. But how do you run out from the toilet, the smell of your own crap clinging to your shirt?

"That's no way to make an impression," Thatcher said. "That doesn't look good on the resume *at all*."

He hit another slug. The stuff was awful but James had no beer and Thatcher decided he couldn't buy any until after the sun went down. Couldn't leave the apartment until the sun went down. Didn't know why, just because. The phone rang, he let it ring, waited for the machine to pick up. Then realized the machine wouldn't be picking up—the machine, in fact, needed to be picked up. The machine lay in pieces on the floor, post bathroom-door *whomp*.

"*Whomp*," Thatcher said. He picked part of the machine off the floor with his left hand, examined, dropped it back to the floor. "*Whomp*." The phone stopped ringing.

"Oh Mama," he said. "Oh Mama I'm in fear of my life from the long arm of the law."

The phone began ringing again. Thatcher crossed to it, lifted the receiver, dropped it back down. Picked it up again, listened. Steady dial tone there. "Keep it steady, baby."

He shouldered the phone, hit another off the bottle, began pressing buttons at random. Hung it up, lifted it again. "Go man go," he whispered. Dialed a number. A man answered.

"Hello?"

"Yo, Stanley."

"Hello?"

"Yo. Stanley."

"Thatcher? Is that you, Thatcher?"

"That's me, baby."

Silence.

Then, "Thatcher, are you drunk?"

"Hey, is Mona there?"

In the background Thatcher could hear: *Who is it?*

"Hey, lemme talk to Mona."

"Absolutely not. You're disgraceful."

Who is it, Stan?

"Yo, Stanley. Lemme talk to Mona. Put her on."

The phone clicked in his ear. Stanley had hung up on him.

"The fuck?" Thatcher said. He dialed the number again. Heard it ring. No one answered. Machine picked up. "The fuck," Thatcher said into the phone, hung up, crossed the room, opened a window, leaned out. "The fuck!"

he yelled. Sat on the ledge. Lit a cigarette. The phone rang. He let it ring.

Thing was, he couldn't help it. Couldn't have done it different, he didn't think. What happened, well. It hadn't meant anything—how's that for lame and predictable document number one? But there it was. He didn't want Jo. He wanted Alice. Would be happy with Alice. Happy, happy in Queens like a couple of church mice, curled up in her little apartment with her books and her sweaters. But this thing, this Jo thing, it had been all this time, all this time, and what was he supposed to do. Had to finish it, had to finish it. There was the chance to finish, be done, and he'd taken it, and—

"Bullshit," he said.

He flicked his smoke to the street, lit another. The rum was sinking rapidly. "Down with the ship," he said. "We go down with the ship."

Maybe we don't get mad, ever, maybe. But no question: we go down with the ship.

THE FOYER OF A DEATH HOUSE

Marsh's phone rang; Carla picked it up. In the kitchen. "Hello?"

It was Mary Ann. She'd made a tray of brownies. Could she bring them over?

"You're so sweet," Carla whispered. "Maybe in the morning? Alright? Marshall is sound asleep on the couch. Dash is curled up next to him."

Stranded in his chair for the whole last gig, but Marsh had about floated home after. As much as you could float in his condition.

Floated home, but woke the next morning feverish and aching, and his leg inflamed like it had been over the winter after his fall.

"Jesus Christ," he'd whispered, then drifted back to sleep. He'd finally gotten out of bed today, but not far. He'd been asleep on the couch by six.

Carla laid the phone gently down on the base. She poked her head around the corner of the kitchen, to where her husband and son lay asleep in the living room. She watched them a moment, then flicked the light off and stepped back into the kitchen. She'd wait another fifteen minutes for Dash to be fully asleep before she moved him off to bed. Then she'd gather up Marsh and get him off for the night, too.

Orris was feeling much better.

"I'm feeling much better," he said, from beneath a blanket on the couch. "I'm feeling much better, Bill Pin."

Bill Pin nodded and hurried back to the kitchen for a ginger ale. He chewed his nails on the way. Nervous, Bill Pin was. Orris said he felt better but just an hour ago he'd been calling Bill not Bill but Dad and asking him stuff that Bill didn't know and then he'd called him another name altogether. He'd called him Bill Pin now, good enough, but—

Bill Pin was scared.

He had some idea of what was going on. A pretty good idea. A very good idea.

So far he'd been trying not to call the hospital.

"Don't you do it, Bill Pin," Orris had said, when was that? A few days ago? A few weeks ago? "If things get—whatever. Look, you just leave it alone. Don't worry about me. I'll pull through it, Bill Pin."

They were both just a little bit worried about how things might be for Bill Pin if Orris wound up admitted for a stretch.

Well maybe the bad was done now. Maybe.

In the kitchen, Bill poured a glass of ginger ale over ice, brought it back to the living room. Orris was standing. "Bill," he said, "I think—" and then a funny look came on Orris's face and his loose eye stopped still. Orris looked around, then up, and then the big man fell straight forward, like he'd been pushed hard from behind, straight forward onto his face without so much as a grunt. Bill Pin watched, then dropped the glass to the floor and screamed.

"Oh!" he yelled and then he screamed again.

Bill Pin knelt, put his hands around his friend's head. "Orris!" Orris's good eye was rolled back. "ORRIS!" Bill Pin jumped up. "I'll call! I'll call!"

He ran to the kitchen, to the phone on the wall in there. "My friend!" he yelled into the phone. "My friend! He's—he's on the floor! My friend! His name is Orris. He's on the floor!" Bill Pin was crying now, his glasses crooked on his face. "Oh please!" he yelled into the phone. "Please send someone for my friend!"

THE STORY

The fucking phone wouldn't stop ringing.

Mona, baby—is dat you?

Thatcher should have been asleep by now. He'd certainly consumed enough alcohol, no question, he should be out. But for the fucking phone that wouldn't stop with the ringing.

Maybe he should pick it up.

Hey, Mona. Tell me your story. Tell me all about your story. Raise a glass and give a giggle and talk about it all. Talk about me, if you want. I'm as good a supporting character as any for your story. The kid who never gets mad.

Do I embarrass you, Mona? Do I?

Hey didja hear: Mona Smith's son joined the army.

He did what?

Why would he do that?

It's alright Ma. You can use it over cocktails, this story. Just another slice of your story. And you can keep using it because I never get mad.

Maybe the story was getting stale. Maybe that's why Randolph got thrown into the mix this late in the game. Thrown into Mona's story.

That fucking phone. It just wouldn't stop.

Thatcher sat still on the couch and he thought for a minute he was Bill Pin. This is how Bill Pin would sit, if Bill Pin was sitting here.

That Bill Pin, Thatcher thought. He's some kid, isn't he?

Phone again.

C'mon Mona.

He'd never not answered her before. She didn't call much, but when she did—well, the phone rings, you answer, right? Doesn't matter who's on the other end.

Maybe that's not Mona.

Holding for Mona.

Yeah, but perhaps not.

Perhaps we're all just a little bit drunk and that's not Mona. What if it's James.

Thatcher leaned forward.

What if it's Alice.

Oh, Christ, oh boy did he fuck that up or what. Oh Alice I'm so sorry.

Phone again.

"The fuck!" he yelled. Who said he couldn't get mad? He definitely could yell. Definitely.

Thatcher answered the phone.

It was neither Mona nor James nor Alice. It was Thomas Barnes. The one, the only, the Trenton Liaison.

"Yo, Thomas. Sorry I didn't pick up."

"What?"

"When you called before. Sorry."

"I didn't call before, Thatcher. I just called now."

Well.

How about that.

"Thatcher?"

"Yes."

"I was calling to—"

Silence.

"Yes."

"Thatcher—holy shit. You don't know, do you? Oh man. I'm at Carbone's Diner, I just found out and was calling to see if you needed—. But you don't even know."

"Thomas Barnes?"

"Look, man—"

Thatcher was sitting still again. He'd registered the old boy had something powerful to lay down, and he appreciated the guy was struggling, but still—you'd like someone to cut to a chase. If there's going to be a chase, yo, just cut to it and be done and—

"He's dead, Thatcher."

foyer of a death house

"Say that again, Thomas Barnes?"

Thomas Barnes was quieter than quiet on the line. Then he took a breath. And than he said, "I'm so sorry, I thought you knew. He's dead, Thatcher."

And then Thomas Barnes proceeded to tell Thatcher a story.

· · ·

On the second floor landing Mrs. Quatrone was stacking newspapers on the pile. It was late, too late for her to be awake let alone out here stacking newspapers on the pile, but she couldn't sleep tonight and Carson was on in a few minutes so she'd watch, maybe—that was always a good sleep aid.

Bent over the newspapers, her back was to the stairs so she didn't see the young man when he came flying down them from levels above. She heard him coming, someone running down, more rolling than running almost it sounded, and she turned as he hit the second floor landing and jumped to run down the last flight and he tripped and flew down, halfway down the next level, landing on his side.

"Oh!" she yelled and looked over. It was the young musician from upstairs, not the nice Italian boy but the other one. He stood from where he fell, turned, ran, fell again, and rolled down the last set of stairs.

"Oh!" Mrs. Quatrone yelled again, pulling her house coat around her. He must be dead, she thought, his body sprawled at the bottom of the stairs, but as she moved to go down to see to him he stirred, moaned, vomited.

Mrs. Quatrone held tight the rail and tried the stairs as fast as she could which was not fast at all.

The young man lifted himself up, and before she could yell again he ran out the front door, far too fast for her to catch. Which is why she didn't see the car hit him as he sailed through the front door, across the sidewalk, and into the street. Mrs. Quatrone didn't see the car hit him, but from halfway down the last flight of stairs she heard the tires squeal and the horn.

"Jesus, Mary, and Joseph," she whispered and crossed herself.

Mrs. Quatrone didn't see the car hit Thatcher, but the accident wasn't without witness. Out on the sidewalk a man with peachfuzz on his cheeks but a boyish aura surrounding saw the whole thing. Jimmy had leaned his bike against the wall of Sixth and Clinton and was just thinking through how he might get out of trouble for being so late in coming home when the whole thing happened. Jimmy took a hard look at the body sprawled on the road. It was a Toyota Corolla that did it, and when the driver's door flew open and an old man in a gas station shirt jumped out Jimmy yelled at him, "Pretty sure you killed him dead, Mister."

The old man was leaning over the body, shaking it. Jimmy strolled over, hands in pockets. "Good chance he's dead, I'd bet. Pretty sure you killed him dead."

Jimmy took a glance at the killer Toyota then pointed in the direction of the windshield. "Hey, is that an air freshener? Can I have that? For my collection."

PART III

POSITIVELY PULASKI

You could argue what's the front door to Hoboken, resulting verdict depending on where your head's at. The New York-centric will say the front door to Hoboken is the Holland Tunnel (in fact the Tunnel entrance is on the Jersey City side of the Hoboken–Jersey City border, but still). The New Jersey-centric would label Hoboken's front door as the Eastern Spur of the New Jersey Turnpike, curving grandly from I-78 at the Newark Airport, past Liberty State Park, then down into the general muddle before the Manhattan-bound Tunnel entrance. Stay left then hang left, shoot away from the Tunnel traffic, and through the door you go, under the overpass, a right onto Observer Highway and into the City of Hoboken.

Those are your choices for front door, and no end of choices on back door: rights then lefts then rights out of Newark and Weehawken.

No question, though, really, on Hoboken's side door. The Pulaski Skyway, the 1/9 (from Newark, just like the Turnpike Spur, but older, the old way, the diagonal way, once the only way). U.S. Route 1 from the bottom of the country, U.S. Route 9 from the bottom of New Jersey (same thing, to some), laid on top of each other for the elevated trip across the swamps of Jersey, across the Passaic and Hackensack rivers, across the lots of Kearny. Mornings in, the Pulaski will save you the crush of the Turnpike if you're lucky, zoom you in the side as you wave at the less-informed on the Turnpike—if you're lucky. If you're unlucky—well, all it takes is one car, on the Pulaski. Just one car. Limited lanes, nothing on the sides, just one car to sink it for everyone. Stars align, and you sail into town. But if shadows cross, one car spins, it all sinks. That's how they did it, old school, that's how they built them—1930, they began the Pulaski, two years to string her up, two years and sixteen deaths (fifteen accidents, one murder; about right for New Jersey construction). It looked magnificent in 1932; sure. And looks magnificent still—if you're lucky. Odds are you're more lucky than not. They sure felt lucky in 1932. Slapped the name of a Polish brigadier general on the thing, cut the ribbon, fly across the Pulaski, descend to Jersey City, a left at the light and welcome to Hoboken.

• • •

Front doors, back doors, side doors. Sure enough. And here's your picture window. Pretty as a picture. The Hudson, wide and deep, lapping on the rocky shore and in some cases under, up underneath Hoboken. You're down from the Palisades, you know; it's all at the mercy of the water here, and where she will go. The Hudson goes where she wants.

Fast and cold, the Hudson, even down here already clear of Yonkers, clear of Fort Lee, passing Hoboken; even now, this time of year. And maybe the cold makes her faster; *go go go*, the water says, *let me down, get me out.* You can sit on a long pier and drop pebbles and sometimes they won't fall straight, the current so fast it'll push the pebbles along, push them forward even as they go down, rock or no rock, doesn't matter to the Hudson, she's pushed heavier things out of the way, kept it moving.

Drop your pebble and watch her go, down and forward, forward and down. Sooner or later it's bound to sink—really, isn't everything? But the current passing Hoboken might push you along, scootch you forward just a little, just a bit, before the inevitable.

CONSUMMATION

Joanne's long finger pushing thick hair behind a delicate ear. "Guess I can't smoke in here," she said.

"No." Thatcher's calloused finger, tapping his opposite forearm, then stopping, hands in place. "Since when do you smoke again?"

"You know."

"Yeah." Yeah, he knew.

"It must be hell on you," Jo said, "not smoking for a week."

"I know the nurses. They let me go out back."

"Is that weird?"

"What?"

"Having them all know you?"

"Everyone here knows me."

"That's what I meant."

"It's—" How to say? It is what it is. "Yes. It's a little weird."

"I don't understand why you're here and not in the real hospital."

"The ER was of the opinion that the trauma to my bloodstream was worse than the trauma to my bones." He looked up at the ceiling, then looked back down at Jo. "They asked, and I didn't feel like arguing."

Trauma—they'd said that. And insult. Blunt insult to the body. Blunt equates with Toyota. Body equates with folksinger. Blunt insult. To the body. Insult. Significant. Appropriate. Consistent. Decompensate.

"I look worse than I am."

"You look like shit."

He did, too; his face and torso a mass of black and purple mushrooms.

"How much longer do you have to stay here?"

"The memorial service is tomorrow. Either way, I'm out of here shortly. Have to be. I won't miss the service."

"I'm sorry I didn't know him. You talked about him a lot, this past year."

"Yes."

"Do you need a ride or anything, tomorrow?"

"There's nothing broken here. I can walk."

"The service is in town?"

"Yes. Thanks for offering."

She put her hand on top of his.

"What are you doing now?" he said.

"Since—"

"Yes."

"Barry moved in with his brother. In Metuchen."

"I'm sorry."

"That's us—pretty sorry."

"Yes."

"I meant you and me, buddy boy."

"I know, Jo."

"So what do we do with this?"

"We—"

"I mean, really."

What to say to that.

"I don't think there's much we can do," he said. We do what we do.

"I don't think so either."

"Really?"

Joanne nodded.

"You used to say you'd marry me, Jo, but you said it would never work out. How come?"

She didn't answer that. Instead she said, "This is our big chance, Thatcher. Here it is. We could take it. We pulled it off and scared everyone else out of our lives. Do *you* think it would work out?"

"No."

Jo's hair had fallen loose, and she pushed it behind her ear again. And smiled.

"You're right," she said. "I have to go now, Thatcher."

"Take care, Jo."

DEUS EX MACHINA

In Hoboken, it was early evening. Might as well be summer what with the warm hanging on like this, daytime not giving in easy, not going down without a fight. The light was gone from the sky but it all happened so subtly you almost didn't notice. Just looked up at some point and realized: day's gone. How'd that happen?

• • •

By sundown, Thatcher was out near the warehouse district, out where no one ever went and no one real really lived.

Only the insane, Thatcher thought. *Only the mad live out here.*

Those with charts. Those with records in a records room, their lives meticulously recorded. Their day to day so meticulously recorded, but their living, breathing interactions completely out of sight.

Out here in the fields.

There was a man sitting on the steps of a stone church. The man was late forties maybe, hard to tell. In shorts and work boots, Hawaiian shirt, thinning long hair slicked back and a goatee. Thatcher stopped at the bottom of the stairs, a little winded—not quite as untouched as he'd made out to Jo during her visit this afternoon; he had a heavy limp, probably would for a while he guessed. The guy on the steps nodded.

"Hey," the man said. He held a bottle of water in one hand, took a swig from it. There was book on the step next to him, Thatcher noticed, thick dark blue hardback. The guy said, "I hope you have the key."

"What's that?"

"The key." The fellow turned his wrist, imitating. "You bring a copy? Of the key?"

Thatcher touched his chest. "Me? I, uh—"

"You here for the fellowship?"

What does that mean? Thatcher thought. "For the, uh, you know—steps. Thing."

"Christ. You're new? First time?"

Thatcher nodded.

"Christ. Then you definitely ain't got the key." The man took another swig from his water bottle. "You look all beat up. You sober?"

Sober? Thatcher thought. *You mean in general?* Then figured the man meant now, right now. He nodded, "Yes. Mostly."

"What do you mean, 'mostly'?"

"I was in the hospital a few days. I got hit by a car."

"Ouch. You have a drink today?"

"No."

"Then you're sober. Good for you. Me, I had me a drink this evening."

Thatcher wasn't sure about all this.

"Yeah," the guy answered his thought, "I wasn't expecting just you, either, my friend."

Down the sidewalk, a man in an overcoat came toward them, stopped. An old guy, seventies, tan overcoat and blue turtleneck sticking up from it—*a lot of clothes*, Thatcher thought, *for the weather*. The two apparently knew each other, nodded. The old man said, "Kenny."

"No key, George," Kenny said.

The old man's hair was shaggy; combed, but shaggy. His hands real old, Thatcher noticed. Curled. The old man showed his teeth now, said, "What do you mean, no key?"

"No damn key, George, is what I mean." Kenny pointed behind him. "No one with a key showed up."

"You been drinking, Ken?"

"A beer or three."

"Are you drunk, Ken?"

"Does it matter?" Kenny shook his head. "No, I didn't say I was drunk. I'm just not sober. Had me a beer, shagged ass over here."

"Good lord," George said. He noticed Thatcher, for the first time. "Who are you?"

Thatcher introduced himself.

"You have a car?" the old man said.

"What's that?"

"Do you have a car, I asked. If you have a car we'll hold the meeting in your car. Ken's got a book, we can sit in the car."

Thatcher shuddered involuntarily. "I don't have a—" Thatcher began, but Kenny cut him off.

"Ain't having a meeting in a damn car, George," he said.

George hissed: "I *need* a meeting. We *have* to have a meeting."

"Well, listen—"

"We *have* to have a meeting. Check again," George said.

Ken shrugged, stood up, walked up the stairs and lifted the mat. Stood a moment, then bent over. "Oh shit," he said. "Here it is."

Deus ex ma-key-na, Thatcher thought, and wanted to laugh and realized he was just whiskers away from crying.

• • •

The room was just inside the church door, inside and to the left. "C'mon," Kenny said, tapping Thatcher on the elbow, and led him to a closet with two bright blue plastic toolboxes inside. Thatcher took one of the boxes, followed Kenny into the room. There was a round table in the middle, chairs pulled up, and George was already seated, his overcoat still on, leaning forward in his chair. He was clicking his teeth again. "I *need* a meeting," he said.

"You'll get your meeting, George," Kenny said. He opened the two boxes, began pulling out pamphlets, books, stacking it all on the table. George leaned back, closing his eyes. Thatcher thought he might say it again—"I *need* a meeting"—but he didn't. The old man just sighed, holding his eyes closed. "Watch this," Kenny whispered, and nodded his head toward George. Kenny closed the two empty tool boxes, clipped them, placed them on the floor. Thatcher watched, waiting. Kenny hooked a thumb at George. The old man's eyes remained closed. Kenny sat down at the head of the table, opened a white notebook and began leafing through it, looking for a page. The last one standing, Thatcher pulled out a chair, sat down across from Kenny. A loud noise burped from George's open mouth. Thatcher eyed the old man. George was snoring.

"Here's the thing, guy," Kenny said. "Three of us, this meeting." He held up three fingers, wiggled them. "You can't lead it because it's your first meeting. I can't lead it because I'm not sober." Kenny allowed himself a small smile, now. "Old George can't lead it because old George is asleep."

"Should we wake him up?"

Kenny shook his head. "Can't. No use trying."

"He won't wake up?"

"He won't wake up." Kenny tugged on his goatee. "And I don't feel like listening to him if he does."

Thatcher crossed his hands on the table, one atop the other. "No shit," he said.

"Yep. No shit."

"Maybe I ought to go, come back another time."

"No time like the present, guy. I'm here to keep you sober tonight. And you're here for me. We'll stumble through."

"I, uh—"

But Kenny cut him off, reading monotone from the open notebook in front of him.

"Welcome to the Friday-night twelve-steppers. This is a closed meeting. Any newcomers in the room, please raise your hand."

Thatcher realized Kenny had looked up at him. He raised his hand. Kenny nodded and began narrating again. He droned on for five minutes and when he was finished he thought they should do a reading so he opened a thick hardback and read for another ten minutes. Then he closed the book, looked around the room. George was still sleeping. The snoring had stopped, but the old man was still sleeping.

"The floor is open for sharing," Kenny whispered.

"What does that mean?" Thatcher said.

"Sharing. It's all you, man," Kenny said. "I'm all ears."

"What do I share?"

"Whatever you own, man. Whatever you own."

Thatcher sat back. Then he leaned forward. "Hi, my name is Thatcher?" he said, but asked it, to make sure. Kenny nodded, waved at him.

"I don't know what I am," Thatcher said, "or how long I have or haven't been, but I do know one thing: A friend of mine died this week. Five days ago." Kenny sat back. "I'd like to talk about him," Thatcher said. "Is that alright?"

Kenny nodded. "It's your show, man," he said. "Whatever you own. It's your story."

. . .

After the meeting the three stood a moment together on the sidewalk. George seemed to have no idea he'd slept through the meeting. He put his hand on Thatcher's shoulder. "Keep coming back," he said. "It works if you work it—so work it, you're worth it."

"Thank you, George," Thatcher said.

The three went their separate ways, Thatcher headed off alone down the sidewalk. Slow going. His leg hurt like hell. They said there was nothing broken in there but it was hard to believe. He lit a cigarette and limped along. Three blocks down he reached Beginnings Behavioral Health— both his former employer as well as sight of his recent hospitalization. He'd told Jo it was weird being in there, knowing everyone, but in fact that wasn't quite true. For the staff's part, he was hardly the first employee to find himself on the receiving end of their business. And it wasn't really uncomfortable for Thatcher—it wasn't like Herm came in to visit him, and Thatcher had never felt particularly solid on his designated side of the workplace sanity divide anyway.

Thatcher stopped at the main entrance, the gate to the smoking courtyard. It was closed, this time of the evening, locked. He put his hands on the iron bars, put his face up to the metal. He'd stood in there on his first day here, smoking and watching the piss-test failures suffer through the ten-minute break in their weekly group session. He'd learned later that one of the other requirements of the program was attendance at AA or NA meetings, at least weekly. Which he didn't quite understand. No one said they were all addicts—they'd just come up hot on a piss test. Herm had explained it:

"But they *are* addicts. They all knew their employer utilized random drug screenings. So to make a decision to partake in something even at night, even occasionally, marks them as out of control and on an addictive path—it's an irrational thought process. To put yourself at risk like that in the face of sure knowledge of the chances…well." Herm had smiled. "Do you see how it is?"

That was Stanley logic, straight out of the book. Thatcher didn't see at all.

He thought about his current circumstances, the recent series of events in his life, and wondered if it changed how he viewed Herm's explanation. He found it did not. He didn't buy the book of Stanley and Mona, or the logic that went along with it.

As for me, though, he thought, *I am clearly an addict.*

Thatcher didn't know if that knowledge changed anything about himself, or even about how he planned to live his life. But the knowledge was something in and of itself. Almost, in a very strange way, a comfort. Better knowledge than vacuum.

He rattled the iron bars a little bit. Out looking in.

Over there was Orris's bench. That's where he'd first seen him, and that bench was where they'd passed most of the last year together. A great storyteller, Orris was. For a madman. Never a dull moment on Orris's bench.

Thatcher rattled the bars again. He was done here, at Beginnings Behavioral Health.

"Goodbye," he said. Then turned and limped down the sidewalk, due east.

It took Thatcher ten minutes to walk the blocks between Beginnings Behavioral health and St. Francis Hospital. The St. Francis ER was where he'd been taken after the accident.

Some accident, he thought. Accident in its purest meaning, as in mental-health speak. Accident in the way of a toddler peeing his pants. *I was drunk and ran into the street,* Thatcher thought. *Truly an oops on my part.*

The front door locked for the evening, Thatcher went in through the ER entrance and limped as unobtrusively as possible through the floor then down the long hall to the main elevator bank. He pushed the button and rode a car to the fifth floor.

Leaving the elevator he thought of Mona and wasn't at first sure why. Mona didn't like elevators any more than she liked phones. She didn't like feeling out of control, and Thatcher thought it funny that someone who so hated to feel out of control of the public events in her life would essentially hand her private life over to someone else. But then Stanley had long ago learned how to make his ultimate control seem like her choice and her doing.

The main thing is her story, Thatcher thought. *Mona holds the strings on her story.*

At the meeting tonight Kenny had said to Thatcher: "It's your story." And the story Thatcher had told *was* his story. His story of friends, living and deceased, liked and disliked and liked again; his compadres, his compatriots.

My motherfucking people, he thought. And smiled.

Alice thought Mona had co-opted Thatcher's story, and maybe Alice had a point. But maybe that was okay, what Mona had done, what Mona had always done. Not okay, but now irrelevant. If he wanted it to be.

She can have that story, he thought. *I walk away.*

• • •

Thatcher found the name he was looking for halfway down the ward, the single occupant of a double room. He opened the door. There was silence as he stepped into the darkened room, then a greeting from the bed near the window: "Hello, young Thatcher."

And with that, Thatcher began to cry. He couldn't stop. He stood there, soundless, tears streaming down his cheeks.

"Was it something I said?"

Thatcher wiped his eyes on his T-shirt sleeves, limped over to the bedside. They had the poor guy restrained, black straps holding limbs in place. Thatcher reached down and put his hand on one of the restraints, then slid his hand up until he was touching skin, cool skin.

On the bed there was a shift of discomfort, then a sigh.

"Hello, Marconi."

"Hello, Orris." Thatcher gripped his arm. Leaned down. "It's me, Thatcher."

"Yeah, sorry. I know who it is."

Thatcher gave Orris's arm another squeeze. Then he said, "I'm sorry I didn't come before. I don't know if anyone told you—I was in the hospital, too."

"Yeah, Bill Pin said. Whaddya, hit by a car?"

Thatcher nodded. "Yeah, hit by a car." They both laughed at that. "They had me at in-patient, though. At our place."

Orris narrowed his good eye. "How come?"

"I was drinking too much."

"You always drink too much."

"You think so?"

"Yep. Why'd you drink so much this time?"

Alice—how to explain Alice. Instead, he said, "My friend died, very suddenly."

"That's terrible."

Thatcher nodded.

"What'd he die of?"

Thatcher paused a moment, then said, "Heart attack."

"No kidding. Just like me."

"You didn't die, though."

"Nope. Ticking right along."

"You have to be careful, though. Heart attack's no laughing matter."

"It was just a little one, doctor says."

"Still."

"Yeah. Your friend died, though, huh? I'm really sorry, Thatcher."

"Me, too. I think you would have liked him. His name was Marshall, but we called him Marsh."

"I know I would have liked him."

"I feel like I was just getting to know him, but I'd been waiting all my life to meet him."

Orris thought about that.

"I'm sure he's in heaven now."

"Do you believe in heaven, Orris?"

Orris closed his eyes, the good one and the bad. "I do," he said. A moment later Orris opened his eyes. The crazy one jiggled, the good one searched until it found Thatcher. "Funny thing—the nuns used to tell us that heaven was in the sky but that heaven was also all around us. I never really knew what the nuns meant by that, so one day I asked Sister Gilly, 'Do you mean Hoboken? So like, Hoboken is part of heaven?'"

"Heaven is here in Hoboken," Thatcher said. "Imagine. What did the sister say to that?"

"She whupped me," Orris said. "She whupped me and said I was a smartass."

"You are a smartass, Orris."

"I know it."

IN HOBOKEN

In Hoboken, three friends sat on a roof and felt the sun on their faces.

"It's all very small from here," James said, holding fingers up to the Manhattan skyline. "I could squish it all under my thumb."

Lou passed clove cigarettes around, lighting two of them. "Marsh always liked second-hand smoke," she said. She took a puff and blew a smoke ring, then Thatcher blew a ring to match. The two rings drifted in the breezeless sky, holding and drifting then losing cohesion, framing the Empire State Building for a moment, gone and apart by the time they reached the World Trade Center.

James and Thatcher were in suits, Thatcher for the first time since Jo's wedding. Lou wore a long skirt and Thatcher was sure he'd never seen her in a skirt before.

The access door opened behind them, Quatrone stepped out, also in a suit, black and double-breasted.

"Thought you might be up here," he said. "My mother wants to go, so I called a car. You can join us. We're stopping to pick up Bruno on the way."

James smiled. "Thank you," he said. "I think we're going to walk."

Quatrone nodded. The man looked haggard. Marsh's death had violently rattled all of them—it seemed, indeed, to have rattled every soul in Hoboken—but some worse than others. Quatrone wasn't just the same age as Marsh (a sobering thought, the first natural death he'd experienced in a peer); he'd known Marsh for more than ten years, and had considered him as good of a friend as he was ever likely to have. Losing him was intolerable.

And Quatrone said that now, staring out over the skyline: "This is intolerable." He coughed once. "I want someone nailed to a cross for this."

He broke his stare then, and hugged each of them.

"*Salud*, youngsters," he said. "Mama and I are off. We'll meet you there."

· · ·

A nurse had opened the windows in Orris's room so the smells and sounds of the beautiful day were in the room with him, which was good—he'd been thinking a lot about death this morning. Specifically, he was thinking of someone he hadn't thought of in a long time, months even. A friend he'd known for years, Larry Ritzi. He and Larry had grown up just a few blocks apart from each other, had gone to school together. Larry was the only person from Orris's childhood who'd ended up as part of his adulthood. They were in Day Hospital together, two days a week. Larry kept his own apartment and even had a job at Pathmark but he came to Day Hospital two days a week. Orris and Larry Ritzi hadn't really been friends as kids, but they knew each other and because of that would sometimes hang out together at the pool table in Day Hospital, and they got to know each other pretty well.

Larry, Orris remembered, liked to point out that Orris was crazy. "Me, I'm just depressed," Larry would say. "Super depressed, but still."

Orris didn't mind. He knew it made Larry feel better to say so, to say that someone else was crazy.

Thing is, in the end, Larry hung himself. A terrible thing. Hung himself in his apartment and no one knew for three days. The stink was how they found out. Terrible.

Orris had gone to Larry Ritzi's service. The doctors hadn't wanted him or any of the Day Hospital clients to go, worried they might get disturbed by it.

"Disturbed?" Orris had said to Bill Pin. "They think the funeral might be disturbing." Orris was combing his hair, or trying, as he said this. He stopped then, and circled around with his arms out. "Tell me, what part of any of this *isn't* disturbing?"

• • •

In Hoboken, this side of Clinton Street is awfully nice to walk down on a warm morning, no matter the circumstances. The three friends walked it slowly. They had to stop twice, once so James could re-tie his shoe, and once a few blocks later when Lou started crying. Later, Lou stepped out ahead, smoking and walking alone. She had an eye out for her sister, and Mary Ann joined them as they turned onto Washington Street.

Half a block back, Thatcher and James walked side by side. James put his arm around Thatcher's shoulder, said, "I'm glad you're still with us, Thatch."

"Not as glad as I am."

James pushed his hands into the pockets of his suit jacket. "You mean that?"

"Mostly," Thatcher said. "Hard, on a day like today. Right?" James nodded. "But yes."

They walked in silence for a block. Thatcher, for his part, felt unreal, ethereal. People passed them—kids and suits and janitors and cops—going the other way on the sidewalk, and he wanted to grab each one and shake them and say *Where are you going? Don't you know Marsh is dead? How can you just go about your business?*

Thatcher wanted to ask James if he felt the same way, but he couldn't work up the breath. Instead, he said, "Everything decays. But it's still art."

James looked over at him. "I think you've gone mad, son," he said.

"No, I'm not mad, James. I'm angry."

Before Thatcher could say more—and he had more to say, yes sir, he had a lot to say, a whole world to talk about, and he planned on saying it all sooner rather than later—they were stopped short, cut off by a bicycle swooshing in front of them, from between two buildings then out onto the street.

"Hi James!" a voice yelled. It was Jimmy, on the bike. He circled back, and waved. Jimmy had Walkman earphones on, nodding his head to the beat. On the handlebars the Mr. T air freshener swung back and forth, and Thatcher noticed another air freshener had joined the decorations, two big groovy fingers flashing a peace sign. Jimmy circled again, stopped in front of them.

"Nice," Thatcher said to him, pointing to the new air freshener. "Where'd you get that?"

Jimmy said, "This guy got run over by a car. Couple days ago. I got it from the car. Driver give it to me."

"Run over by a car?" Thatcher said. "You're kidding."

"Nope, I wouldn't kid," Jimmy said. "Got run over by a car. Right in front of your building, James. Sixth and Clinton."

"You must be kidding," Thatcher said. "How could that happen in Hoboken?"

"Wouldn't kid!" Jimmy said. "Guy got hit by a car! And I got a new air freshener. It happened right here. Right here in Hoboken."

AUTHOR'S NOTE

Two sections of this novel appeared previously in other works of mine, in slightly different form: Part of the chapter "Matthew Broderick and Tools of the Trade" as a radio essay titled "First Day on the Job" on National Public Radio's *All Things Considered*, broadcast May 14, 2006 (Martha Wexler has been my patient and encouraging editor at NPR since 2003; thank you, Martha); and part of the chapter "You Put the Ho in Hoboken" as an essay titled "The Commute" in the anthology *Living on the Edge of the World* (edited by Irina Reyn; Simon & Schuster/Touchstone, 2007).

There are many real songs mentioned inside this novel, and a few have had their origins fictionalized. I owe a debt of gratitude to the real authors and/or heirs for indulging me. The songs are: "Gone" by Don Brody (Chase Me Dog Music, BMI), Richard Grula (Big Happy Tunes, BMI), and Gregg Cagno (Cagnotes Music, ASCAP); "Mingus Died in Mexico" by Gregg Cagno (Cagnotes Music, ASCAP) and Christian Bauman (BMI); and "99 Years" by Don Brody (Chase Me Dog Music, BMI).

The quote at the front of the book is both the key line and the title of "God Damn Everything (But the Circus)" by Jonatha Brooke, probably my favorite song recorded by The Story (the duo of Jonatha Brooke and Jennifer Kimball), from their first album.

• • •

There is a residential building on the northeast corner at Sixth and Clinton Streets in Hoboken, New Jersey, but not the one described within. Mrs. Quatrone, her son, and her tenants—indeed, all of her Hoboken neighbors, known and unknown—reside only within these pages; likewise the staff and patients of Beginnings Behavioral Health, and the management and roster of Zippy Records.

This novel began life not on the banks of the Hudson but across the state in Lambertville, New Jersey, along the Delaware River, in 2004; most of the book was written in 2005 and 2006, a good chunk of it scrunched over a laptop on planes to Chicago and Los Angeles and trains to Baltimore and Boston—two years of much motion, backward and forward, in more ways than one, for more reasons than one.

There are a handful of people without whom I could not have properly written this novel. For reasons varied and in many cases years old, my thanks to: Gregg Cagno, Linda Sharar, Karl Dietel, Matt Angus Williams, Richard Grula, Connie Sharar, Carol Sharar, Jack Hardy, Charlie Hunter, Nora Guthrie, Alan Rowoth, Tom Neff, Bob Conway, Cheryl Welch, Brian Wheeler, C.T. Tucker, Amanda Patten, Frank Cotugno; also, Matt Borondy and Robert Birnbaum, et al at IdentityTheory. Many thanks to Dennis Loy Johnson, Kelly Burdick, and David Bukszpan at Melville House for their careful and thoughtful efforts in getting this novel from my hands to yours.

There is nothing new under the sun, lives come and go, and in Hoboken there has been no shortage of amazing and colorful characters. But to those of us who knew him, Don Brody was one of a kind. As was once written about another great spirit: It is not often that someone comes along who is a true friend *and* a good writer—Don was both. I thought of him often while writing this book.

—Christian Bauman
  finished Spring 2007
  Villas, New Jersey